Truth or Dare

Lance Litherland

Copyright © 2023 Lance Litherland

All rights reserved.

Acknowledgements

Since writing my first book "A Darker World" my inspiration for writing has grown. Writing my second book has been a fantastic journey, and a wonderful fulfillment, but none of this would have been possible without the support and encouragement of the people around me. So, I'd like to give a special mention to the following people.

I have to start by thanking my wife, Sharon for believing in me and of course my family, Luke, Ryan, Sam, Reece, Paul and Layla.

I'd also like to acknowledge the other special people in my life. My adopted daughter and partner, Shanice & Kieran Baily-Smith.

My best friend, Paul Greening, who is the closest person I have to a brother and a constant source of drama and entertainment.

I would also like to mention my editor, Amy Coombes of Gemini Editing. Her valuable input, honest critique and attention to detail have been fantastic in helping me develop and evolve my novel.

...

Contents

MARCIA 1
   CHAPTER ONE 1
SUMMER 1996 6
   CHAPTER TWO 6
MARCIA 15
   CHAPTER THREE 15
1996 24
   CHAPTER FOUR 24
MARCIA 30
   CHAPTER FIVE 30
1996 34
   CHAPTER SIX 34
MARCIA 41
   CHAPTER SEVEN 41
1996 50
   CHAPTER EIGHT 50
MARCIA 54
   CHAPTER NINE 54
1996 58
   CHAPTER TEN 58
MARCIA 66
   CHAPTER ELEVEN 66
1996 75

CHAPTER TWELVE 75
MARCIA 79
CHAPTER THIRTEEN 79
1996 86
CHAPTER FOURTEEN 86
MARCIA 95
CHAPTER FIFTEEN 95
BECKY & AUSTIN 110
CHAPTER SIXTEEN 110
1996 128
CHAPTER SEVENTEEN 128
BECKY & AUSTIN 136
CHAPTER EIGHTEEN 136
1996 142
CHAPTER NINETEEN 142
BECKY & AUSTIN 148
CHAPTER TWENTY 148
1996 163
CHAPTER TWENTY-ONE 163
BECKY & AUSTIN 167
CHAPTER TWENTY-TWO 167
1996 180
CHAPTER TWENTY-THREE 180
DR ARTHUR TOE 197
CHAPTER TWENTY-FOUR 197
DOCTOR ARTHUR TOE 202

CHAPTER TWENTY-FIVE	202
DR ARTHUR TOE	209
CHAPTER TWENTY-SIX	209
DR ARTHUR TOE	214
CHAPTER TWENTY-SEVEN	214
DR ARTHUR TOE	219
CHAPTER TWENTY-EIGHT	219
DR ARTHUR TOE	223
CHAPTER TWENTY-NINE	223
THE HOST	227
CHAPTER THIRTY	227
THE HOST	239
CHAPTER THIRTY-ONE	239
THE SPECIAL GUEST	245
CHAPTER THIRTY-TWO	245
THE SURPRISE GUEST	252
CHAPTER THIRTY-THREE	252
THE STING IN THE TALE	257
CHAPTER THIRTY-FOUR	257
CHAPTER THIRTY-FIVE	264
A LAST THROW OF THE DICE	264

•••

MARCIA

CHAPTER ONE

Marcia could feel the weight of her anxiety rising with each hurried step, hindered by her high heels and black pencil skirt. Her footsteps echoed off the rows of corrugated shutters, which were like heavy eyelids, signalling that the world was very much asleep.

The dim fluorescent streetlights did little to make her feel any safer. But it wasn't the empty streets nor the darkness that had her picking up the pace. She'd walked these streets from Bennies Wine Bar a million times, a swanky, uptown place brimming with city slickers, expensive suits, and designer accessories, where Pinot Noir flowed like water and bulging wallets were waved around in sweaty palms. She would often meet her clients there.

But tonight was different. Tonight, she was being followed. Marcia focused her sights on the T-junction, which crossed the backstreets of London a few hundred yards past the boarded-up shops.

She didn't know how long the person had been following her. Was she just being paranoid?

She glanced sideways at the only glass-fronted shop without shutters, hoping to catch a glimpse of the figure she feared may be following her. But the feeble light denied her any chance of that.

Her heart rate was now matching her pace. Quick and heavy. The footsteps got closer. Her breathing became more erratic, and the pulsing in her throat became more noticeable. She knew this area well. Her place was just a few minutes walk – a converted industrial building, 1250 sq. ft. of innercity luxury living space. But at this moment, it felt a million miles away.

She crossed the road. An excuse to look over her shoulder and catch a glimpse of the figure following her.

Maybe it was nothing. Nothing more than paranoia conjuring up scenarios born from her fear. After all, it wasn't the first time someone had walked behind her from the bar. However, it was the very first time her intuition had raised its ugly head walking home. Was it because the footsteps were matching her changing pace?

She wasn't supposed to be walking home tonight. She was supposed to be riding shotgun in a black Maserati, then sip cocktails in an opulent hotel room in silk contour-hugging lingerie before satisfying all her client's fantasies.

Instead, her client was a no-show, and she was left walking home with her purse a grand lighter than it should have been.

She drew her long black coat around her. The late January air was now a biting breeze, strong enough to make her eyes water. The pavements mirrored the luminous-coloured neon signs above.

She turned to her right, stopping briefly on the edge of the pavement. As she flicked her head, she saw the figure approaching—a middle-aged woman in a black parker. Grey fur framed the hood, almost the same shade as her hair tucked neatly under it. The woman locked eyes with her. She didn't say anything for a moment, her breath bellowing like an overworked industrial chimney.

Marcia felt the fear starting to slip away from her throat.

Her fears of a hooded attacker retreating.

"I believe you're Marcia?" the woman asked.

Marcia frowned, pausing for a second. "Yes, I am. Why?" she inquired.

The woman placed her gloved hand on Marcia's arm and turned a smile so subtle you could easily miss it. "Does the name Dr. Arthur Toe mean anything to you?" she asked, squeezing Marcia's arm ever so slightly.

Marcia's heart skipped a beat. She returned a smile all the same, but it was more out of politeness. "I'm sorry, lady. I don't know who you are or know anyone by that name."

Marcia tilted her head. "Did you follow me from the bar?"

The woman stood awkwardly, watching the late-night stray cars drive by before returning to Marcia's question.

"As a matter of fact, yes, I did, and I still believe you are the person I'm looking for." Her voice was clear and free of any accent.

"Did you have anything to do with my date not showing?" she asked directly.

The woman smiled. This time it was more obvious. "A date.

Is that what you call it?"

"Excuse me, but who the hell are you?" Marcia said impatiently.

Marcia pulled her coat tighter around her. The bitter January chill had caught up with her now that she had stopped moving. The background volume was tempered by a few late- night stragglers, high on the evening's nectar, weaving their way down the street opposite, exchanging some youthful banter.

"Look, if you're some jealous wife, hoping to find out where all his expenses have been directed to, then here I am. I make no apology for what I do. I offer a service, and they call me. It's just business."

The woman focused on the stragglers for a second, then on to another passing car, before landing back on Marcia.

The woman grinned, her piercing blue eyes were dancing with humour. "Oh dear, I think you've completely misunderstood. I'm well aware of what you do. I'm certainly not jealous, married, or even interested in how you make your living."

Marcia shook her head in confusion. "So, what's this all about?" she asked impatiently.

The woman stood momentarily, glancing up and down the street before pulling a large brown envelope from her bag, which she then held out to Marcia.

"Take this, go home, pour yourself a glass of wine, sit down, and read. Let's just say that this could change your life."

Marcia hesitated for a while, confused about the woman's intentions. Maybe she *was* a private detective hired by a jealous wife. Maybe there were photographs that involved her husband she wanted to confront Marcia with.

"What's this all about? Because if you don't mind, it's late, and I must head home. I'm not interested in playing mind games," she said in a harsh tone.

"Oh, but you do like games." The woman's stare remained.

She glanced up and down the street like some kind of Cold War spy. "It's a one-time offer for a very rich client. Everything you need to know is in the envelope. Good night."

The woman disappeared into the shadows and Marcia was left holding the envelope. She felt confused. She'd never conducted business this way before.

She held the envelope tightly. Apprehension started to surface.

Marcia pondered momentarily on her past – a past that held more than a few skeletons she preferred to keep buried. She lived in a world where the lines of pain and pleasure were blurred. It was a world where she was in control and got paid very well for it. Whenever she was asked what she did, Marcia felt the phrase *"I'm in the entertainment business"* was much more palatable than saying she was a high-class escort. She avoided the low end of the game with sweaty overweight perverts in the back seat of a car, feeding the profits of seedy pimps. She aimed her sights higher than that. She focussed more on rich businessmen, opulent settings with all the benefits, and of course, a four-figure rate. For that, she gave them their very own fantasy. She was not only blessed with beauty but also form. But this path hadn't always been a steady one.

She had little memory of her mother after being put into care at the age of two. Life after that became a numb sensation of self-destruction and the abandonment of responsible behaviour, inevitably ending up in the custodial services of a secure unit when she turned seventeen.

However, she carried a secret. There was a young man, a meticulously dressed, smart young man, who was the only visitor she'd ever had at the unit. He was polite and discreet, and would sit opposite her in a tiny repressive room, not unlike an interrogation room, with little colour, security doors, and metal furniture bolted to the floor.

She remembered that he'd asked short and purposeful questions, all intended to engage her attention. But at seventeen and full of resentment and anger, she evaded anyone in authority.

That was until he slipped her a piece of paper with a name on it.

Dr. Arthur Toe.

"Remember this name, memorise it, because it will be your calling one day," he told her.

She never saw him again.

That calling now lay clutched in her icy hands. Did she really want to open Pandora's box?

Marcia slipped the envelope inside her coat and headed home.

SUMMER 1996

CHAPTER TWO

Laura Myers was nervous. But it was an excitable nervousness, just like the time her dad took her to a theme park. She was twelve back then. The excitement of the thrilling rides was coupled with a healthy fear of the unknown. This is how she felt as she navigated the narrow country roads. It was not something she was used to doing, living in a big city. But a new job and a fresh start were just what she needed, even if it meant uprooting to the depths of Cornwall.

Female live-in housekeeper required in a country cottage, enjoying local views and access to a large lake—own room with ensuite. Various duties required. Must be flexible. Some early mornings and late evenings are involved. Please call Mrs Monroe on the above number.

Laura envisioned the beauty of working in such a peaceful place with the calming surroundings of the quiet countryside, free from the spoils of ugly tower blocks, endless streams of traffic, and artificial white noise which bombarded her senses on a daily basis.

Then there was the constant chatter of humans, half conversations on a continuous loop.

She was done with the unsociable hours of waiting tables, with very few tips, then jostling through the crowded underground station like herding cattle.

Eat, sleep, travel, work, repeat.

She steered her red Mini through the narrow arteries of the rural countryside, singing at the top of her voice to "Killing Me Softly," which was blaring out from Radio 1, pushing her speakers to the brink of distortion, and occasionally glancing at the handwritten directions taped to the dash.

It was warm too. The scattering of white cotton clouds only added to the picturesque backdrop, along with the scented breeze from the freshly cut fields and an assortment of sounds that she'd never experienced in the city.

Eventually, Laura came to a narrow track that snaked its way across Bodmin Moor. Wild sheep wandered around carefree, meandering across the track, oblivious to her movements. Although, at first, she was quite amused at such a sight, she soon grew impatient at the crawling pace and aimless stop-start to the point that she honked her horn, which made them flee in various and uncoordinated directions. She even found herself leaning out the window, shouting "sorry" to them.

The track ultimately wound its way to an open gate. Beyond that, there was a gravel drive and a border of lush green well- tended shrubs and candy-coloured flower beds – an image Laura had conjured up in her mind many times.

Maybe it was the multitude of pictures she occasionally browsed in *Country House & Garden* magazine, the ones that lay in numerous waiting rooms, along with *Hello* and *Good Housekeeping*. She often thought these were fanciful images staged by wealthy homeowners to draw in the holiday clientele, giving a false impression. In reality, they rarely met the expectations of the pictures. By the time you realised, they already had your money.

However, on this occasion, her preconceptions matched her imagination perfectly, much to her surprise. She then saw the white-washed stone cottage. It was the most beautiful house she'd ever seen, with leaded windows and a sea of emerald green lawn so well-tended that it made her wonder if it was all real. It was way larger than she'd imagined. Slightly proud of the building was a protruding entrance that housed the large oak door. Sprouting from the thatched roof were two annexes on either side of the main front and a large glass orangery at the gable end.

She sat for a second, taking in the beauty of her newfound surroundings. She was so busy eyeing up the house that she hadn't noticed the owner appearing in the doorway. A woman, who she'd only spoken to on the phone, didn't resemble the image she'd formed in her head at all. She was shorter than Laura imagined, with a fuller figure, wearing a bright floral pinny over a grey shirt and flowing pleated skirt. Her greying hair was up in a bun and she had a radiating smile.

Laura had already decided that she liked her.

The woman stood with her hands resting on her ample hips and a blue checkered tea towel over her left shoulder. Even her slip-on shoes were the same shade of grey.

"You found me okay, then? You better come in, my dear. I reckon you could do with a cuppa. I'm Mrs Monroe, we spoke on the phone," she said with a broad Cornish accent.

Laura grabbed her two small suitcases from the back seat.

She expected the house to be as romantic on the inside as it was on the outside. What she didn't expect was another person standing at the back of the hallway, who wasn't as welcoming as Mrs Monroe. A young girl, maybe in her late teens, she guessed, stood in the shadow of a tall antique sideboard, with her arms straight by her sides in a red flowing dress with mosaic white and yellow flowers, dark hair and a straight-cut fringe. There was no warm smile or a welcome gesture. Whoever she was, Laura was sure they'd get acquainted eventually.

Mrs Monroe led Laura into the kitchen. They both sat at a large, oblong wooden table in the centre of the room, surrounded by pine wood cabinets and a large, black double Aga. The room was cluttered. An assortment of items all seemingly abandoned. Even the terracotta floor tiles were home to a multitude of papers, books, and magazines, including several volumes of the Yellow Pages, cookbooks, and encyclopaedias. The fridge door was a mosaic of postcards, notes, and pictures. It was clearly a lived-in house. Laura made her mind up; she was going to convince Mrs Monroe that a good sort-out was needed. She may have only come from a one-bedroom flat, but she was fastidious about everything being in its rightful place. Tidy house, tidy mind.

Mrs Monroe placed a fresh pot of tea on the table, complete with a floral cosy and cups to match.

"This was my mother's set, you know. Got a few cracks an' all, but just don't feel right replacing it. Sugar?" she asked, pouring the tea.

"No thanks. You've got a lovely house," Laura said, her eyes still scouting the busy room.

"Been in the family three generations. I was born in this house. Reckon I'll be leaving this world in here too. I don't go far, rarely venture anywhere these days. Oh, ark at me going on.

"So, you'll be wanting to know more about the job then. To be honest, I haven't really thought it through yet," she said, spooning some more sugar into her tea.

Her smile was radiant. Every time she smiled, her cheeks would swell up like two small lumps. It reminded Laura of her nan, who had an animated smile so wide it almost distorted her face.

Laura sipped her tea; it was stronger than she liked, but she did so out of politeness.

"So, the advert said that you need a cleaner and general helper. Is that right?"

"Well, more of a live-in housekeeper; since I lost Jack, things round here have been tough. Left me in pieces, it did, I mean, what with my arthritis an' all, 'tis a big place to keep on top of an' all, but if I'm honest, it's more the company I'm craving."

"Mrs Monroe, who's the girl I saw earlier in the hallway?

"Ah. That's my daughter, Becky, just turned seventeen last

month. She don't do strangers very well. She's..." Mrs Monroe paused mid-bite of her toast. "Well. She ain't what you call easy." Her smile faded and her eyes drifted to the table.

"Doctors came up with all sorts of fancy letters to describe her. In my day, you were just hyperactive, not labelled with letters. It's all foreign to me. Poor girl's moody one minute and happy as Larry the next. Me and Jack had our difficulties with her, she was expelled from school, so we home-taught her for a while, but that didn't work, long story, then my Jack arranged a special school for her. She just got back – for summer break. Reckon we ain't done her no favours, being she's isolated an' all, but she don't do crowds either very well. She none too happy about your arrival, I can tell you, but that's my business to deal with. She spends most of her time with Greer, the gardener, or Molly, some girl she met last year. Likes to be outside though."

"You've got a gardener?" Laura asked.

"Jack took him on, young lad, bit of a loner I think, spends all weathers out there, but what he's done with this garden is nothing short of poetic. Help yourself to some toast, dear. Always have tea and toast late afternoon, we have our proper cooked meal at lunchtime here," she said, sliding the toast rack across the table.

"Does he live on site?" she asked.

"Goodness, no. He lives on the other side of the lake, small village. That's where I get most of my supplies. Anyway, let's talk about why you're here, dear. I wasn't sure I'd get anyone. Fact is, you're the only person who applied, I mean, it was only a small ad back one of those English travel magazines you pick up in Lunn Poly. Figured if people like Cornwall so much, they might want to stay. But obviously, you took a fancy to it."

"I was looking for a break, to be honest. I'd had enough of the city life. And then your ad caught my eye, and I had this crazy idea about leaving and not going back. The more I thought about it, the more appealing it became." She slurped her tea. "So, here I am," she smiled.

Laura felt the sun land on her face from the adjacent window; its touch was almost hypnotic. It made her squint slightly, but not annoyingly so. It felt different here somehow. Maybe it was the stillness and the absence of any fumes distilling its qualities like in the city.

"The thing is, I'm twenty-three and still not sure where I want to be." Laura beamed and threw open her arms. "But this place. I think this is where I want to be."

"So, you were working then, in the city?" asked Mrs Monroe, licking the jam from her fingers.

"Bar work. It was boring, crap pay and I was on my feet all day. Same old routine. But I was saving up to go travelling."

"And your parents, if you don't mind me asking. They keen on you being here?"

Laura turned her cup around in the saucer, lining up the pattern. It was an OCD trait she often did when she felt nervous. "Well, my mother was, or is an alcoholic. Dad struggled with her addiction. She ended up moving up north. My dad travels a lot for his business. He's in Australia at the moment, doing some big deal. We're close, I just don't get to see him as much as I'd like."

"You poor bird, reckon you're a strong sort, going through that with your mother an' all."

"I'm better off without her, to be honest. So is my dad. I like my own company – never been one for lots of fuss. I concentrated on college. I was on a typing course, fancied being a posh secretary somewhere," she said, dismissing the subject of her parents.

"Drink up dear, plenty more in the pot, likes to keep it going, I do," she said, stirring the teapot for the umpteenth time. Laura imagined Mrs Monroe's insides to be the colour of mud with the amount of tea she consumed.

"So, what happened?" asked Mrs Monroe.

"With what?"

"College, becoming a posh secretary."

"It was bad timing. I mean, with everything at home, then a friend of mine who worked in a bar was looking for more staff. Not what I really wanted, but it served the purpose. I just saw it as a way to escape home, especially with my parents arguing all the time."

Laura turned her cup again, matching the pattern on the saucer. She hated dwelling on the past.

Mrs Monroe perched her arms on the table. "Well, I can't say I can offer a king's ransom, dear, it'll be a basic wage, cash in hand and free accommodation. 'Tis a big place to clean an' all, be some laundry, cleaning out the fireplace, especially in the winter, mind you, and general duties."

A sudden knock at the door startled Laura and she turned to see a young man in a flat cap and dungarees stroll in, cradling an armful of chopped wood.

"For the Aga," he said, dropping the wood in a wicker basket by the door.

"Ah, young Greer, come and meet our new resident, Laura."

Greer nodded to her. "Hi there," he said, offering her an earth-stained hand.

Laura remained seated and reciprocated with a handshake. His hands were large and rough. Laura guessed he was maybe the same age as her. He had a handsome face and black curly hair sprouting from either side of his brown cap.

"You met Becky yet?" he asked, leaning against the worktop and brushing the grass cuttings off his trousers.

"Oh, can you not do that inside please?"

"Sorry, Mrs Monroe," he replied, removing his cap and ruffling his hair.

A few moments later, Mrs Monroe's daughter came barging through the door cradling a dead blackbird in her hands. A small trickle of blood oozed from its beak.

"I found it by the lake. It was injured, Mother, so I put it out of its misery. It's kinder that way, don't you think?" she asked, completely ignoring Laura.

"Take that off her, Greer, will you?" Mrs Monroe asked

with a disapproving expression.

Greer threw up his hands like he was surrendering to the enemy. "You kidding? Go and chuck it in the woods, Becky."

"Becky, dear, this is Laura," Mrs Monroe said, gesturing at her. "She's taken the job I advertised."

Laura stood up. "Hello, Becky." She avoided offering Becky
her hand, having seen the dead bird nesting in her palms.

Becky gave her a fleeting smile before dismissing her just as quickly. "Yes, I saw her arrive."

"How about I give you the guided tour, get you settled in? Reckon you could do with an early night, after all that travelling an' all. We can chat more tomorrow. That sound good?" Mrs Monroe asked as she picked up the teacups.

"Yes, thank you. That works for me."

Laura's eyes drifted towards the doorway as she watched Becky slip out of the kitchen. She sensed that her relationship with Becky could be a difficult one—something that would require a great deal of patience.

Mrs Monroe led Laura up the narrow stairs to a long landing that ran the full length of the house and disappeared around the corner. She opened a pine louvre door and showed Laura the first room at the top of the stairs.

"Hoping this will fit your needs, young lady. Fresh towels in the double wardrobe and en-suite off to the left. Plenty drawers and storage, too. There's a telephone, but I'll have to charge you for all your calls, you understand, less you have one of those fancy portable phones."

"I've got a Motorola my dad gave me, but I'm guessing it's not much use here."

"I don't understand those fancy phones, but like I say, landline's available."

Laura set the two cases by her feet and smiled.

"I'll leave you to unpack an' all, get settled in."

"Thanks. It's a lovely room," she said, admiring its unique character.

Mrs Monroe paused at the doorway. "You'll get used to Becky, she ain't too good at new folk. Hoping you'll be a better influence than her friend Molly."

Laura nodded with a smile. She set her cases down on the bed and scouted the room, exploring all the pine wood drawers and wardrobe. The en-suite bathroom was adequate, with a cubicle shower, toilet, and small hand basin, surrounded by lemon yellow tiles with a floral border.

The room was large. Certainly bigger than her one-bedroom flat in the city and much more appealing, with its exposed beams and curved walls. The sloping ceiling ran down to two large windows at the front, giving her glorious views of the landscaped gardens and, beyond that, a border of woods. A single, large window on the end wall enjoyed a view of the lake, just a stone's throw from the house. Even from here, she caught sight of the birds skimming the surface of the water before disappearing into the nearby trees.

She pulled open the window and inhaled the scent of summer—a welcome change to the everyday aroma of city fumes.

She fell onto the bed, swallowed up by the soft mattress, her head sinking into the feather pillows. She revelled in the peacefulness of the moment. Only the chirping of the birds and the distant sound of a lawnmower could be heard in the background. It wasn't long before her eyes surrendered from her long and tiring journey.

MARCIA

CHAPTER THREE

Marcia entered her flat. It was an open-plan, converted industrial building with slim, full-length windows down one side, looking out onto the heart of the city. There were seven in total. The fine oak flooring had a scattering of ivory-coloured modern contemporary furniture, all mixed with whitewashed brickwork and exposed industrial steel girders just like a huge metal skeleton. Only the bedroom was separated by the original unpainted red brick wall.

She had done well for herself, surrounding herself with nice things—expensive and exquisite things. She shopped in boutiques and designer stores, living her life exactly how she wanted. Except she wasn't. There was always an enormous hole that she just couldn't fill. No family, few friends, and affection that only came with money. She desired something more.

She kicked off her killer heels and did what the woman had suggested. She reached for the fridge and grabbed an open bottle of wine, though it wasn't an expensive one. Besides, she only drank that if her clients were paying. She knew her wines very well. It gave the impression she had class and made her look as if she moved in higher circles. The higher the circle, the more contacts with money. It was better for business.

This life she had now was nothing more than an elaborate

game. A facade for a lost life. She was unable to face the truth about her past. The more she stared at the envelope on the glass coffee table, the more she feared its contents—even if it was a job.

It was the name that unsettled her.

Marcia circled the table, sipping her wine. Her tired mind was conjuring up all sorts of possibilities.

She glanced at the large wall clock; it was almost two in the morning. She wandered over to one of the large, full-length windows, glass in hand, studying the empty streets below. They were empty except for a single car parked below with its headlights on.

She took another sip of wine and followed the car as it slowly pulled away to the end of the street. It was a Rolls Royce.

The following morning, she woke to her phone vibrating its way off the bedside cabinet and landing on the wooden floor. She reached down and stared at the screen for a second before answering. Her voice wasn't in sync with her mind yet.

"It's me, Philip. You're supposed to be downstairs, remember? Nine a.m. pick up. I can see your blinds are still down, you okay?"

"Shit, sorry, bad night, hold on."

She leapt out of bed and slipped on a pink satin robe as she made her way to the window. She raised the blinds. The low January sun caused her to squint.

"I'm still here."

Philip, a regular client, was standing by his BMW in the street below, wearing a dark suit and a bright tie, with his hair slicked back. He was one of her first customers from a few years back. He was one of her few clients who weren't married, although he'd constantly tell her that his job as a detective left very little room for a relationship. But for five hundred pounds, he got the undivided attention of Marcia for the afternoon. Sex, affection, and a companion who didn't moan at him about the menial and trivial stuff that most relationships get tied up in. He also knew how to switch from business to friendship when required.

"We can rearrange if you like. It's no problem. I can always go to work."

"Actually, can you come up?" she asked. She'd never had clients in her own place before. It was outcalls only and expensive hotel rooms. This was her private space. But she knew Philip well enough. She trusted him.

She buzzed him in through the security door downstairs, and he made his way up.

"Wow, nice place you've made for yourself," he said, standing in the doorway and admiring the décor.

"Do you mind if I take a rain check today? Bit of strange night last night." She ushered him in.

Philip noticed the lack of her usual warm, welcoming smile. He'd also never seen her in her natural state, minus her makeup and sporting a bedhead.

"You know, you're a very attractive woman, Marcia. You don't need all that muck on your face, and I have to say, I'm quite digging the satin gown." His eyes wandered over her.

"Let's leave that conversation for when I'm on the clock, shall we? Coffee?"

"Sure."

Philip took a moment to wander around her apartment, admiring her taste in décor—the strange phallic wooden sculptures and minimalist artwork. He was especially drawn to a painting of two blue circles on a white textured background named *Visions*.

"Never understood this rubbish, and I bet you paid a fortune for it as well. Hell, I'm sure I paid for some of this, you know."

Marcia scowled at him from the open kitchen. "I need some professional advice, not a joker right now."

"Sorry, what do you need?"

He removed his jacket and took a seat on the cream sofa.

She wandered over with two mugs of coffee fresh from the espresso machine, conscious of his eyes already removing her satin robe as she retied it around her narrow waist. She

looked after herself. Even in her early forties, she was aging well. In
a couple more years, she'd jack it all in, move to Spain, and enjoy the spoils of her ill-gotten earnings. But until then, she'd make the most of her beauty while she still had it.

She picked up the brown A4 envelope from the table and handed it to Philip. "Open this, will you? Take a look."

Philips's expression changed from a schoolboy crush to an inquisitive detective.

"What's going on? Why aren't you opening it? Anything I need to know?" he asked, loosening his tie.

"I need you to trace a name for me, and I wouldn't ask if it wasn't important. Last night, a woman followed me from the bar. She gave me this envelope and told me it was a job offer. She was shifty, and I had never seen her before. At first, I thought it was some jealous wife. I reckon I would have handled that better…"

"Hold on, Marcia," he interrupted. "You're worried about a job offer? One where you actually pay tax and all, or are we talking about a job for a client who just wants to hire you for his own ends?"

Marcia's temple wrinkled.

"Did I sense a tone of judgement? Because then you're treading on thin ice."

"What, no!" he said, raising his hands.

"I hope you're not jealous because it's the one thing I can't have in my line of work."

"Jesus, Marcia, it was a simple question, that's all."

She slurped her coffee. At home, she didn't need to be graceful, charming, or have etiquette. And she made no apology for it. She ignored the awkward silence. Instead, she decided to get to the point of why she'd invited him up.

"It's the name that has spooked me. Not the job," Marcia stated.

"Do I need to guess what it is, or…"

"Dr Arthur Toe."

Philip smiled.

"A doctor. Figures, I suppose."

Marcia placed her mug on the glass coffee table and sat up.

She stared at her lap, twisting her gold rings around her fingers nervously. She felt a vulnerability she'd never experienced before. Sure, she'd felt it as a neglected child, but certainly not in her adult years, even less so in front of her clients. But here she was, exposing herself.

"Back in late'96, I had a spell in a young offender's detention centre, and no, I don't want to discuss my past," she added.

Philip raised his hands again. "Wasn't going to try."

"I had a visit from a man, I guess in his twenties, can't really remember why or even what his name was. He asked me a bunch of questions and handed me a piece of paper with a name on it. Told me to remember it, and one day, I'd hear the name again. He said it would be my calling. Well, that one day arrived last night."

She tapped the envelope on the coffee table.

"And you've no idea who this Dr Arthur Toe is?"

Marcia shrugged.

"And the woman?"

"Never seen her before, didn't even give me the courtesy of a name. To be honest, I was freezing my tits off and just wanted to get home. That's another thing. I think she sabotaged my date with a client."

Marcia peeled herself off the sofa and paced the wooden floor before making her way to the middle window and gazing down at the world below. There was a pang of disappointment that stabbed at her every time she viewed the world from above. A sense of belonging that she knew she'd never have. Marcia pined for a normal life. Most people dream of escaping the rat race, but she was different. She wanted in. The 9 to 5 and two point four kids. But her past had different ideas.

"Tell me, Philip. Do you ever look back on something you did when you were younger, something despicable and so wrong, and wonder why you did it?" she asked, still drawn to the world below.

"Not sure what you're getting at. I've done some stupid stuff in the past, but it's just history. Don't we learn from our past mistakes? Isn't that what we're supposed to do?"

"I guess so."

"Something you want to share?" he asked.

"No, no, I don't."

She didn't need to turn around. She could hear the tearing of the envelope behind her. She closed her eyes, anticipating its contents. She imagined the fear of standing in a courtroom, the black robes and the white wigs, facing twelve unconnected people all about to decide her future. The second before the verdict was read; that was the crest of all fear. The pinnacle of where incarceration and freedom hinge in one moment frozen in time. That's how she felt at this exact moment.

"Well, it's a letter. Typed, but signed by hand. Shall I read it?"

Marcia turned from the window and nodded with a slow blink.

Let me introduce myself. My name is Dr Arthur Toe. I trust that this letter finds you well, and please forgive the rather unconventional contact, but I am a rather private person. I would very much like to employ your company for a murder mystery party this weekend. Please find enclosed a cheque for £2,600 to cover any inconvenience for the short notice. Furthermore, you will be handsomely compensated for this coming weekend. My driver will pick you up and take you to the venue. I very much look forward to you accompanying me. Please indicate your acceptance by texting either yes or no to the number on the top of the letter, and further instructions will be sent.

Yours sincerely Dr Arthur Toe

"Shit Marcia! £2,600, are you kidding me? I'd sleep with him for the weekend myself for that kind of money."

"For God's sake Philip," she snapped. She made her way

to the fridge and pulled a bottle of Chateauneuf Du Pap from the shelf. She then grabbed a crystal glass and poured it.

"Don't say a fucking word about how early it is. I need a favour. I need you to investigate this Dr Toe; I need to know who he is and why the name has come back to haunt me after all these years."

She marched back into the lounge area and grabbed the cheque.

"You've got to be fucking kidding me."

"You want to take a minute, catch your breath, and tell me what the hell is going on in that pretty little head of yours?"

Marcia perched next to him.

"Do you believe in coincidences?"

"I believe in the right place, right time, and the wrong place, wrong time. Depends on what you're referring to, I suppose."

She held out the cheque in front of him, almost thrusting it in his face. She mouthed the figure.

"£2,600, is that not a strange amount? And when are you going to consider the fact that the first I heard this name was back in '96?"

Philip dropped the letter and grabbed the cheque from her hands. He caressed it like it was a Willy Wonka golden ticket. His eyes locked on hers. "Twenty-six years ago?"

Marcia downed her wine in one gulp.

"So, will you find out who this is for me? I need to know exactly who I'll be spending the weekend with."

Philip relaxed into the sofa.

"Well, I'm guessing you won't be alone since it's a murder mystery weekend. Sounds kinda fun."

"Fun?"

She stood up and then sat straight back down again in one motion, animating her words with her hands.

"I don't give a shit about the weekend or the money. It's the name that concerns me. Don't you realise this name has been with me for twenty-six years, and now I've got to face it? I'm just not that comfortable with it all." She went to the full- length window again and watched the dull city sky drifting by on the winter breeze. "I need you to look into the doctor for me. I need to know everything about him."

"Look, I understand, but it doesn't work like that. I need to have a good reason to investigate someone. I can't just type a random name in. Everything's logged, and unless it's connected to a case, I could lose my job. I'm sorry, but I just can't."

Silence interrupted them for a minute.

Marcia turned from the window and instantly switched to seductive mistress, her face full of amorous desire as she catwalked towards him, dropping her satin robe on the way. She knelt in front of him, placing her delicate hands on his inner thighs. She used the only tool she had. She knew all her clients very well—their inner secrets, desires, and wildest fantasies. She could switch roles to suit each client's desire at the flick of a switch. She knew what to wear, how to touch, and, more importantly, how to please them. She had always dreamt of becoming an actress, but circumstances and bad choices left that dream long behind. But here, in this life, in her world, she was the leading role, and she played it so well.

Philip shifted position on the sofa, avoiding her Medusa-like glare, soft eyes, and subtle licking of her lips. His eyes wandered towards her firm breasts, despite making a clear and conscious effort to avoid them.

"Marcia. I appreciate what you're trying to do, but my hands are tied. It's not like it is in the movies. Everything I do has to be justified. I can't even take a shit without my senior knowing about it. I'm sorry, I really am."

Marcia switched again from seductive mistress to angry maiden in the blink of an eye. She grabbed her robe from the floor and marched into the bedroom, slamming the door behind her. Philip stood up, straightened his tie, and grabbed his jacket, pulling his car keys from the pocket.

"Look, Marcia, there's someone I think can help you," he yelled towards the door.

Philip fiddled with his keys, waiting for her to appear from the bedroom. A few minutes later, she emerged in a white cotton robe. Less seductive and more stern matron.

"So, who can help me then, Philip, if you won't?"

"Can't help, not won't, Marcia, big difference. Look, it's clear that something or someone has got to you. It's written all over your face. You don't need to be a detective to figure that out. I just thought you might want to be a bit more forthcoming about whatever twenty-six years means to you."

"I don't want to talk about it. Look, okay, I get it. You can't help. So, who can, then?"

Philip scribbled a phone number and an address on the envelope.

"Bernie. He's an old-school private detective. He's a bit forward, maybe even a bit rude, but he's ex-police. A little unorthodox in his methods, but if anyone can help, it'll be him."

She peered at the address. "I'll give him a call, thanks."

Philip touched her shoulder. "Call me if you want to talk."

He slipped on his jacket and juggled his keys in one hand. Marcia ignored his last comment.

"You better go. I need a shower."

She went to the window and watched him disappear in his BMW.

1996

CHAPTER FOUR

A noise woke Laura up. It was dark, and she could hear muffled voices below. She turned on the small table lamp and glanced at her alarm clock. Just gone midnight. She climbed out of bed and made her way to the window on the end wall. Peering down through the glass roof of the orangery, she could see that the light was dim, but it was enough for her to see Mrs Monroe engaged in an argument with her daughter. Maybe it was about her being here. Becky seemed an odd girl. Closed off. Distant.

Whatever it was, Mrs Monroe wasn't shy about sharing her daughter's problems. Laura decided to concentrate on her job and leave any family matters well alone. For now, at least. Realising she'd fallen asleep in her dress, she changed into her night clothes and went back to bed.

The next morning, Laura woke to silence rather than the continuous sound of tooting horns and the relentless noise of car engines. Only the sound she could hear was of a wood pigeon and birds chirping. Something obviously not present in the city. She peered out of the window to see Greer, the gardener at the side of the house, chopping wood. An odd name, she thought.

She showered and got dressed, wearing a pair of Jeans, a black T-shirt, and white trainers. Clipping her blonde hair up out of the way in preparation for her chores, Laura headed downstairs to the kitchen.

Mrs Monroe was sitting at the table in the same floral pinny with a large mug of tea, rack of toast, and various jars of homemade jams to boot.

"Morning, dear. I trust you slept well," she asked. "Help yourself to toast, less you be one of those girls who skip breakfast. Most important meal of the day, so they say."

Does this woman live on tea and toast?

"Yes, I did, thank you," Laura replied, reaching for the toast and homemade jam.

"Is Becky not joining us?" She decided to pry just a little.

"She's out with Greer, fetching more wood for the Aga. I'm sure she'll make an appearance at some point. That girl doesn't go long without food," she said, stuffing some more toast into her mouth.

"The gardener, Greer, is that his first name or last?" she asked.

"No idea, I'm afraid. He just calls himself Greer. Not for me to pry, Jack might have known."

Laura stood up from the table, collected the plates and cups, and filled up the sink. She stood working her way through the breakfast dishes, gazing in awe at the picturesque view of the lake. A far cry from the dismal sight of redbrick tower blocks and the gritty city air. She took pleasure in the way the morning sun shimmered across the water.

"If you ask young Greer, he might take you across the lake later, pick up some groceries."

Laura turned from the sink and frowned. "Across the lake?" "Happens it's quicker by boat than a car, much more pleasant in the summer too, give you two a chance to get acquainted an' all."

"Sure, that sounds lovely."

Laura suggested giving the upstairs rooms a good spring clean.

"Better you talk to Becky first. She ever so funny about folk going into her room," she said, rising from the large wooden table and dumping her mug into the sink. "Happens even I don't dare cross the line." She raised her eyebrows. "Likes her privacy, does that girl."

"Of course, Mrs Monroe, I'll be sure to talk to her first. I wouldn't want to get off on the wrong foot with her."

"I think that happened when I put pen to paper. That girl already made her opinion known long before you even arrived."

Laura placed a bucket of cleaning products at her feet. Her eyes side-tracked to a sun-scorched picture taped to the fridge door.

"Is that your Jack?" she asked, crouching towards the picture of Mrs Monroe and her husband, clad in winter jackets and surrounded by a flurry of white.

"That was a difficult winter, likes of which we hadn't seen in a while," she replied.

Laura paused in the silence that followed, realising Mrs Monroe was enjoying a moment, stirred by the memories in the picture. Something maybe she hadn't done in a while. Laura felt sorry for her and gave her the time she needed.

Mrs Monroe gently pulled the picture from the fridge door and thumbed the image of her late husband. "Oh, Jack, you silly fool," she muttered with longing eyes.

Laura found herself asking the obvious. "May I ask what happened to him?"

Mrs Monroe put the picture back and took a tissue from her sleeve before sitting back down at the table.

Laura pushed the bucket to one side and joined her. A dark shadow swept across the room; the sunlight was hidden by a passing cloud. Its timing almost seemed orchestrated for this moment.

Mrs Monroe dabbed at her eyes. "I honestly don't know what happened, dear. Said he was going birdwatching. His hobby, you know. That man spent hours roaming them woods with his camera and binoculars tracking wildlife. He'd come racing back like he'd found gold. Bless him. It was just another bird to me, but he couldn't wait to go into town to get his pictures developed." She glanced at the picture again.

"Early this year, it was. That morning I'd made him a packed lunch: ploughman's, his favourite. A big slab of pork pie and a lump of cheddar, not good for him, what with his heart problems, but well, anyway, he left here early, say about seven, the sun was just waking up too. I watched him wander off into the woods from the landing window. He never came back."

Silence followed. The room filled with light once again.

"Did you call the police?"

"They told me they couldn't do anything, what with him only being missing for eight hours an' all, but I knew something was wrong when he didn't return after four. He doesn't normally go for more than a couple hours, three at most."

"So, what happened? You must have been sick with worry.

Did you go out and look for him?" she asked softly.

"I couldn't, not with my arthritis an' all. I walked to the edge of the woods, which took me a good twenty minutes, and I shouted his name, but nothing. Then half an hour later, young Greer came back across the lake with Becky. So, I sent them out to look for him. They seemed none too bothered, though. Reckon they'd argued an' all as they hardly said two words to each other or me."

"I'm so sorry, Mrs Monroe."

"Do you know the worst thing?"

Laura shook her head.

"Seeing his footsteps in the snow for days after. Every time I looked out, all I could see was his footsteps. Didn't want it to thaw. I didn't."

"Could the police not track his footsteps in the woods?"

"Wish it were that easy, see, them woods is dense, not a single flake landing in there, just like one big, thatched roof, unfortunately."

"So, nothing then?"

"Hell, dear, there's a good hundred-odd acres of dense wood out there. Police reckon he must have had a heart attack based on his medical records. See, Jack had a heart attack five years ago, angina. So, it makes sense, at least, that's what I believe happened. It helps me sleep. It does."

Laura reached across the table and took her hand. "But Mrs Monroe, I don't want to talk out of turn, but haven't you considered getting someone to find his body? I mean, wouldn't you like to bury him?" she quizzed.

"The police looked; the local Bobby in the next village rounded up some folk to help. They searched for hours and days, but nothing."

"What if I looked? I could go out after my chores each day, take a different path."

Mrs Monroe patted her hand. "Oh, bless you, dear, but I've come to terms with it now, he's where he enjoyed being, in them woods, that's his resting place. Gives me peace— it does. Looking out the kitchen window to them woods, I feel connected to him. Silly, I know, dear."

Laura rose from the table and filled the kettle. "Brew, Mrs Monroe?" she asked, dropping a scoop of tea leaves in the ornate China teapot.

"That be lovely, dear, you're such a caring child. Wish my Becky had half the heart you do, bless her. But she ain't built that way."

"And how did Becky take the news? It must have been hard on her."

"Truth be told, she wasn't that close to him, especially after he sent her to boarding school. Clashed on everything, they did. Jack said there were folk that could help her there, understand her sort. That girl doesn't get attached to anything unless it benefits her."

Laura served the tea. An ark of birds across the lake stole the mid-morning silence, reminding her of the peace that this place brought. She turned and glanced through the kitchen window. She couldn't imagine looking out towards the woods, knowing that someone she loved lay dead and undiscovered. Mrs Monroe was more flippant than she could ever be.

"Did Becky agree with your assumption that he just collapsed in the woods?"

"Truth is, thinking back, she didn't say much, fact, she spent a lot of time with that Molly and Greer. Maybe they helped her through it, and she didn't speak to me much, still doesn't really."

"Who's this Molly you mentioned last night?"

"Oh her, she's trouble, I reckon. Never seen such inappropriate behaviour from a young girl. Becky don't say much about her to me. Bad influence, if you ask me, surprised she wanted to go birdwatching with Jack, the last thing I thought a young girl would want to do, but he enjoyed her company, talk to anyone about nature, he would."

Laura frowned. "How old is she?"

"Not sure, similar age to Becky, I reckon."

"And she was interested in birdwatching?"

"Apparently, she just asked Jack out of the blue if she could tag along one morning." Mrs Monroe looked at the wall clock. "Best I get a move on."

"Of course, and I've got rooms to clean," she said, picking up the bucket.

MARCIA

CHAPTER FIVE

Alone with just her thoughts, Marcia stood in the steaming- hot shower. Her memory was dragged back to a time she'd long since buried. A past she had all but disassociated herself with, casting her previous life aside and emerging as a new soul. But this life was just a manifestation of old habits and wayward traits which she would always be chained to.

She hadn't uttered her birth name in over twenty years. She was Marcia now, or whatever her clients wanted to call her during her working hours.

She emerged from the bathroom in a cloud of steam and a white toweling robe to answer her mobile, which was vibrating its way across the coffee table.

"Hi, Lisa."

Marcia pinched her eyes, heavy in thought. "Yes, hi, Derrick," she replied, finally remembering.

"Can I pick you up at two?"

She'd forgotten about her appointment. And why didn't Derrick's name come up on her phone? Marcia had a list of regulars who were all in her phone by name. Her behaviour was matched to each client's needs. Derrick enjoyed the surrender of her authoritative voice. Others required a more meek approach. This time, she'd been sharp.

"Is everything okay, Lisa?"

"What number are you calling from? Your name usually comes up," she asked.

"Sorry, I've got a new number. Are we still on for later?" he asked, his voice full of excitement.

She paused, staring at the envelope on the coffee table.

"Derrick, can you do me a favour? Can you drop me somewhere? I need a lift to Noak Hill."

She'd never taken advantage of a client outside of the agreed period. Asking for favours only led to unhealthy working relationships. Quid pro quo. Owing favours was just the position she didn't want to find herself in. Playing to a client's desire would be an easy leap to make, an extra half hour, a discount there.

But this was just once. This was for something far more important to her than her rules. She didn't have a car. Like most Londoners, the need for one didn't arise often enough for it to be an economic and viable option.

She could take a cab. But somehow, the circumstances had fallen into place, and Derrick was a submissive and pliable man. He'd helped her in the past, and he was the only person she'd ever opened up to about money and investments.

Derrick stumbled over his words. "Oh, well, I guess that should be okay. Shall I pick you up outside Waterloo Station, as usual? Oh, and Lisa, can you wear the black figure-hugging outfit I gave you, please?"

Derrick's voice was an excitable mix of hopefulness and expectation.

Marcia slipped into her role. "Oh, Derrick, of course, if that's what you want. You know I'm always eager to please my Lord. I mean, being head servant, I find it such a privilege to serve you," she answered seductively.

Derrick cleared his throat. She could almost hear his juices flowing. He was one of her older clients, a financial advisor from the city; neat, tidy, and well-turned out. Behind closed doors, his desires took on something grittier, him playing the Lord of the manor and she the sexy servant; innocent, soft, and obedient.

"Perfect, my dear, see you at two p.m."

Marcia picked up the envelope again and took out the letter. *Fuck it.* She decided to call the number, despite the letter giving instructions to text. Her curiosity had been piqued, and with only three days to go before the weekend, time was not her friend.

Disappointment struck. Voice message only.

She typed *Yes*, but her finger hovered over the *Send* button. She read the letter again. Each time she did, she formed a different picture of how this might play out. She didn't like not knowing. It was out of her control. She despised the vulnerability of being denied control. But here she was. Hanging on a ledge. Then there was the name. A name that she'd carried through life with her and which, at some point, had buried itself deep inside her subconscious, only for it to
raise its ugly head again now.

Was this an opportunity or something else?

She got dressed, slipping into the sexy, black outfit Derrick had bought her. With makeup and nails done and her hair styled so her silky, flowing, blonde locks were falling over her face, she was ready.

Marcia's wardrobe was organised and categorised according to each client's preferred outfit or item of clothing, from leather-studded belts with silver chains to a more conservative look. Everything was labelled with each client's name, ready for her to slip into the role she was expected to play. Except for today! Her professional performance wasn't at the forefront of her mind.

She waited for Derrick in the usual spot outside Waterloo Station. Her long, flowing winter coat gave no signals of what lay beneath. The air was sharp, and the sky a deceptive blue for winter. It wasn't long before a white Porsche rolled up, and she stepped in before whisking her off to a five-star hotel.

A few hours later, Derrick pulled up to the kerb in his Porsche, and Marcia stepped out. He was keen to make some

future arrangements, but her swift exit left him high and dry, much to his displeasure. It wasn't something she usually did. Her typical routine of rounding up with lingering goodbyes and
setting up future appointments was cut short.

1996

CHAPTER SIX

The following day started very differently, this time with a spell of summer rain. Even the rain smelt different than it did in the city. It was sweeter here, and it felt purer, somehow. But it wasn't long before the rolling clouds made way for brighter skies. Laura set about taking the opportunity to get acquainted with Becky and Greer. She anticipated Becky being difficult, given what her mother had said. But if she was to spend any length of time here, then she needed to try.

Morning tea and toast came and went. A natter with Mrs Monroe and several chores later saw her making plans to visit the lake and some possible bonding. She filled a small flask of iced juice to use as a greeting gesture and headed down to the edge of the lake.

Greer was attending to a small wooden boat moored at the end of a boardwalk.

He was crouched inside the boat, head buried, fixing a loose oar. Laura's footsteps on the wooden boards briefly drew his attention before he returned to the job.

She stood at the end of the boards with the silver flask in her hand, squinting in the dazzling sun.

"Thought you might like some refreshments," she said, offering him the flask.

"I'm good, thanks. I'll wait until lunchtime." His eyes returned to the boat.

Laura sensed some awkwardness in his manner. She was used to awkward customers at the bar she worked at, but then she'd never tried to build any kind of relationship with them, except for Jonny Kirk, a regular who'd caught her eye on more than one occasion. He tipped well and would always wink at her with his left eye when she came to collect the money. He always wore the same dark suit and black open-necked shirt with a starched collar. The only meaningful conversation she'd ever had with him was over his black shoes, which looked like they'd been thrown under a bus. She'd constantly catch him dipping his serviette in his beer and then wiping the tops of them.

"You try keeping these creepers clean riding the tube at rush hour," he'd say.

Apart from an exchange of names, the conversation never progressed any further, much to her disappointment.

She wondered if Becky would be any less challenging than Greer.

"You busy?" she asked, standing awkwardly at the edge.

"Fixing the rowlock."

"Ah, okay." She pretended she knew what he meant. She looked up and watched the cormorants gliding gracefully just a few feet from the surface of the lake, like a squadron of bombers on a low-flying mission before they swooped up into the nearby trees.

"I bet you never get bored of this. I can't get over how peaceful it is here," she said, trying to break the ice. Greer stopped for a moment and acknowledged her.

"Yeah, can be peaceful, except in winter, then it becomes a different beast."

"Try living in the city, even just for a week. You'd soon come to appreciate a place like this."

"You can keep your city life, not for me, ta. Too many folks." He went back to fixing the ore lock.

"Mrs Monroe said you'd take me across the lake sometime." "Can do. I'm going tomorrow morning, fetch a sack of potatoes from Rawlings, twenty-minute row, lunch halfway. Be here about nine. You spoke to Becky yet?"

Laura grunted. "I'm not sure she sees my presence here as a good thing. I already feel like I'm stepping on her toes."

Greer climbed out of the boat and wiped his hands on his dungarees, then removed his cap and rearranged his hair.

"She don't get on with her mum. And her dad, well, he just carted her off to boarding school, hoping to fix all her problems, but that just made her worse. You being here, well, it just kind of told her that her mum don't want her help. So, yeah, she's a bit cranky, but she's company. Gets mardy a lot, but hey."

Laura nodded.

Greer checked his watch. "Tell you what, you wanna go now instead? I've fixed the oar lock, so be a good excuse to try it out. If it doesn't work, we'll be rowing in circles the rest of the day."

Laura grinned. "Okay, why not. I'm sure Mrs Monroe won't miss me for an hour."

He offered Laura his arm, and she took it, stepping into the boat, her balance not quite functioning as she would have liked. A sudden movement found her on all fours.

Greer laughed as she tried ungainly to compose herself. He untied the boat from the boardwalk and set off across the lake.

"Maybe I will take that drink."

Laura handed him the flask. She adjusted herself on the wooden seat, her hands gripping the edges of the boat tightly on each side.

"You look nervous," he said.

"Never been in a small boat. It just feels unstable."

He laughed.

"Only if you try and stand up."

Laura leaned back, letting the late morning sun pour over her. The calming sound of the disturbed water was mesmerising, and the gentle rocking of the boat was all too tranquil.

"So, what did you do in the city?" he asked, rowing at a gentle pace.

"I worked in a busy bar in the West End, just trying to earn some money to go travelling."

"You got any family?"

Laura was slightly annoyed at his questions. She wanted to savour the peace and quiet, but she knew it was a good opportunity to get to know him.

"It's just me. My mum's not around anymore, and my dad's in Australia on business. But we're quite close, me and my dad. You?"

"Same, I mean, only child. Grew up around here, Mum and Dad divorced, but I still see them occasionally."

"Do you live close by?"

"Rawlings wholesale. I rent out a room in his place. You'll meet him. Bit of a character, runs a farm across the lake. That's where Mrs Monroe gets all her veg. It's easier to get to by boat than drive, plus it keeps me fit."

"That's what Mrs Monroe said."

Laura allowed her hand to drag in the cool lake water. She closed her eyes again, taking in the choir of local birdlife. "I could stay out here forever." She sat up suddenly as if pricked by a question. "What's your take on Becky's friend Molly?"

"Why do you ask?"

"Just something Mrs Monroe said. I got the impression she didn't seem to think she was a good influence, that's all."

Greer huffed and stopped rowing for a second.

"Only met her a few times. Bit of a flirt. She and Becky got drunk once and took the boat out. They were gone a while. Mrs Monroe wasn't happy at all. She had to wait to have the groceries delivered by Rawlings."

"I hear she used to go birdwatching with Becky's dad. I can't imagine that being very exciting for her."

Greer removed his cap, messed with his hair, and then replaced it. "Jack was Becky's stepdad. Him going was a good thing for her." I don't know anything about Molly ever going birdwatching with him."

Laura noted his cold and dismissive response. "Jack's presumed dead, right? Surely that's not a good thing?"

Greer stopped rowing and cast his eyes across the lake.

"Look, things were complicated between them. Now he's not around, things are better for Becky. Just leave it at that, please." She noted the tension in his voice. She let the silence linger, then asked, "So, what happened to her real dad?"

"He left when she was like five or six. Look, best if you don't tell Becky I told you any of this. She don't like new folk knowing her business."

Laura nodded. "Of course. So, what's with Becky? Mrs Monroe seems to think she's got some problems, although that's not the word she used, but she implied it. I get the impression Mrs Monroe doesn't understand her daughter very well. I heard them arguing last night in the orangery."

"Why are you so interested in Becky?" His question was sharp.

Laura looked him straight in the eyes. "I'm here for the long haul. I'm just trying to get to know the people I'll be spending a lot of time with, that's all."

"There's always two sides to every story. Best you make your own mind up after you get to know her. Don't listen to everything her mother says. Yes, Becky can be a bit hot and cold; we get on well, though. Somehow, she finds it easier to talk to me. Her mother don't have much time for her. Her stepdad had even less."

He picked up the oars again. "So, what does your dad do? Sounds like he has a good job."

"Hotels. He refurbishes them. His old business partner has just moved to Australia, so he's over there, closing a big deal." Laura watched the signets tailing the white swan as

they moved in a regimental line across the lake. It was a golden moment.

Greer removed his cap and ruffled his hair again. He then got a small, white lunchbox out from under his seat, leaving the boat to drift.

"How long have you worked for Mrs Monroe as a gardener?"

Greer took a bite of his pork pie. "Couple years now, I only came to help Mr Monroe to cut the lawn one day. After that, he offered me a full-time job. Should have gone to college, really, but the opportunity seemed too good to turn down."

"Is this what you were looking at doing as a job?"

Geer offered her a piece of cheese from his lunch box, but she declined. "No, it wasn't. I wanted to be a writer. I like writing stories."

Laura raised her eyebrows. "Didn't see that coming."

He put down his lunchbox and turned his attention to the approaching mooring. "Grab the mooring rope, will you? It's under the seat."

Laura turned to see the wooden jetty approaching behind her. She passed him the rope, and he maneuvered the oars, turning the boat side-on before lassoing the rope around the wooden post.

An hour later, they returned from Rawlings with the supplies. Standing at the end of the boardwalk in a yellow floral dress and dark glasses was Becky, silhouetted against the midday sun. Arms folded, fingers drumming against her pale skin.

"I get the sense she's had her nose pushed out with me being here," whispered Laura.

Greer rolled his eyes. "She'll come round," he said in a tone that suggested he was trying to convince himself rather than her.

Laura put on a smile. "Hi, Becky. I'm glad you're here. I was hoping to see you."

Becky blanked her, resting her eyes on Greer. "You never said you were going across the lake."

"I asked him if he'd take me. I thought it would be good to get acquainted," Laura said, stepping out of the boat.

Becky turned to Laura, her eyes masked by her dark

lenses. "I think my mother would rather have you help her in the house than joyriding in the boat all day."

Greer ignored the hostility between them and focused his attention on tying up the boat.

"Look, I'm aware that I may not be welcome here, but your mother hired me to help. If you feel that I'm stepping out of line, then please talk to your mother. I'm not going to apologise for doing what I was asked to do. I'm sure you understand." Laura's voice crept up higher than she'd intended, but Becky's comment had tested her patience.

"I'd better fetch the wheelbarrow, carry the sacks up to the house," Greer said, scurrying off.

Becky turned and followed Greer. Laura was left wondering if there would ever be an opportunity to have a civilised conversation with her.

MARCIA

CHAPTER SEVEN

Marcia stood in front of the weathered, red front door housed between two shops on a less-than-busy road, a couple of streets back from the high street. The fragrant smell of blossom and other strong scents she couldn't quite place wafted out from the small hair salon to her right. The large window offered little in terms of privacy, but the two young girls mid-cut seemed at ease with being on display for passers- by.

She pulled a slip of paper from her coat pocket and double- checked the address. A small, tarnished brass plaque on the door indicated the name she was looking for, "Bernie Goodman PI."

How very American.

The crisp January air was cold enough to expose Marcia's breath, spurring her to draw her long, black coat around herself before pressing the bell.

A large, middle-aged woman weighed down by two large shopping bags in a black puffer coat that was much too large for her stopped behind her.

"He won't come down. You know, love, I'd go on up if I were you. It's open. I reckon he'll have a heart attack knowing he might actually have some work." She grinned, revealing a black tooth.

The woman placed the heavy bags at her feet, taking some

time to catch her breath. Her round face was made more obvious by her dyed blonde hair, which was pulled tight into a bun.

"You know him?" Marcia asked.

"I should hope so. He's my brother."

Marcia held the women's gaze, expecting her to elaborate, but the awkward silence only prompted her to speak first.

"Is he still taking jobs, do you know? You implied that he's not busy."

The woman stepped closer to her, allowing a passing family with a pushchair to squeeze by on the narrow pavement.

"You do know he's not your typical investigator, right?"

"Meaning?" Marcia asked curiously.

"He doesn't always follow the rules. That's why the idiot's got no work. The ABI shut him down once. They're the people who check he's acting professionally. Oh, but look at me, daft sod, trying to talk you out of giving him work." She smiled and arched her back to alleviate her pain.

"Maybe that's why I want to hire him."

The woman raised her eyebrows, accompanied by another smile.

"Oh, well, you'll make his day then. I say you're not a reporter, are you, or from the ABI?" she asked, looking Marcia up and down, her attention resting on her well-manicured red nails and matching shoes that were so glossy you could catch your reflection in them.

"I can assure you I'm not."

The woman pulled out a small mobile and fumbled with the keypad, texting, "Bernie, you got a customer waiting down here."

"Thanks, I'm Marcia, by the way."

"Janice," said the woman, meeting her with a hand full of gold rings. "So, what line of work are you in then?"

"You could say I'm in the entertainment business," Marcia replied coyly, slightly side-tracked by a woman exiting the launderette to the left of the red door with two young kids in tow. One was clearly throwing a tantrum about something, his legs barely able to keep up with his mother's large steps and fast pace.

Janice looked up at Bernie's office above the shops before meeting Marcia's expectant expression.

"Anyways, he's waiting for you now." Janice picked up her shopping bags before smiling and nodding goodbye.

Marcia entered the building to a narrow, wooden staircase that appeared to ascend beyond the height of the building. Once at the top, she was greeted by a well-rounded, middle-aged man in his fifties. He had a welcoming face with a horseshoe-shaped ring of hair and sporting a dark blue suit which clearly hadn't seen the inside of dry cleaners for some time. Not the kind of suit she was used to seeing.

He extended his hand to hers. "Please, sit down," he said, gesturing as he lifted a pile of paperwork off a rickety wooden chair and dusted it down with his hand.

She glanced around the office; it was cluttered up with old cardboard boxes stuffed with paperwork on metal Meccano-style shelving from floor to ceiling. This wasn't what she'd imagined when Philip recommended him. Maybe she should have paid more attention to the phrase "old school." But still, she was here now.

The room was long and narrow, almost like a carriage on a train, but with fewer windows, allowing a limited view of the street below. The single flickering strip of light down the middle was feeble. It failed to cast any light to the far end of the room. The back walls were strewn with pinboards, each containing a collage of newspaper clippings about various missing people and even a few photos of owners' beloved dogs. *A pet detective as well, maybe,* Marcia thought. But he was no Jim Carrey in the looks department. A middle-aged barrel of a man with slitty eyes and half-rim glasses. His unkempt blue suit evidenced a struggle with an unhealthy diet. To the point that the middle button would have popped off at any time, had it been fastened.

Marcia sat on the slim, padded wooden chair, very aware

that his eyes were drawn to her curvaceous figure. Something she was very much used to in her profession.

Bernie sat forward in a high-back leather chair, making some last-minute room on his desk. It was clear that he wasn't an organised man.

"Well, I've been here nearly twenty years, lady," he started, "And I think you're probably the most attractive client I've ever had in here. Sorry if that makes me seem a little forthcoming, but I tend to say what I think and observe."

"Well, Mr Goodman, first off, I'm not your client yet, and secondly, please don't call me 'lady.' Marcia will do," she replied, crossing her long legs.

Bernie smiled. "So how can I help you then, Marcia?"

She handed him a brown A4 envelope. "I need you to find out about the name on the letter and trace the number if you can."

Bernie sat up and pulled the letter out, taking a moment or two to digest it. He swung from side to side, his tired leather chair creaking loudly. He tapped his lips.

"You want me to find this, Dr Arthur Toe, is that correct?" he asked, peering over his glasses.

"If you can. And the venue, anything that may help."

Bernie rubbed his double chin. "Hmm, I can certainly make some enquiries. I'm sure a well-to-do person such as him will have what we call in the business a blazing trail and should be simple to track down. Not sure about the venue; with no address, it's a dead end. Seems rather an odd invitation, don't you think? And a very handsome reward to boot. Can I assume this name throws up some concerns for you? And I'm guessing the very cloak-and-dagger circumstances surrounding this make you feel cautious?"

"I'm always a cautious person, Mr Goodman, but I have my reasons to be overcautious this time."

"You've certainly got my attention, and I'm intrigued to know more. But before I get into that, I need to get the ugly business of money out of the way, you understand."

"Which is?" Marcia asked.

Bernie stood up from his desk and reached for the coffee pot, which by the smell of it, had been stewing all day. "Coffee?"

"No thanks."

"My standard fee is two hundred a day plus expenses, which I have to point out can be significant depending on travel and whatever third-party resources I need to bring in."

Bernie placed his coffee-stained mug on the desk, which just added to the collection of numerous other coffee-stained rings already there. He pulled a magnifying glass out from the desk drawer and studied the letter more intensely, giving Marcia time to consider his offer.

"Interesting."

"What is? It's just a letter," she said.

"That's where you're wrong. You see, it's not the usual white 80gsm printer paper. No. This is more your exquisite variety, much like a politician or a lawyer would use. I mean, goodness, with what they charge, I'd expect it to be of a decent quality."

Bernie swung in his chair. This time more swiftly. "Dr Arthur Toe. Dr Arthur Toe." He repeated the name to himself several times, almost chanting it, prompting Marcia to give him strange looks.

Philip wasn't wrong. He is odd.

She pulled a wad of fresh notes from her Prada bag and threw them on the desk. "There's two thousand there. Is that enough to get started with?"

Bernie's eyes nearly leapt out of their sockets, and he stumbled over his words. "That's, well, very generous and unexpected, but thank you," he replied, sliding the money into the drawer. "Receipt?" he asked.

"Do I need one?"

Bernie smiled and raised his greying eyebrows. "Unless you're going to submit it to the tax man, then no."

"I'm happy to deal in cash," Marcia replied. She'd lost count of how much tax she'd avoided in her line of work.

Bernie pulled out a writing pad from the same drawer and

started scrawling.

"Mind if I ask a few questions to help get a perspective of what I'm looking for?" he said, taking a sip of coffee.

"Fire away."

"So, how did you come to be in possession of this letter? I ask because I can't see a postmark, so I can only assume it was hand-delivered, and if so, then I'm guessing while you were out. Otherwise, we wouldn't be having this conversation, would we?"

"Very good, Mr Goodman. I was handed it by a woman when I was on the way back home from a bar. She implied that she knew who I was, despite the fact I'd never seen her before, although it was dark, and she was hidden by a large parka coat. She dashed off before I had time to even comprehend what had happened."

"And that's it, she just vanished?"

"Pretty much, I'm afraid. Look, I've got no idea who she was, but you need to know something, something about me that might put a spin on this. We're going to arrive at this shortly anyway, so let's just get it out of the way."

Marcia leaned forward, smoothed her long blonde hair, and played with her rings, turning them like worry beads.

Bernie clicked the silver pen. "I'm all ears."

There was a momentary silence that Bernie had experienced before with clients, knowing they had to open up about their most intimate lives. The more information he had, the better chance he had of understanding them and assisting in reuniting them with their loved ones.

"I was pretty much abandoned as a baby, so I don't have any family. I was told my mother killed herself shortly after I was born in 1980. The midwife apparently found me screaming in my cot on a routine house visit. She told the police that the front door was left open, and a suicide note was found on my mother's dressing table. I bounced from foster home to foster home, had a spell in a secure detention centre until my home became the streets."

"Chanel, I believe."

"Sorry?"

"Your perfume, it's Chanel, I believe. Just an observation. Carry on."

Philip, who have you sent me to?

Bernie fell back into his tired leather chair, locking his hands behind his head.

"The name on the letter, I've heard it before when I was in the young offenders' centre for three weeks, back in late '96. I had a visit from someone, a man, not sure how old, twenties, maybe. Anyway, I can't remember who he was or what he was. You have to understand that I was mixed up back then. I was a different person. But I do remember what he said before he left. He handed me a piece of paper with the name Dr Arthur Toe on it and told me to remember it, and one day I'd hear that name again. And that was it until last night. So, there it is. I have to know what I'm getting myself into if I go there. Does that help?"

"I'm sorry. It sounds like you've had a tough time, and please don't take this the wrong way, but looking at you now, you seem like you've done okay for yourself, turned your life around. Just an observation, Marcia, that's all," he replied, holding up his hands.

Bernie scribbled some more notes, slurped some more coffee, and sat back in his chair again.

"I've got a few questions; I hope they're not too intrusive, but it's important that I build a picture."

Marcia nodded.

"Well, I've got a list of questions we need to work through, but I think the obvious question I need to ask first is, did the police look into your mother's suicide? I'll need her name and any other bits of information you've got relating to her because if there was an investigation, then I can get a copy of it. That'll give me a location to narrow things down. It may even throw up some names and addresses. Secondly, do you know your father's name or anything else? I believe this name you were given could be someone from your past. A family member or someone with connections to you. What

I haven't figured out just yet is why the cloak-and-dagger drama and the very specific way they handed you the name. It was done very purposely. It's significant. Something for me to ponder over later."

"I've got no idea. I don't know my father; All I've got is what my social worker at the time told me. But I was a rebellious teenager who hated anyone in authority, so I never paid much attention. Graham Best, if you're after a name. North Central London social services. Used to visit me in the Feltham detention centre. He'll be retired now."

"Well, that's a good start. I'll also look into this murder mystery weekend, narrow it down, and find out how many hotels or venues are hosting one this weekend."

Bernie sat forward and removed his glasses, pinching the bridge of his nose. "If this isn't a relative, do you have any idea who it could be?"

"I guess that's why I'm paying you, Mr Goodman."

Bernie smiled and stood up from his desk. "Touché. One other question, did you try calling the number in the letter?"

"I did, yes, but it just went to voicemail."

"Okay, Marcia, I appreciate you being so forthcoming. Leave it with me, and I'll make some preliminary enquiries. And one more thing, the cheque you were given. Cash it for me today if possible. It might give me a lead."

"Oh, I intend to," she said, smiling.

Bernie extended a hand. "I'm pretty confident I can have this wrapped up in forty-eight hours."

Marcia smiled. "Thank you, Mr Goodman. I look forward to hearing from you."

"You will, Mrs …?"

Marcia handed him a card. "It's Miss. You can contact me on this number."

Bernie flicked the card over and then back again. "Marcia Cole and a number. Hmm. Usually, business cards list the business. I'm just curious."

"I'm a high-class escort, Mr Goodman. Not something you want printed," she smiled.

Again, he stumbled over his words. "Err, no. No, I suppose not," he replied, looking slightly awkward.

"Don't be embarrassed. I'm not. We both offer a service. Keep me posted on what you find."

1996

CHAPTER EIGHT

Laura returned to find Mrs Monroe at the side of the house, standing under an arched pagoda of fully-blossomed purple wisteria, hauling a large wicker basket of laundry. The pagoda framed a black, rusted wrought iron gate which led to a small wire-fenced vegetable garden.

Mrs Monroe's stroppy teenage daughter emerged, complete with a blank expression and a bottle of Sunny D in her hand. Laura hadn't noticed earlier by the lake that Becky was wearing an oddly matched pair of Dr Martens, one in a peculiar shade of cherry red, the other black. Laura had never been in any "phase" in her teenage years, but given Becky's attitude, it was obvious that she was most definitely in the rebellious phase.

Laura seized another opportunity to break the ice with Becky. She'd just ignored her previous attempt. She'd said her piece. Made a stand. With her mother present, maybe Becky would keep her attitude in check. Laura was the adult here.

She nodded to Becky. "Sorry about earlier. I'm not here to interfere with your or Greer's routine. I'm just trying to help your mother, and, of course, I want to take advantage of these gorgeous surroundings. I'm happy to leave the lake journeys to you in the future if you like." She smiled through gritted teeth.

Becky shrugged. "Yeah, whatever."

"What's with you now, Becky dear? Come on, we talked about this when …"

Her daughter jumped in. "No, *you* talked about it. In fact, you just decided, like you always decide, what's best for me, like interfering at my school, and then Jack carting me off to some boarding school because I wasn't your perfect little angel."

Becky stormed off, leaving Laura to fill an awkward silence with Mrs Monroe. Sympathising appeared to be the best solution.

"I was a stroppy teenager once. My father cursed me so many times. I guess she's just adjusting to me being here. It's going to take a little time, I think." Laura was lying, of course. But her opinion about Mrs Monroe's daughter wasn't something she felt she could share at this time.

Mrs Monroe perched her hands on her hips, shaking her head. "Pretty sure that outburst was for your benefit, likes to stick the knife in, does that girl. She don't know she's born. I'm taking it you two had some words to say. I'm sure she'll come round to you. Like I said, peculiar girl when it comes to new folk."

"I'm sorry if she embarrassed you," Laura said.

Mrs Monroe changed the subject quickly. "Be a dear and hang this out for me."

Laura picked up the basket and felt its weight pulling at her slender arms. She still had more questions. She had a thousand questions. Some were around the relationship between Becky and Greer, judging by the response to Laura's trip with him.

She placed the basket down on the grass and set about pegging out the clothes.

"Do you have much to do with Greer?" she quizzed.

"How'd you mean, dear?"

"I mean, how often does he work for you? Is it just in the summer or …"

"Don't really keep tabs, be honest. It was my Jack that sorted the arrangement out. He just sees what needs sorting and gets on with it. Got amazing green fingers, that lad. Keeps this place looking proper nice, he does."

Laura worked her way through the laundry and fired out more questions.

"Does Becky not pitch in at all?" she asked, hoping to explore a conversation she had in her head while trying not to come across as judgemental. But that was precisely what she was doing. *Why is your daughter such a moody, rude, and cantankerous bitch?* That's what she wanted to ask. Mrs Monroe seemed like a woman who appeared to be completely oblivious to her daughter's social failings. That became obvious in the first conversation they had about her.

Mrs Monroe tutted and pointed to the small vegetable patch to the right. "What in God's name?" She knelt ungainly in front of a small patch of cabbages. "Must be those darn foxes. I mean, look at the state of the soil. Looks like a stampede's been through, it does."

"I can sort that for you if you like," said Laura, offering her an arm.

Mrs Monroe's agility was laboured. Laura almost felt sorry for her. She guessed this over-proportioned woman couldn't be older than her late forties, but she looked far older.

"Thought this garden was fox-proof. Had chickens in here last year, I did. Not one got in so much as a fight. State of those cabbages." Mrs Monroe perched her hands on her hips again. "Oh well."

Laura jumped in. "Like I said, I can sort it for you. I mean, I'm not a gardener, but I can level out the soil if you like. I'm here now. Maybe there's a trowel in the shed." Laura felt sorry for her. Besides, being outside was much more pleasant. It was all a new experience for her. It was bliss.

"That be kind, dear, bothers me, it does. Greer usually tends to all this; he'd be livid if he knew what the foxes had done. Ruined me cabbages, I reckon."

Laura might not have been clued up about wildlife in the countryside, but she was sure that foxes had no interest in cabbages.

Mrs Monroe waddled off to the house, leaving Laura to sift through the weathered shed for gardening tools. She found a trowel, some gloves, and a kneeling pad, so began to repair the mess and replant the cabbages squarely. But as she started to dig, she struck a solid obstacle. *A stone?* she thought. Maybe.

The more she dug, the more resistance she met. She widened her dig area, displacing more soil. A few moments later, she found herself staring at a round, metal biscuit tin. By the lack of rust, it couldn't have been too old.

Laura pulled the tin from the ground and brushed off the damp soil. Something inside rattled. She prised open the lid. Inside was a small, square, silver digital camera. She pressed the power button. It was dead.

Laura's head was suddenly clouded by confusion. Her first thought echoed back to a conversation she'd had the day before with Mrs Monroe, and more specifically, the story about Becky's stepfather birdwatching in the woods. *Was this the camera he used to shoot birds with? And if so, why is it buried in the garden?*

She knelt over the hole she'd dug, silenced by her thoughts. She weighed up her options. Keep the camera, find some batteries, view the contents. Or put it back. The power of her curiosity was too strong. She pocketed the camera, reburied the biscuit tin, made good the soil on top, and hurried back to her room.

She placed the camera under her pillow and rooted through her belongings for batteries. But she found none.

MARCIA

CHAPTER NINE

Marcia left Bernie's office full of confidence and a sense that the enigma would be solved before the weekend. Bernie might have been just as Philip described, but he seemed to make a lot of sense. She hailed a cab back to town, cashed the cheque, and returned to her apartment, this time feeling some sense of control returning.

Despite the mid-afternoon hour, Marcia poured herself the remainder of the wine from earlier and stood gazing out from one of the tall windows. The clouds were low and moody.

She grabbed her mobile from her bag and texted "Yes" to the number on the letter. This time, she didn't hesitate or allow any thoughts to cloud her actions.

The moving scenery calmed her mind. She found the view from her apartment to be a therapeutic one, much like the fascination of staring at fish in a tank. She took the same approach by observing the world from five storey's up—an ever-changing picture of human behaviour.

But her attention was drawn to the silver Rolls Royce parked at the end of the street. Like the one, she saw the other night. She was familiar with all the cars in her street. Each car was allocated its own parking permit and was paired with the apartments on her street. She pressed her hands against the glass, peering below. A single occupant in dark clothes was sitting in the driver's seat.

She raised her phone and took a photo. Maybe it was just an innocent car, albeit rather lavish for this street. Despite the newly converted industrial buildings and middle-class wealth, it stood out all the same.

Maybe a visitor to someone in the apartments?

She picked up her phone again. This time she called Philip. "You busy?" she asked.

"I am at the moment. Why?"

"Just thinking about earlier. I was stressed and I snapped at you. I just want to apologise and maybe you can come over, and I can finish what I wanted to start." She could hear voices and phones ringing in the background.

"Did you speak to Bernie?" he asked, his voice louder this time.

"Yes, I went to see him. He thinks he can have it all sewn up in a couple of days."

"That's good news. How about after work? I'm knocking off in a couple of hours, I'll pick up a bottle of red, how's that sound?"

"Sounds good, but you're on the clock," she added.

"Okay, guess that's fine, see you later."

She sensed a wave of disappointment in his voice. She was aware that it sounded like a date. The very thing she avoided in her work. Attachments and feelings were the complications she didn't want clouding her job. Attachments were a sign of weakness, like one big patch of quicksand, drawing you in more each time you struggle until you reach the point of no return, and before you know it, you're influenced by emotions and attachments: guiding, shaping, and inevitably becoming a prisoner of them.

Philip was a good man. He was a handsome and thoughtful client. But that was all he was—all she'd allow him to be. She'd already broken one of her rules; allowing clients into her apartment. But seeing as she'd already let him into her private world, she saw no harm in a second time.

She ran a bath with juniper and coconut salts and set

about unwinding with the rest of her wine until Philip arrived.

It wasn't long before her buzzer sounded, and she pulled herself out from the comforting bath, wrapped herself in a towelling robe and buzzed him up.

"Wait in the lounge, I'll be out soon," she said.

She would make him wait… wait until she was ready to slip into her role, in just the right outfit. Red, lacy, and see-through. He liked her blonde, so she slipped on her blonde wig and arranged the flowing locks before slipping on her six-inch black stilettos. With just the right amount of rouge and smoky eyes, she greeted him at the bedroom door, posing seductively and beckoning him in with a wink and a pout.

Philip placed the bottle on the kitchen countertop, removed his jacket and orange tie, and entered her bedroom full of promise.

Early evening came and the outside world had slowed to a changing picture of lights and neon. Even the heavens were a backdrop of passing planes, with red flashing lights crossing the sky.

Philip stood at the window. "Looks even more beautiful lit up; I'd never get bored of that view. Just a shame it's tainted by all the scum that live in it. Sometimes I wonder if we ever make any progress, it's almost like we're just treading water. But hey, someone's got to do it," he said.

Marcia stood next to him. "If you think about it, you're a hypocrite. On that basis, I'm a criminal, and if you want to use the ugly word I hate, 'prostitute', then you are, aren't you?"

"You're right. It is an ugly word, but one where you offer a service, much like anything else in life—the oldest profession in the world. Personally, I see no harm in it. We tend not to criminalise 'working girls'," he said, gesturing with his fingers. "In fact, they help us a lot. Eyes on the street. We leave them alone, they help us to see things, and some even work with us. And before you say anything else, your clients aren't the usual lowlifes."

Marcia squared her shoulders and turned to him, his eyes

still drawn to the flickering lights of the city. "No, my kind of criminals are more sophisticated. Trust me, I could tell you some stories. I don't question how they make their money, but I know some are very much criminals."

Philip nodded. "I imagine you hold some important missing pieces we'd love to get our hands on. But don't worry, I wouldn't ask you to do that."

"Good, because there's no way I would."

Marcia picked up the bottle of wine from the kitchen and held it out to Philip. "Maybe next time we'll get to drink it," she said as he slipped on his jacket.

Philip took the bottle. "Kicking me out already," he said, laughing.

"When your time's up, your time's up," she said, opening the door.

Philip stood in the doorway hesitantly for a moment. "I was thinking …"

"Whatever you're about to say, save it until next time."

She paused for a second. "Actually, Philip, can you trace a number plate for me?"

Philip leaned on the doorframe and dropped his head. "Marcia, you know the answer to that. You know I can't, not without good reason. Look, maybe Bernie can. I'm not even going to ask why. Goodnight, Marcia."

"Goodnight."

She closed the door behind him.

1996

CHAPTER TEN

The following week progressed as normal. Laura settled into a routine of chores, with afternoon tea still being very much part of that. Despite her urge to chisel away at Mrs Monroe and, most intriguingly, the history surrounding her daughter, she resisted for now.

Her desire to find out what was on the camera occupied her mind. The opportunity to cross the lake to the local shop for batteries now became her main focus.

The afternoon sun made an occasional appearance through small patches in the steel-grey clouds. It wasn't strong, but it charged the air and made it mildly pleasant for late afternoon. Laura learned that her chosen outfit, jeans and a t-shirt, wasn't a sensible choice, given the summer heat, so she changed into her cream shorts and a white vest.

Mrs Monroe had discharged Laura for the day and given her the afternoon off. So, she focused on taking the opportunity to cross the lake. Greer had mentioned earlier in the day that he and Becky had planned to have a picnic at their favourite spot. Laura gathered an assortment of snacks – jam sandwiches, fresh fruit, and a bottle of cherryade. She borrowed a wicker picnic basket and an old blue and red tartan blanket. She hoped Greer would take her across the lake. She was desperate for the batteries. Her curiosity had been lingering for far too long.

She set off. The long grass struck her open sandals and felt like a million paper cuts on her feet. When she arrived at the lake, Becky was standing over Greer by the water's edge, holding a large, black plastic bag.

Becky turned to her with her dark-framed sunglasses. Much to Laura's surprise, she removed them and gave her an unexpected smile. If Laura didn't know any better, she'd assume Becky was directing her unusually pleasant demeanour towards someone behind her. She even considered turning around to check but settled on the moment being very much in her favour.

"I brought some food and cherryade," she said, holding up the wicker basket.

Greer held up the black plastic bag. "I've got something better."

He stood in the boat with his brown dungarees dropped to his waist, sporting a Jaws t-shirt.

"Reckon, there's any of those in the lake?" Laura laughed, pointing at his t-shirt.

"Who knows?" he shrugged.

Laura watched him tie some orange baler twine around the neck of the plastic bag. He then tied the other end around one of the rowlocks and dropped the bag into the water. "Keep the beer nice and cold," he said, winking.

Laura nodded. "Nice one."

Becky pulled out a bottle of gin from a hessian shoulder bag. "The old bag won't miss this," she said, punching the air with it.

Laura was nervous. Alcohol was her kryptonite. She'd witnessed the mess it made of her mother. She'd been around drunks in her job. Now she was around it again. But if she wanted to build any kind of friendship with them, then this was her chance. So, for now, she took the situation as a win.

Becky stepped into the boat and patted the wooden seat next to her, "Come on, girl, let's party."

This wasn't what Laura had in mind. A quiet trip to the village across the lake for batteries was looking like a mission failure. Still, she decided that this could be a golden opportunity to build a rapport with Becky.

Laura removed her white sandals before stepping in and fell onto the seat next to Becky.

"Officer on deck. Isn't that what they say?" humoured Becky as Greer took the oars.

Greer smiled as he pushed off from the boardwalk, rowing with his back to the sun, which had now made another appearance from the clouds.

Laura lay back, her eyes closed, facing up to the sky. A sudden breeze blew over the lake. She listened to the sound of the mallards close by, quacking their displeasure as Greer crossed their path.

"I see why you come out here, Becky," Laura said, her eyes still closed tightly against the bright sky.

"We have a laugh, don't we, Greer?"

Laura opened her eyes and looked over at Becky, necking a mouthful of gin. Becky offered her the bottle. "Gin?"

"Thanks, but no thanks. Not my tipple."

"Of course, you like cherryade," Becky said in a condescending tone.

Greer stopped rowing for a second. He removed his cap, ruffled his hair, and replaced it. "Come on, Becky! Play nice."

"What? I ain't done nothing. Besides, there's more for me now." She took another gulp.

"Where are we going anyway, Greer?" asked Laura, ignoring Becky's behaviour.

"Just further across the lake. There's a decent spot around this corner, and it's shaded by the trees."

"Not the village, then?"

"Not today. Why?"

"No reason," Laura said, disappointed.

She watched him pull up his t-shirt and wipe his blotchy, red face. She smiled at the contrast between his tanned arms and white belly.

Becky was quiet. At least for now, lying back across the

seat with the bottle of gin cradled in her arms like a baby.

Laura dragged her hand in the water like she did the other day. Her mind wandered off.

Greer steered the boat around the corner of a small headland and turned to get his bearings. He spotted someone on the bank, lying down. "Look out, looks like someone's got me spot on the bank."

Becky sat up and removed her sunglasses. "Fuck's sake."

"Isn't this a public lake?" Laura asked.

"Well, yeah, but it's a bitch to get to sometimes. The local sailing club uses it, a few canoes, but ain't too many tourists. Besides, you can only get to that part across the barley fields or by boat, like us."

Becky pointed to the figure on the bank. "Looks like a girl. I can see her tits sticking up."

Laura tutted but couldn't help a smile creeping in. The more time she spent in Becky's company, the more she understood what Mrs Monroe meant about her moods. The other day Becky seemed like the devil incarnate; now she was playing the joker. The girl had issues. But it was the buried camera that still concerned Laura the most.

Greer allowed the boat to drift towards the bank. A row of tall grass fenced the small cove. He navigated the boat, standing in the centre, and used the oar to move the boat like it was a gondola.

Becky whistled at the girl lying on the bank in bleached, frayed denim shorts and an orange crop top. "Hey, it's Molly," she shouted.

Molly sat up and watched as Greer beached the boat on a shallow mudbank.

"Hiya," said Greer.

Laura stood up, feeling the cramp take hold in her legs and stepped onto the soft banking. Within seconds, her feet were submerged in the mudbank. She cursed.

Greer laughed and noticed Molly sniggering at their inept attempts to disembark. Becky was clearly at the mercy of the gin as she stumbled from the boat, falling face down on the grass and dropping the bottle into the edge of the lake. Molly leapt to the bank, plunging her arm into the water and retrieving the bottle.

"Don't lose that, girl."

"Hi Molly, didn't expect to see you here," Greer said, dragging the boat onto the bank and gasping.

"All right, handsome?"

Laura pulled her feet from the soft mud and washed them in the water, thankful she'd removed her white sandals earlier.

Becky tried to brush off the grass stains from her dress and snatched the bottle from Molly.

"All right, girl, and you're welcome, by the way—for me saving your drink."

Becky tutted, more concerned with her grass-stained dress.

"Your mum might think you've been shagging in the grass with Greer," Molly joked.

Greer shook his head. "Very funny, Molly."

"Who's the new recruit?" Molly asked.

Becky took a swig and passed the bottle to Molly. "Laura. Apparently, the old bag needs a servant."

Laura felt awkward. "Hi Molly," she said, raising her hand.

Greer pulled out the plastic bag he'd hung from the oar lock and tore it open. "I brought beer. Anyone for a can?" he asked, cracking open the ring pull.

Laura retrieved the basket from the boat and pulled out a jam sandwich. "Food anyone?"

Molly peeked into the basket. "I'll take the crisps."

"Drink?" asked Molly, offering up the bottle to Laura.

"She don't drink," snapped Becky, lying back on the grass bank.

"What the hell!" Laura took the bottle, filling her mouth with the awful taste and swallowing quickly, hoping the afterburn would be relatively mild. She figured if she wanted to be part of whatever this was, she'd need to loosen up. She was wrong; it made her cough harder than a forty-a-day smoker until her eyes swelled with tears.

Simultaneous laughter followed.

"Respect girl," Molly said, holding her hand out for an air slap. But Laura was too busy trying to catch her breath.

"Have a beer instead," offered Greer.

Laura decided if she wanted to save face and keep her lungs from exploding, then beer would be the safe bet. "Thanks," she said, reluctantly taking a can from him.

It wasn't long before the intermittent afternoon sun and copious amounts of alcohol had lured them into a tranquil state. Space and time became a blur and conversation soon turned to whimsical dreams and carefree talk.

Greer lay on his back, chewing a grass stem. "I think I want to be a writer one day, something like that. Horror, I think. Scary stories."

"Shut up, you big gay," said Molly.

"I used to write short stories, you know. At school. Didn't much bother with other subjects, but I loved English," said Greer.

"I'd like to teach. I like being bossy, no good at being told what to do but doing the telling, that would be cool," said Becky.

Laura gazed up at the clouds, trying to associate a cloud with an animal, pointing to the sky. She felt the inner child in her escape for a moment. "That one looks a bit like an elephant, don't you think?"

"What do you want to do Laura, apart from running around all day for Becky's mum?" giggled Molly.

Laura ignored her comment. "I want to travel the world; experience new things, see new places. The world's too big just to stay in one place."

"Well, that's not a job, unless you're going to be a trolly dolly on an aeroplane."

"You mean a stewardess."

"That's what I said."

Laura ignored the urge to argue with her. "What about you then, Molly?" she asked, turning to her through the long grass

"Fuck knows, look out for number one. No fucker else

will, it's the way of the world. Haven't figured out what I want to do yet."

"Molly's going to shag her way through life, ain't that right?" laughed Becky.

"Fuck you, Becky."

"Do you live far from here?" asked Laura, trying to redirect the conversation to something resembling a half-intelligent exchange.

"Does it matter?"

"Just making conversation, that's all."

There was a short silence before Molly replied. Molly tore up a handful of grass and twisted it around in her fingers. "I live where my social worker decides. He's a dick. Thinks he knows what's best for me, but he don't know shit. That's when he can be bothered to come and see me."

"You live in a foster home, then?" Laura asked.

"She lives with the other misfits, don't you, Molly?" Spouted Becky.

"Fuck off, Becky."

"Ignore her. I live in a residential home, and yes, there are two others there. Jacob, he's all right, buys me alcohol. He's only sixteen but looks older."

"In exchange for a blowjob," joked Becky.

Greer turned to Becky. "That's a bit harsh," he said, laughing as he cracked open another ring pull.

"I might just sleep here tonight, can't be arsed to go back," yawned Molly.

Becky sat up quickly. "Come back to mine. The old bag will be in bed by nine. Laura won't mind, will you?"

Laura felt pressure to agree. "Okay, yeah, why not."

"Cheers girl," said Molly, smiling.

This wasn't Laura's scene. Drinking neat gin from a bottle was something she'd never usually entertain. Her dad would be mortified. She was mortified. But here she was, stuck between fitting in, but staying far enough away from their devious behaviours. Getting close enough to understand them, but far enough away to stay safe. She was learning all about Becky's behaviour. Mrs Monroe's observations about her friend Molly were spot on. Another damaged girl. Certainly not a good influence on an already-angered teen. All this, and it was only week two.

What about the camera? Who buried it? Why bury it? These and a million other questions continued to float around Laura's head.

MARCIA

CHAPTER ELEVEN

Marcia woke to a buzzing, faint at first, but it became louder as she withdrew from her slumber. She hurried to her intercom, her eyes still heavy and foggy, slipping on her pink satin robe on the way.

The small black and white screen showed a courier, and she buzzed him up.

A young, skinny lad in dark trousers and a yellow shirt with shifty eyes handed her a small envelope.

Marcia took the envelope hesitantly while the young lad's hypnotic gaze lay on her thinly veiled breasts. Marcia's usual attire for visitors was a thick, white towelling robe, but in her quickness to answer the door, she'd grabbed the most convenient one, left from her night with Philip.

"You're not my usual postman or courier," she said, noting the absence of any badge or emblem.

The young lad blushed as his eyes engaged with hers, standing awkwardly, with his spotty face seeping. "Oh, I'm not, Madam, I was …" He shifted from foot to foot and wrenched up his baggy trousers. "I mean, I was just told to give you this. Thanks, bye."

The young lad turned and descended the stairs two at a time.

Marcia dashed to the window, parting her blinds, and saw him emerge onto the street below. She followed his movements as he jogged to the end of the street, stopping to pull up his trousers again. She watched a silver Rolls Royce nudge into view. Her skin pricked. The young lad became obscured by a parked car. But a subtle movement in the reflection of the Rolls left no doubt that there was a connection.

She pulled away from the window and stared at the white envelope in her hand. She poured a glass of orange juice from the fridge, gulping it to wake up her sour mouth before tearing the envelope open.

She took out a printed card with gold lettering.

Thank you for accepting the invitation via text.
Dr Arthur Toe requests the pleasure of your company for a weekend of fun and games.
A chauffeur will pick you up on Saturday, 21st January at 3p.m. and will drive you to my residence for an 8 p.m. evening meal.
As previously mentioned, you will be handsomely compensated.
I look forward to meeting you, for what promises to be an unforgettable evening.

Marcia dropped the card on the worktop and hurried to her bedroom. She grabbed her phone from the white bedside table and dialed Philip as she paced the room.

"It's me," she said before he even had the chance to real off his title of Detective Inspector Morgan.

"Marcia?"

"I need you to do something for me. I've had another card and …"

"Slow down. Look, I'm in the middle of something right now. Why don't I drop round in a bit? I'll be free in, say, an hour. We can chat then."

"Thanks. I'll see you in an hour."

Marcia dropped the phone on her bed and turned on the shower. She stood in front of the tall mirror, gripping the sink and staring at her reflection before watching it fade away in a cloud of steam.

Her mind was a merry-go-round of dead-end questions and nervous uncertainty. Yet again, she felt the control slipping away, the one feeling she feared the most. But there was also a crushing curiosity inside her to ride this rollercoaster and face the name she'd only ever seen on a piece of paper.

Maybe Bernie was right. Maybe it was a relative.

Maybe it was her father, who she'd never met and had little information about. That would be the fairy-tale scenario. But would that be any better than the unknown, a father who abandoned her and her mother? Love and hate. Sitting side by side. Another confusing and emotional proposition. But she crushed that fairy tale with logic and reasoning. If this was her father, then why would he invite her to a murder mystery weekend with other guests?

It's not my father.

She showered and slipped on her lounging clothes: baggy joggers and a sweatshirt. When she wasn't working, she preferred to dress for comfort and the relief from the usual tight-fitting outfits and crippling high heels. She didn't want to work today, so she cleared her appointments, politely cancelling her clients via text. Her mind wasn't on work today. She opened the blinds, filling the room with the low-lying winter sun. On the streets below, a thin veil of frost was draped over the cars and nearby lawns, and a horizon of bellowing steam rose from the multitude of tower blocks. She fired up the coffee maker and waited for Philip to arrive.

The hour soon came, and Philip was standing at her door in a sharp, grey suit and three-day stubble, this time sporting a bright yellow tie, something of a trademark for him.

"Coffee?" Marcia asked.

"Black, two sugars, please."

She handed him the mug and gestured for him to sit. She sat cross-legged on the end of the sofa, cupping her mug. Philip loosened his tie.

"That's a look I never had you down for," he said, smiling.

Marcia reciprocated a smile.

"So, what's this card you mentioned?"

She handed it to him.

"So, you replied then? Weren't you going to wait and see what Bernie threw up first? Looks all ok to me. I mean, it's just another date, right? I take it you've had similar dates like this," he said nonchalantly.

"Not like this. Most of my clients tell me exactly where I'm going; there's no cloak-and-dagger drama around it. They give me an address, they pick me up, and that's it." Marcia uncrossed her legs and sat up. "The card was delivered by a young lad who I followed from the window, and I think he got into a silver Rolls Royce. Incidentally, this is the third time the car has made an appearance on my street."

Philip watched her go to the bedroom and return, handing him a piece of paper.

"What's this?"

"The registration of the Rolls Royce. I need to know who owns it. I'm pretty sure it's connected to all this. Maybe it's this doctor."

Philip blew out a sigh and stroked his tie.

"I really can't see what the problem is here. I mean, you're getting well paid for a quite frankly fun weekend with other guests, a nice meal, and maybe he doesn't even want to sleep with you. Maybe you're just the plus-one for a lonely man. And a wealthy one, by the sounds."

Marcia held out the piece of paper. "So, can you do it?"

Philip stood up and adjusted his tie. "Look, Marcia, I can't just type a car reg into a computer for my own agenda. Like I said before, everything I do has to be logged and justified, so unless you witnessed the car committing a crime, then I can't. I'm sorry," he said with open hands.

"Ok, ok, I get it."

Philip moved to the door. "Talk to Bernie. He may be able to help. And stop worrying. It'll be a great weekend." Marcia forced a smile.

It seemed that Bernie was the only person who could shed some light on all of this. He appeared pretty confident about the whole thing, and given it had been two days since she'd seen him, she was keen to learn what he'd found out. If she was lucky, he might even be able to trace the registration of the Rolls.

She picked up her phone to call him and stared at it momentarily before slipping it back into her bag. She felt the urge to escape her apartment and always favoured a face-to-face approach when she could.

She swapped her loungewear for something a little more discerning, somewhere between flattering and conservative. She toned down her usual makeup and picked a pair of sensible shoes. She was always aware of her dress code when she wasn't with a client. She never dressed like a working girl when she was off the clock. She disliked the association with the way some escorts dressed. It was obvious to most men a mile off. She was never like that, at least not in the last ten years, not since she'd fled the streets from cheap fumbles with eager men in the back of their cars. Something she was forced to do in the beginning.

Escaping the streets had its price. With no money or place to live, it was only a matter of time before she fell on the sleazy side of survival. Her attractive looks and perfect form were soon noticed by a preying pimp one evening when she was begging for food. Desperation has no room for self-respect or morals.

Survival was what she called it. Getting noticed and becoming very much wanted in the working girl circles gave her the edge she needed. No more pimps. No more being told where and when to work. She made her way up the food chain, educating herself in social niceties and etiquette, expanding her intellect, and achieving a higher standard of living.

Marcia made the forty-minute journey by taxi across town to visit Bernie. She stood at his door once again. This time, filled with some hope and a sense that whatever this enigma was, she'd have the answers she needed to face the weekend and ultimately regain some control.

The afternoon air was now biting with the absence of the weak winter sun. She pulled her camel-hair coat a notch tighter around her as she pressed the bell.

A voice from above shouted from an open window, and she ascended the narrow stairs to his office.

Bernie greeted her at the doorway, dressed in the same drab blue suit with matching stains and an aftershave that resembled more of a disinfectant than a tasteful cologne. Marcia unbuttoned her long coat and sat down, full of anticipation, as he hobbled around the wooden desk to his chair.

"Miss Cole, I was just thinking about you," he said, his broad smile revealing a row of smoker's teeth.

"I hope those thoughts are about *your* work and not mine," she joked.

Bernie raised a finger. "Yes, I see what you mean, of course. Well, it's definitely about my work, and I have to say, Miss Cole
..."

"You can call me Marcia. I'd prefer that," she interrupted.

Bernie nodded, leaned forward, and dropped his glasses on the desk.

"It seems, Marcia, that your case isn't as mundane and straightforward as I'd assumed, and I feel rather embarrassed by the whole thing."

Marcia tilted her head and threw him a narrowed look. "I'm not sure I follow."

"Well, in short, there is no Dr Arthur Toe, certainly not on the GMC or any other register. I even contacted all the major universities to see if an Arthur Toe had attended but failed the exam or dropped out. But it seems this name escapes even my extensive resources. Have you considered that it may be an alias?" he asked.

Marcia sat silently, hit by a huge wave of disappointment. "So, not even a close match?"

"Well, it gets even stranger because I can't find any murder mystery events going on anywhere in the country.

Certainly not this weekend or even for the next few months. And then there's the phone number which, unfortunately, was disconnected as of this morning. I've got a contact in the comms industry who I rely on for this kind of detective work, but it was an unregistered sim like a lot of pay-as-you-go phones, so it's untraceable."

Marcia closed her eyes and took a deep breath. "Can't you ping the phone, get a location?"

Bernie smiled and squared up some papers on his desk.

"I think you've been watching too many police programmes. I'm afraid that's a privilege even I don't possess. Only the police have the resources and legal backing to do that in very isolated cases."

"Well, this is turning out to be a waste of time, isn't it, Mr Goodman?"

Bernie grunted, clearly perturbed by her statement.

"You never got back to me with any of your mother's details. As I said, I can do some digging around your family. Maybe someone's trying to reach out. Admittedly, it's a rather bizarre way of doing it, but nothing surprises me in this job. Just last month, I had …"

Marcia interrupted him.

"Mr Goodman, I'm not interested in the other cases, just the one I'm paying you for. And I'm not convinced that it's a long-lost relative, but just so I can feel like I'm getting my money's worth, then yes, please look into it."

Bernie picked up his silver ballpoint. "Ok, what have you got for me?"

Marcia took a moment.

"My mother's name was Victoria Cole, and she never married. I was born in Truro, Cornwall, on 8 April 1980, and she died on 12 September 1980. I don't know the exact address, just the place. As I said last time, my social worker was Graham Best. He's more than likely retired now."

"And your father?" he asked, picking up his glasses.

Marcia shrugged. "I've no idea, never bothered to find out. Like I told you, I ended up in the system."

Bernie removed his glasses again and leaned heavily on the desk.

"Give me a few days, and I'll do some …"

Marcia jumped in again.

"I don't have a few days. I've got the rest of today and tomorrow before I'm picked up for the weekend." She picked her bag up off the floor. "If it's more money you need, then fine."

"Miss Cole."

Marcia rolled her eyes.

"It's not about more money. It's about time. It may take some time to track this Graham down, and it'll take a couple of days to obtain a copy of the death certificate or a report on your mother's death."

Marcia stood up and fastened her coat.

"So, I'm not likely to know anymore by the weekend?"

"I'll do my best to get something for you, but I can't promise anything."

Marcia reached into her pocket and took out a piece of paper which she handed to him. "At least trace this reg for me, then. I need to find out who owns it."

Bernie smiled and extended his nicotine-stained hand. "That I can do. I'll call you when I've got something." Marcia declined his hand, favouring the door instead.

"I look forward to hearing some news by tomorrow. Oh, and I'm being picked up at three p.m.," she said, holding the door open and feeling a rush of cold air in the stairway.

"I'll keep trying to get to the bottom of this doctor too."

Marcia nodded, gave him a smile, and left.

She spent the rest of the day focusing her thoughts on her job. She'd already turned down two clients in favour of her personal pursuits. However she pieced this together, nothing made sense, and journeying into the unknown wasn't something she'd ever felt comfortable with. Most of her life had been dictated and decided by the system she was put into. Venturing into her past served no purpose, especially memories from twenty-six years ago. A time she was at her most disruptive, volatile, impressionable, and dangerous phase. She was afraid of what Bernie might uncover, hoping his detective skills in digging up her family's past were just as useless as they'd been in finding the doctor. It wasn't a relative. She was sure of that. And that left one unimaginable possibility she refused to consider. But even that didn't fit the clues. Whatever reservations she had about the weekend ahead, it was the name that enticed her most and the only chance of finding out who this Dr Arthur Toe was.

1996

CHAPTER TWELVE

Laura lay in bed staring up at the cracked ceiling, stirred by thoughts from the day's escapade. Their immature behaviour wasn't attractive, and she was slightly annoyed with herself. Consuming alcohol mid-afternoon to fit in and build a rapport was below her. She couldn't help but think that the buried camera had something to do with one of them. Something didn't sit right with her. The answers she sought lay in the camera that had been buried in the garden. Why would someone bury a camera? She couldn't shift the question from her head.

Vague shadows manifested by the full moon squeezing through the ill-fitted curtains danced across the room. She turned to her alarm clock. It struck 1:20 a.m.

Surrendering to a night of insomnia, Laura climbed out of bed, slipped on a thin cotton gown, and made her way silently downstairs to the kitchen. She poured a glass of water and stared out towards the lake. Its surface glowed like a silver platter in the moonlight. Even the woods opposite carried a hint of colour. It was a bright moon. Brighter than she'd ever seen. Piercing stars blinked in the night sky. Another purity only exposed by the lack of city smog and a million streetlights. Tomorrow she'd make an excuse to cross the lake. With everyone upstairs, the urge to rifle through the drawers for batteries was too risky. She returned to bed full of thought.

The morning sky was no treat for July. Graphite clouds filled the sky, and the air felt charged for a summer storm.

Laura engaged in her morning routine and another serving of tea and toast.

"Don't like the look of that sky," Mrs Monroe said, scooping a mountain of butter onto her toast.

Becky appeared at the doorway in a pink dressing gown with wild hair. Laura wanted to ask about Molly, but knowing Mrs Monroe was oblivious to her staying, she kept quiet.

"Cup of tea?" asked Laura, trying to figure out what mood Becky was in.

"Yeah, whatever." Becky plonked herself onto a wooden chair and buried her head in her arms.

"What's up with you this morning? You're normally up with the larks," asked her mother.

Becky lifted her head, and Laura pushed a fresh mug of tea in front of her.

"Do you mind if I go with Greer to the village later? I need some batteries. For my alarm clock," Laura added quickly.

Becky shrugged. "Whatever."

"Anything anyone needs?"

"See if Rawlings has any slug pellets, bloody things eaten half me cabbages. Oh, that reminds me ..."

Laura jumped in, keen to avoid any mention of her attending to the cabbages. She fixed her eyes on Becky, looking for a reaction to the word cabbages. But Becky wasn't fully functioning this morning.

"Yes, I'll make sure I ask him. Well, I think I'm going to sort out the kitchen first," Laura said as she rose from the table.

Mrs Monroe moved towards the open backdoor and stood gazing at the angry sky. "Don't look like I'm going to get me washing out today."

Becky grabbed Laura's arm. "Don't tell my mum about Molly," she whispered.

Laura nodded. She felt like a huge divide was on the horizon. Keeping secrets between mother and daughter could come back to bite her hard.

Mrs Monroe closed the backdoor and went into the lounge.

Laura jumped on the opportunity to talk to Becky. "Is Molly still upstairs?"

Becky raised her head from the table. "No, she sneaked out earlier."

Laura pulled out a chair next to Becky and reached for a piece of toast. "So, what's Molly's story then? Seems like she's a bit of a lost soul."

"There's no story. She's my best mate. She just doesn't have a proper home."

"Must be tough for her. Has she got any family?"

Becky screwed her face up. "Dunno, I don't ask." Becky then raised her head. "Actually, can you do me a favour?"

"Depends what it is."

"We're all meeting at the abandoned house later. Can you grab some booze from Mother's cabinet and hide it in the picnic basket? You can join us, be a laugh."

Laura's eyes widened. "Come on, Becky, how can you expect me to steal from your mother? This is my job. I'm sorry, but that's just disrespectful. I'm sure if your ..." Laura stopped herself.

"My dad? Is that what you were going to say? And for the record, Jack wasn't my dad. He was just some nasty, arrogant shit who did nothing but try and get me out the way, or into trouble. That witch in there couldn't see it, though," she yelled, pointing to the lounge.

Laura was surprised Mrs Monroe didn't come back into the kitchen with all the commotion. But the thick, stone cottage walls were much more effective at concealing sound than she gave them credit for. Nothing like the paper-thin walls in her flat.

Greer was right. Jack *was* her stepdad. It appeared that there was friction in the Monroe family. Becky's resentment was as clear as day. Mrs Monroe seemed to feel differently. Naive even. She was a troubled daughter and a stepfather who had neither the time nor the patience to manage her.

Laura leaned against the worktop, slipping her hands into her pockets and staring at the broken terracotta floor tiles, pondering over her next question. She could take the soft approach, but that would take time. If she was honest with herself, Becky and her less-than honourable-scruples weren't a trait she'd consider when engaging in friendships. Mrs Monroe's daughter may have been damaged goods, but she was also an intricate part of Mrs Monroe. Her boss.

In the end, Laura threw caution to the wind. "Can I ask about your real dad?"

"Ask my mother."

Laura allowed the silence that followed to linger.

Becky tore the crust from her toast. "He left when I was five. She said he found me 'difficult.'" Becky used her fingers to emphasise the word. "But he didn't want my mother either, so that was just a lame excuse. And no, I don't know where he is, nor do I care. Then she shacks up with Jack; he hated me the minute he moved in, and he slowly turned my mother against me until he could get me shipped off to some boarding school. I fucking hated it." Becky shoved the empty plate away from her. She underestimated the force, and the plate flew off the edge of the table and smashed into several pieces on the floor.

Laura picked up the pieces, dropping them in the bin.

"What do you think happened to your stepdad in the woods? Your mother thinks he had a heart attack."

Becky shrugged. Laura caught sight of a smirk as Becky got up and re-tied her dressing gown. "I'm going for a shower," Becky announced.

Laura's thoughts turned once again to the camera.

MARCIA

CHAPTER THIRTEEN

Marcia decided a night out would distract her from her revolving thoughts, so she chose to strip away her high-class escort role for one night and spend the evening at Bennies bar; her usual meeting place for clients. Except tonight, there were no clients. It was just her in a tight, contour-hugging, black dress revealing just enough flesh to entice the imagination and her favourite killer heels.

Carlo, the barman, hooked eyes with her through the people crowding the bar. "Hey, Marcia, good to see you. What'll it be tonight, the usual?" He yelled above the bustle of conversations.

She'd known Carlo for a few years, ever since she started using this place to meet clients. She was always straight with him and had been completely transparent about what she did from the start. He'd look out for her, making a note of who she was with in case things ever got ugly. They were never anything other than good friends, and Carlo was never anything other than respectful and maintained their boundaries. Marcia was good for business, bringing wealthy clients and starting the evening with nothing less than expensive champagne and wine.

Carlo had a cheeky face, and his olive skin and dark, curly hair helped him maintain his alter ego as an Italian stallion. Something he believed gave him an edge with the ladies. He even had the accent spot on and had learned a few Italian phrases. His real name was Carl, but he preferred the more fitting name of Carlo. She knew the truth, of course, that he was from Hackney, and the closest association he had to an Italian bloodline was a deep-pan pizza from the Little Italy pizza parlour near the West End.

Marcia maneuvered her way to the bar, squeezing past a scrawny-looking yuppie in an oversized suit and a gold watch that appeared far too large for his skinny wrist. His attempts to engage her with his charming smile and schoolboy wink were ignored as she maintained eye contact with Carlo behind the bar.

"Red, something fruity, Carlo, if you will," she replied.

Carlo poured a glass of house red and pushed it towards her. "On me," he said, winking. "You working?"

"Not tonight. I'm taking a break, figuring some things out. How's bar life?"

"It's good. Look, come through the back. I need to tell you something."

Marcia stepped behind the bar, and Carlo gestured for the young bargirl to take over.

The small back room was stacked with silver kegs and crates of drink. It was cool and carried a damp odour.

Carlo closed the door and leaned against a large, upright fridge. Marcia's skin prickled momentarily with the cold; she'd left her coat at the entrance.

"You need to know that a woman came in here a few nights ago asking for you."

Marcia's mouth dropped. *The woman who accosted me the other night on the way home. It had to be her.*

"I figured she might have been the wife of one of your clients. I just said I didn't know you and that I deal with a lot of customers. Just thought you should know."

"What did she look like? Was she wearing a big coat?"

Carlo nodded. "Yeah, like a parka with one of those oversized hoods. But she had the hood up. Even in here, she left it up."

Marcia rubbed her arms for warmth. "Did she leave after?" "Not sure. It was a busy night that night. She just disappeared in a sea of people, so I can't say. You got any idea who it was?"

"Maybe, it's kind of complicated. Have you got CCTV?" she asked excitedly.

"Yes, but it won't help you. It gets recorded over every twenty-four hours if there's not been any trouble."

Carlo placed a comforting hand on her shoulder. "You know this woman, don't you? It's all over your face."

"Not really, no, but she confronted me the other night on my way home from here, she must have followed me."

Carlo looked at her wide-eyed. "And?"

"And it's a long story. Look, I appreciate you telling me, thanks."

Carlo nodded. "You making a deposit this month? Bennie's asking."

"Yeah, I need to lose some cash."

"Cool. I'll let him know."

Suddenly the room was overwhelmed with noise as the young bargirl opened the door and asked for Carlo.

Marcia glanced out at the sea of heads which filled the bar. It seemed her night out to avoid her imposing thoughts had other ideas. Her mood was now quashed by Carlo's news. Another dead end. Somehow, she and this doctor were linked, but trying to make any sense of it only irritated her more. She was now two thousand pounds down from cancelling her clients and was no nearer the truth about the upcoming weekend.

She hugged Carlo. "Thanks for looking out for me. I'll see you some time next week."

"Look after yourself. Give me a bell if you need me, yeah?" Marcia smiled and set about squeezing her way through the
sweaty bodies and spilling drinks towards the exit.

She grabbed her coat and stepped out onto the street.

The walk home was quiet. It was early for her, but with no

client to entertain, she took advantage of the fresh evening air and gathered her thoughts for the next day. She couldn't help peering over her shoulder occasionally, anticipating another stalker trailing her home, scouting the shadows and doorways for lurking figures. It was clear.

She entered her apartment, threw off her coat and heels, and headed to the fridge, staring at the neatly stacked bottles of wine. She closed the fridge door, ignoring the urge to get blind drunk and lose all sense of self. Instead, she favoured the coffee machine, deciding a clear head was the best way forward.

She went towards the window to enjoy the city lights and her mellow coffee, but her attention was snatched away by her phone vibrating on the kitchen worktop.

"Hello, Miss Cole? It's Bernie Goodman here." Marcia's stomach coiled. *Maybe he has some good news.*

"Hi, Mr Goodman, what have you got for me?" she asked, pacing the lounge area.

"Sorry, it's late, but I've got some information for you. But before that, I also need to clear something up with you."

"Yes, go on."

"Well, you've not been entirely honest with me, Miss Cole. You see, I managed to look up a copy of your mother's death certificate, and from that, I was able to track her birth certificate and then your birth certificate."

Marcia closed her eyes. She knew what was coming. She remained quiet.

"It seems your birth name isn't Marcia." She held her breath.

"It's Molly, isn't it?"

Silence.

"You still there?"

"Yes, I'm still here. I'm sure you understand, Mr Goodman, that in my line of work, staying under the radar is part of my role."

"I do understand, but that also changes things because have you considered that this doctor or alias is someone who knows you as Molly and not Marcia?"

"I doubt that very much, Mr Goodman. I stopped using that name when I turned eighteen."

"Forgive my intrusiveness, but I'm guessing you weren't pursuing this type of career back then, so I don't understand your explanation for the name change."

Marcia stepped towards the fridge and took out a half-empty bottle of wine. She put the phone on the loudspeaker and poured herself some.

"Can we just leave that one, please, and move on? What's the other bit of news?" she asked, redirecting any further conversation around the name Molly. She drank it quickly and poured some more.

"As you wish. Well, I managed to trace the car. It's registered to a business, S. L. Holdings. Does that mean anything to you?"

"Not really, no. I don't even know anyone with those initials, so that doesn't help me either," she sighed.

"I'll keep digging, see what else I can unearth."

"Thank you, and yes, please let me know if you find anything else. I'm being picked up tomorrow at 3 p.m., so anything you find before then, please let me know."

"Of course. Good night, Miss Cole."

Marcia sank onto the sofa and scrolled through her contacts. She was hoping it was just an old client, albeit an eccentric one at that. But nothing matched her contacts. Or her memory.

With time running out and no helpful leads, she was compelled to delve into her past and an unsettling assumption that this could be a skeleton she'd discarded a long time ago.

Don't be silly. This is all in your head, she told herself.

Besides, nothing in what Bernie had said gave any indication that this was anything but an eccentric, rich client seeking a bit of adventure and some female company.

She stepped in front of the window again. The place she found most settling. She allowed her mind to clear. She followed the constant moving lights of the city and the figures dashing out of the winter sleet, which lashed against her window and sounded like loud static.

She grabbed a small, designer black and gold suitcase from the wardrobe and threw it onto the bed. She checked her watch. It was late, and she had a long day tomorrow, but tiredness hadn't taken hold yet.

She pushed the suitcase under the bed and sat on the end.

I'll pack in the morning.

She grabbed her phone from the coffee table and called Philip in a single motion.

"It's me, you busy?"

"I was just going over some case files with a beer. Why?"

"Would you like to spend the night here? And please don't mention the ugly word of money," she asked, gritting her teeth. This was the third time now that she'd slipped on her own rules. But this had been an unusual week and possibly an unusual weekend still ahead.

There was an awkward silence for a moment, and Marcia felt judged by her conscience.

"Just so I'm clear here, you're asking me over on a personal level, is that right?"

"Jesus, Philip, yes I am, and just to add insult to injury, I'm using you to take my mind off all the shit that's in my head right now because your so-called private detective has come up with nothing." Her words were blunt.

"Ok, give me thirty minutes."

Marcia swapped her white toweling robe for the pink satin one. Tonight, she was going to lose herself, strip away all the acts and roles, and let the evening take her into something she'd never let herself experience. She would put the control in Philip's hands.

Philip entered the apartment, dressed down from his usual attire of dark suits in favour of jeans and a t-shirt. The low lighting and soft music set the moment, and Philip was careful not to spoil it with questions as he watched her pour herself a glass of red. She stepped towards him with a seductive smile and ran her finger down his chest, hooking it onto his belt. Philip went to speak, but he was stopped by her finger landing softly on his lips.

She pulled him towards the bedroom, and without saying a word, she dropped her satin robe, letting him explore her and lost herself in the night.

1996

CHAPTER FOURTEEN

As Laura's duties came to an end that afternoon, and the smell of the homemade pasties wafted throughout the house, she poured over her earlier conversation with Mrs Monroe. She sat cross-legged on her bed, staring out towards the woods. The vast foliage seeped deep into the horizon.

Somewhere out there lay Becky's stepfather, undiscovered and lost. A tragedy that didn't make any sense. But she couldn't ignore a chilling thought seeping its way to the front of her mind. Becky knew more than she'd ever be willing to say. That tell-tale smirk. It was teasing. Disturbing even. It was also deliberate. A taunt even?

Laura picked up a book she'd started the week before, then dropped it back on the bed, irritated at her distraction. Then she heard the unmistakable tones of Becky's voice under her window.

She peered out to find Becky in jeans and a white crop top, waving two bottles of wine in her hands.

"You coming?"

Laura paused. "Give me five, just grabbing my shoes."

This is a bad idea. She held her stomach. It felt like a coiled spring. *Why are you doing this, Laura Myers?*

"Let's go. Greer's got something to mellow you out as well."

No way am I even entertaining that. Maybe Becky might mention the camera. Maybe I'll ask. Maybe not. I'm not drinking this time.

Laura pulled on her white trainers and a purple hoodie and stuffed some snacks in a small black rucksack. On the way through the kitchen, she picked up a couple of Mrs Monroe's homemade pasties, still steaming on a wire tray.

"Don't mind, do you, Mrs Monroe?" she asked, holding up the pasties.

"Of course I don't, dear, you off out?" She wiped her hands down her pinny, leaving white flour handprints.

"Just the other side of the lake for a picnic."

"Be locking up at ten tonight, extra hour and all for you. Be sure you're back by then, dear."

Laura nodded and took off with Becky across the fields.

Greer was waiting in the boat, sporting a pinstripe shirt and grey jacket. Not his usual dungarees and flat cap. Even his hair was gelled back. He was looking slick.

"Who's the lucky girl, Greer?" asked Laura, handing him her rucksack.

Greer looked confused. "What? No one."

"He's hoping Molly might take his virginity," said Becky.

Laura shook her head and sat beside Becky, wondering if Becky would ever know the meaning of decorum. "Talking of Molly, where is she?" Laura asked.

"The old farmhouse. It's an abandoned house on Bodmin Moor. We're meeting her there. She's getting a lift from a local lad she knows."

Greer set off, propelling them across the lake. A swarm of midges and mosquitoes hovered around the boat like a darting cloud, and Laura found herself waving her arms around frantically.

Greer stopped halfway and took his jacket off. The rowing had brought him to a sweat, and fumes of Kouros lingered in the boat.

"Shit, Greer, you smell like a tart's handbag," laughed Becky. Even Laura smiled.

Twenty minutes later, they reached the other side. They scrambled up the bank and waited by a narrow, gravel road.

After a few minutes, a silver mini-Metro rounded the corner, sporting wide wheels and an ill-fitting body kit. It skidded to a halt on the gravel. A cloud of white dust charged in their direction, causing airborne grit to fill their eyes.

The young lad in the car had a wide grin and was chewing gum. He was skinny with crew-cut hair and a round puppy face.

"You guys here to meet Molly?" he asked, chewing frantically.

They nodded. Dust drifted across the road like a desert storm.

"Get in."

The two girls sat in the back, and Greer took the passenger seat.

"I'm Greer, What's your name, buddy?"

"I'm Aaron. Greer, is that like foreign or something?"

Greer ignored him. "Is it far?"

"Couple of miles, but you'll have to hike, like twenty minutes across the moor. The track is a right bastard, full of holes. No way am I taking this up there. You need a four-wheel drive."

"How do you know Molly?" shouted Greer above the noise of the extra-loud exhaust.

"Same children's home. I left a few months ago to work for my old foster carer on his farm. You guys hanging out at the old farmhouse then, yeah?"

Becky leaned forward between the seats, holding out a bottle of Zinfandel. "You joining us, Aaron?"

"Can't, have to be up proper early, feed the cows. Besides, I don't touch that shit anymore. That's what got me into trouble. Drinking and smoking shit."

"Boring," said Becky.

Laura wanted to commend Aaron for making some good choices, but Becky would only condescend to her comment and belittle him for turning his life around. She was also having second thoughts about tagging along. Maybe it was the desire to get into Becky's head. Curiosity was a powerful draw. Maybe she had it all wrong. Maybe Becky was the victim of over- parenting. A father who disappeared when she was at her most vulnerable, only to be replaced by someone hellbent on having no kids around, especially a damaged one.

Laura could relate to some of Becky's behaviours. Her mum's excessive drinking took a huge toll on her, together with her father's struggle to protect her and keep the family together. She locked herself in her room every time there were raised voices, usually around teatime when her mother was most intoxicated. It wasn't uncommon for her to sneak out of her bedroom window to avoid hearing her parents thrashing it out with each other.

She had resented her father when he kicked her mother out. At the age of fourteen, it was a difficult time. Like Becky, she too nearly got expelled due to unruly behaviour. But with maturity came understanding and clarity on situations that can't be fathomed in hormonal teenage years.

At least now, her relationship with her father was stronger and built on respect. She occasionally thought about her mother but had no desire to contact her. She always believed that if her mother had got herself sober, she'd make contact. Until then, she was better off without her. Laura was stable. Mature. Wiser.

Aaron pulled the car into a turning and pointed to a large pile of slanted rocks in the distance. "Head to that, turn right and follow the moor. You'll see the old farmhouse. Molly said she'll meet you there around seven-thirty."

Greer checked his watch. 6.50 p.m.

The evening sky settled from a sombre grey to a blue and orange hue. The late sun shone on their backs as they marched over the barren grasslands with wild ponies and sheep grazing on the nearby long grass.

"You two been here before?" asked Laura as she stumbled on the uneven ground.

"Nope, Molly has, though," replied Greer.

After hiking for over thirty minutes, which Aaron had

clearly underestimated, they arrived at a large, white, stone farmhouse, sitting within a drystone wall, which was in surprisingly better architectural shape than the house it boarded. The exterior render on the house had fallen away, ravaged by the Cornish weather. Parts of the slate-tile roof were open to the elements. The decaying window frames were boarded up.

Greer prised open a rotten board from a side window and helped the girls through the gap.

Inside, the smell of stagnant water was rife. It was stale and pungent. A small passage of light bathed the room from the open ceiling above, and the concrete floor was an assortment of broken timber and fallen tiles. Sprouting vines made their way up from the damp floor, reaching for the light of the open roof.

Laura screwed her face up. "This is disgusting. Why the hell does Molly want to meet here? The lake's much nicer."

Becky pulled another wooden panel from a boarded-up window. Light spilled across the floor. Greer did the same. Soon, the room was flooded with light.

He forced open the front door, its lower edges eaten away by the elements.

Becky went up the stairs to explore. Her footsteps echoed around the hollow rooms.

It wasn't long before Molly's voice could be heard bellowing from the moor. She entered the house, dressed as usual to attract attention. Hot pants. A short top and a layer of makeup that appeared to be thicker than the render on the walls.

"This is cool, isn't it?"

"It's disgusting. Why would you want to come here?" asked Laura.

Molly grinned. "Me and Aaron come here to shag upstairs. There's still a bed up there and some really cool furniture."

Laura shook her head. "Jesus, Molly, have you got no scruples?"

"You look nice, Molly," said Greer.

Molly caught Greer stepping into the light and sniggered.

"Shit, Greer, what's with the shirt and jacket, and your hair? Dude, you look smoother than a baby's ass."

Becky jumped in, hollering from the landing. "He wants you to take his virginity."

Greer blushed. "Shut up, Becky, you're such a bitch sometimes."

Molly winked at Greer. "Maybe I can, handsome."

Greer turned away and wandered into the next room. Laura and Molly ventured upstairs, where Becky was drifting from room to room, exploring the decaying house.

The large five-bedroom stone farmhouse was once home to the Tregellan family. A working family who made their money in tin mining. It lay abandoned and soulless since the mines closed, and the financial strain of its upkeep became a burden on the already dwindling family funds. It was the bank that eventually pulled the trigger on their fate. Although it piqued the interest of a few select businessmen, its isolated and bleakly situated position made it a difficult place to sell. For the past few years, it had remained at the mercy of the Cornish gods. Left to age unloved.

It wasn't long before the drink was introduced. That and some of Greer's pot. They sat on the damp floor, drinking wine and telling ghost stories.

"Pass it round," said Greer.

Becky held the bottle close to her chest. "Laura's turn next.

You have to tell a story first," she said.

"I'm not very good at ghost stories, and I don't really know any."

"Well, that's a let-down."

Time passed quickly. Adolescent stories were shared, and alcohol flowed. It wasn't long before Laura craved something a little more comfortable than a damp floor. It didn't matter how many times she hinted at this to the group. It seemed they were all oblivious of time. The light was fading. Had it not occurred to anyone else that navigating the moor in darkness would be a roulette game of direction?

Becky and Molly sneered at Laura. She was on her own. Even Greer looked surprised at her willingness to leave. Maybe it was the two bottles of wine they'd had between them. Maybe it was the spliff they kept passing around. Fortunately, Laura didn't smoke. Being around smokers in the bar had put her off. Returning home with the rampant stench of cigarette smoke on her clothes was enough. Greer's sweet-smelling marijuana hanging in the air was repulsive.

She watched them carefully, losing themselves in fits of laughter over childish jokes and stories.

Laura was suddenly struck with an idea. "Can I borrow your torch, Molly? I need to go pee."

Molly tossed her the torch. "Don't piss on your knickers."

Laughter echoed off the walls.

Laura stepped outside into the semi-darkness. She realised that even if she left now, there wouldn't be enough light to find her way back. And not enough time. Mrs Monroe was locking up at ten p.m. It was already ten to ten. She was stuck here for the night. But that didn't matter as she had other ideas.

She twisted the end off Molly's torch and dropped the two AA batteries in her hand, the same size as the ones she needed for the camera, and then slipped them into her pocket.

She returned to find Becky lighting candles and placing them on the floor. Greer was spouting nonsense, fueled by too much pot.

"Sorry, Molly, I lost your torch. Must have dropped it in the overgrowth."

"No worries, we'll find it in the morning. Come, sit, have some wine. We're upping the game now. Wake up, Greer," said Molly, squeezing his cheeks.

Greer mumbled, blinking hard and rubbing his eyes. He stared at Molly's cleavage. "Molly. Me and you tonight. How about it?" He slurred his words.

Molly rolled her eyes. "You're pissed and high. I doubt

you could even raise a smile."

Becky had no intentions of walking home tonight. Even if by some miracle she found her way back, waking up her mother wouldn't be a good idea. But equally, spending a night at Hotel Gross was no better.

"Let's play a game," Becky suggested.

Greer leaned against the wall. His eyes looked varnished. "Hope it's not an Ouija game, I ain't touching that scary shit." His words were slurred.

"Nope. We're playing Truth or Dare! You get to ask three truths and two dares, but if you pass, you've got to do a forfeit."

Molly's face glowed. "Yes, I like this!"

"Who's going first?" asked Laura nervously.

Becky tapped her lips. "Let me think. You can, Laura."

Laura's eyes fell on Molly. "Molly, truth or dare?"

Molly took another swig of white wine.

"Truth."

Laura thought about her question. She didn't want to come across too strong. She wanted to see where all this would lead, so she started with a simple but provoking question for her.

"What was the last lie you told?"

"That she's had sex," Greer spat out.

"Shut up, Greer," snapped Becky. "Wait your turn."

Greer saluted. "Yes, Her Commandant."

"I didn't really sleep with Aaron upstairs. We're just good mates. My turn."

Molly turned her attention to Greer. His vacant expression was obvious. The weed had rendered him less than fully functioning. "Truth or dare?"

"Oh, how about dare?" he said, his eyes brimming with excitement.

"I dare you to snog Becky."

Becky took another swig. "Cow."

Greer leaned towards Becky, his jacket narrowly missing a candle. He met her lips with his. "Was that good, Becks?" he asked.

She pushed him away. "You stink. And it's your turn."

He looked to Molly with a Cheshire cat grin. "Truth or dare."

"Dare," she said instantly.

Greer rubbed his hands together. "I dare you to show me your tits."

Becky shook her head. "You're so predictable. Pervert."

"What if I pass?"

"You've got to do a forfeit," he grinned.

Molly looked at everyone in the circle. All eyes were on her.

She lifted her top. She had no bra on.

Greer's eyes popped out. "Wow, can I have a feel?"

"No, you can't," snapped Molly.

"My turn," said Becky. She looked at Laura. "Truth or dare?"

Laura wasn't as adventurous as the others, and given they didn't know much about her, she opted for truth.

"How long do you plan to stay with my mother?"

Laura felt the seriousness of Becky's question. There was no light-hearted delivery this time. Even Molly getting half-naked was no match for this moment. Just when she thought Becky was feeling more at ease with her. She had thought wrong.

Laura answered honestly like the game demanded. "As long as your mother needs me to."

Becky huffed.

"Is there a problem, Becky? I thought we were past all that."

Becky stood up and brushed the dirt from her dress. "I'm going to find somewhere to sleep. I'm tired."

"You're a party pooper. Maybe we can do this again tomorrow," said Molly, adjusting her top.

Greer dropped his head and mumbled something that made no sense to anyone and fell limply against a stone pillar.

Laura scouted the downstairs rooms and found one with

an old, blue velvet sofa on its back. She turned it upright, brushing off the debris. It was no cosy bed, but it'd do for one night, much to her disgust.

She checked her pockets for the batteries. Tomorrow, she'd view the contents of the camera.

MARCIA

CHAPTER FIFTEEN

The following morning, Marcia woke to a whirling noise and the sound of glass clinking. Just as her eyes and her brain focused, Philip walked into the bedroom with coffee and toast. "I'm guessing you like strawberry jam since it's in your fridge," he said, sitting on the edge of the bed.

She rubbed her face, and the sudden reality of the day struck her. She mustered a smile, but it was short-lived as she rolled out of bed, ignoring Philip as if he were a ghost, and headed to the en-suite, closing the door behind her.

He placed the coffee on the bedside table and stepped towards the bathroom door. "You okay?" he asked, knocking gently.

"I think you'd better go. I'm sorry. I shouldn't have called you last night."

"So, what was that? You playing games with me now?"

Marcia yelled through the door. "I told you on the phone that you were a distraction."

"Yeah, I know, but I thought somewhere in that statement was the genuine side of you wanting something more than just business in favour of something personal."

She pondered his comment for a moment. Maybe he was right, and maybe there was a subconscious desire to experience something more than just acting out a role. But if she admitted to what she thought she might have felt, she'd

be admitting to a weakness.
Cut the head off the snake before it bites you.
"Sorry to disappoint you, Philip. You know my rules," she yelled over the sound of the shower.

Philip thumped the door. "I don't have time for these petty games. You can take me off your list. Good luck this weekend with Doctor Love."

She heard her apartment door slam and cursed to herself. The long shower did nothing to wash away her thoughts of last night. The uncertainty of the afternoon was drawing closer. Her nerves spiked.

She dressed casually. Jeans, a white top, and a black jacket, with just a hint of makeup and her hair pulled into a messy bun, with a couple of loose curls to frame her cheeks.

She packed an assortment of outfits. Nothing too saucy or tacky. Murder mystery weekends weren't her thing, but she took comfort in knowing that other people would be there. She suppressed some of her fear in knowing that. She focused her thoughts on it being just another paying client who she'd be entertaining.

With an hour to go before pickup, she decided to call Philip and apologise. He was a good friend and someone she could see herself with in another life. Maybe.

His phone went to voicemail. She left a message apologising.

She stood at the window again. The city sky was low and sombre. Sporadic white flakes drifted in the breeze and settled on the world below.

She cast a thought to Bernie and the disappointment she felt with the absence of any useful information. It was now the eleventh hour, and the prospect of any new information faded with every minute that passed.

Why was she so scared? It was just a name, she told herself. Probably more times than she could count. But it didn't matter. It wasn't the name, but the significance of when she first heard it. Twenty-six years ago was a time that she almost felt detached from. Because if she opened that

Pandora's box in her head, she'd have to face what happened that summer.

She glanced at the large, silver wall clock. The witching hour had arrived. A black Mercedes pulled up below. A dark-suited man approached the entrance to the apartment block.

Her lift was here. Her stomach tightened. The same way it did before her first client in the early days. She picked up her case, her clammy palms sliding around the handle.

Her buzzer sounded, and she answered.

"Miss Cole, I'm here to pick you up," said a voice.

She descended the stairs onto the street. The driver took her bag and placed it in the boot.

Icy flakes prickled her face as she stepped into the car.

His manner was rigid. There was no formal greeting or comforting smile, just the minimal robotic action required. No more. No less. She settled into the soft leather seats, her first question already burning on her lips.

She leaned forward slightly. "Where are we going?"

His eyes connected with hers in the rear-view mirror. "Don't you worry yourself, Miss. Just relax. It'll be a while. There's some bottled water in the seat pocket." His words were regimental, and she sensed he wasn't going to give anything away. But why would he? The whole thing, from start to finish, was a mystery. Enticing in its delivery but slightly chilling in its appearance.

She watched the familiar city pass by the window and the late afternoon sky descend in a light flurry, wondering where she was going. A multitude of questions was mounting. The low-volume background classical music was almost haunting, and the silence was awkward.

She tried engaging the driver. A tall man. Advanced in years. Snow-white hair and striking blue eyes, which occasionally hooked with hers. But they weren't smiling eyes; these were more like the eyes of a wild animal studying its prey.

She leaned forward again, making sure her question landed above the music. "Can you at least tell me your name? I mean, if I'm going to be stuck in the car with you for however long?"

"Call me Peter," he said with an accent she couldn't place. Not from a few words.

"Well, Peter, since I'm the guest this weekend, can you tell me something about my host, Doctor Arthur Toe? Is he actually a doctor?"

"You'll know soon enough, Miss."

She felt a sense of frustration rise. This was going to be a long journey of relentless questions and evasive answers. That and the annoying drone of classical music trampling on her eardrums to the point of being a form of torture.

"Peter, do you mind finding something else to listen to, something that doesn't make me feel like I'm going to a funeral, please?" She raised a smile just long enough for him to notice in the mirror.

He said nothing as he switched channels to a local station. Something a little more upbeat.

"Thank you," she said.

She pulled out her phone from her bag and selected maps. She turned on her location and watched as the blue dot steadily moved west. She could follow her progress now, at least.

"I see we're heading west," she said, holding up her mobile. He gave no response. This time, his eyes stayed on the road. Darkness was falling fast. Flakes of winter snow were racing hypnotically towards them in the headlights as though they were travelling through space at warped speed. She wondered if they would even make it to their destination.

Two hours had passed in near silence without so much as a grunt from the driver. She glanced again at the blue dot moving further west.

An intrusive thought suddenly made an appearance. Her anxiety came knocking once more.

I hope we're not going to Cornwall.

The urge to ask the question was strong. But fear of the answer was equally so. She was side-tracked by her phone pinging a message. It was Philip.

"Got your message, thanks. I think you need to take some time to figure things out. I can't do mixed signals. Hope you have a good weekend. Chat after, Philip x"

She broke the monotonous silence. "Is it much further, Peter? I mean, what with the weather coming in, the last thing I want is to get stuck in the snow."

"Let me worry about that, Miss." Another evasive answer fell from his lips.

Marcia turned to the window. But the darkness just reflected her deflated expression.

"Where are you from? I mean, your accent, I can't quite place it," she asked, hoping to make a connection.

"Oz, Miss."

"So, you're the wizard," she joked.

"Not sure I follow, Miss."

"*The Wizard of Oz*, the film?"

Marcia wasn't sure which was most frustrating. His ability to evade a question more times than a politician or a complete absence of any sense of humour. She needed a break from this guy. And the car.

"Can you pull over as soon as you can, please? I need the ladies."

The driver grunted. "Aha."

A few miles passed, and he indicated off the motorway and

into the services. Marcia stepped out onto a thin covering of virgin white snow and wrapped her thick fur coat around her.

"Ten minutes, Miss, I've got a schedule to keep," he said, turning from his seat.

"You want a coffee or something?" she asked, holding the door.

"I'm good, thanks."

Marcia closed the door and dashed to the atrium entrance, shaking off her coat. She got her phone out and called Bernie, hoping for a last-minute clue to help with her burning curiosity. This was probably the last chance she had to change her mind before getting back in the car. She waited for an answer, her heart racing in anticipation but equally in the disappointment that would crush this last-ditch attempt for answers.

Bernie picked up.

"Hi Bernie, it's Marcia Cole. I'm sorry if it's after hours, but

I just wanted to see if you'd made any progress. Anything at all for me?" She chewed on her bottom lip.

"To be honest, I've exhausted all my contacts. The only thing I can tell you is that S. L. Holdings is a company registered in Australia, but I can't find any links here in the UK. No progress on the doctor, though, not even close. The only Arthur Toe I can trace is from 1809; there's nothing recent. Have you arrived yet?"

Marcia closed her eyes for a second. Her disappointment was almost physical. "No, not yet." She took a deep breath and let it go with a long sigh. "Don't worry. It's probably all in my head, anyway. I'm sure it'll all make sense, and I'll be back home on Monday laughing about it. Sorry to have bothered you."

She ended the call. The intrusive thought popped once more into her head. She tried again to rationalise it.

This is just a rich client who wants to remain private and is using an alias to protect himself. Stop fretting, Marcia.

She freshened up and jostled her way back out, avoiding the wet slush churned up by the hundreds of footsteps in and out of the atrium entrance. The snow was lighter now, and the soft flakes seemed to hover in the air, drifting sideways in the soft breeze. She clambered into the back seat and removed her coat. The cabin was pleasant, with a steady stream of warm air feeding through the vents by her feet.

Peter looked at her in the rear-view mirror. "Comfortable, Miss?"

"Actually, can you drop the 'Miss,' Peter? Marcia is fine, and yes, I'm comfortable. Can we just get to wherever we're going, please?" There was urgency in her voice.

Peter said nothing. He maneuvered out of the car park and back onto the motorway.

She closed her eyes. Tension darted across her temple back and forth like a ball bearing ricocheting around in her head. Her thoughts were jumbled, and she gave up trying to make sense of them. The doctor's name was the only thing from her past that troubled her. Maybe it *was* a relative reaching out. But she had no family. None that she knew of. Another thought quashed.

She flinched and opened her eyes to her mobile ringing in her bag. She glanced at the luminous screen. It was Bernie.

Peter's eyes felt heavy on her. She could sense his stare.

"Marcia, I forgot to tell you before you hung up. I managed to track down Graham Best, your old social worker."

Her heart skipped. "What did he say? Does he know who came to see me?" she asked with a hint of excitement.

"Sorry, another dead end there. He's been retired for the past ten years and can't remember, but I can get hold of the records relating to your case; social services have to keep them for seventy-five years, but it'll take a while. But he does remember that you had no traceable family. Even your father was a dead end. Sorry."

Another arrow of disappointment struck Marcia hard. It was clear she was heading into this unarmed with no useful information. She always had a plan. 'Know where you're going and know your client' was her motto. For extra protection, she always called her answering machine with the client's name, number, and destination, just in case the unthinkable happened.

This was a first. Doubts were now seeping in. Her anxiety heightened, and one look at the blue dot opened the floodgates for every memory she'd tried to suppress.

They were now in Cornwall.

This was the one place she had no intention of ever visiting again. Was this a pure coincidence or something else?

She felt a wave of nausea rising in her throat. She inched

the window down just enough to allow the biting draft to douse her face and stop the sickness from rising further.

Marcia attempted another question. "So, whereabouts in Cornwall are we headed to? I used to live here, so I'm just curious," she asked nervously.

"It's a surprise."

She shuffled in her seat. "Have to say, I'm not big on surprises. Can you give me a clue, at least, Peter? C'mon, don't leave a girl hanging. I won't tell if you don't," she said, trying to hide the desperation in her voice.

"I'm afraid it's against my instructions."

"Well, I'm not too good with all this secrecy." Marcia sighed and grabbed her phone. The blue dot was gone.

Well, this just gets better.

She looked closely at the icons at the top of her phone. No signal.

The Mercedes made a right turn from the main road onto a gravelly road, barely wide enough for a single car.

She turned and stared out the rear window into the vast darkness, watching the roadside lights disappear into the horizon. A flurry of flakes danced in the headlights.

Only darkness. This was Bodmin Moor.

She'd returned to the scene of a once-forgotten nightmare. The only blanket of comfort came from the thought that this was nothing more than a big coincidence. Her fizzled brain churned out pieces of logic. She'd told no one about the events that happened twenty-six years ago. If Bernie Goodman was as good as Philip had suggested, then he would have picked up on it. Changing her name was an easy piece of information for him to find. It meant nothing, and Bernie appeared to accept it.

She spared a thought for the other two people whose lives were also anchored to that awful night. The summer of '96 was as exciting as it was dreadful. She wondered where they were now. Were they also prisoners to those awful memories? They were the only other people who knew what happened. That was the last time she ever saw them.

How could anyone know what happened back then?
There was one piece of the puzzle that still didn't fit. Dr Arthur Toe. The only connection that linked the past with the present. She figured she'd get the answer to that this weekend. She shut the window and relaxed back into the leather seat.

The snow persisted. Heavier and with worrying persistence.

It wasn't long before a set of bright lights appeared from the darkness. She sat forward. Her hand squeezed the front headrest as a large house appeared from the white haze.

The car pulled up to a set of iron gates, which opened almost immediately. The driver turned in. The sound of crunching gravel could clearly be heard amidst the deadly silence. A lit porch light bathed the large oak front door.

Marcia peered out of the window. The house was large and imposing. Moments later, Peter opened her door, and she was hit by a wave of chilled air.

"Please go into the hallway, where you'll be greeted by your host. I've got another pickup to make," he said as he climbed back into the car.

Marcia entered the house and was immediately drawn to the staircase in front of her. She threw her fur coat over the leather sofa at the end of the hall and started to explore it. Her eyes leapt around the room and followed the large wooden staircase and polished ornate balustrades, weaving their way to the top. This was a place that she felt at home in. She was used to opulent settings and the kind of environment that exuded class and wealth. Her anxieties were subsiding, for now at least, and hopes of a fine evening with fun and games were beginning to appeal to her.

The house was quiet. There was no sound of activity and certainly no sight of this Doctor Toe. Her host.

Her phone vibrated in her bag. She answered. "Hello?"

"It's Bernie again. I've managed to find out why I couldn't trace this doctor."

Marcia moved around the room, trying to get a clearer

signal. "You traced him, you say?"

"No, it's not a person it ..."

Marcia plugged her other ear with her finger. "Did you say not a person? Hello?"

Her phone cut off. She cursed. Another disappointing blow. Another half-answer hung in the shadows.

The double doors to the lounge opened, and a man entered the hallway, casually dressed in blue cord trousers and a black roll-neck neck jumper. He was tall and stocky, with dark hair the colour of coal and a neatly trimmed beard. He wore thin framed silver glasses. Immediately, the scent of his aftershave filled the space. Powerful but pleasant. She couldn't place it. She knew her wines well but was less educated on men's aftershave.

"You must be Marcia. Please call me Steven," he said, gesturing her to go into the lounge.

So, you're not Dr Arthur Toe?

Marcia stepped into the lounge, and the warmth of a large, roaring fire welcomed her. Its opulence matched the hallway with its new-look wooden panelling and an ornate chandelier suspended from the middle of the ceiling, surrounded by a cast plaster rose wreath.

"Drink?" he offered, pouring himself a whisky.

"Red wine, please. Pinot Noir, if you have it."

He turned from the drinks cabinet. "I certainly do. You have good taste in wine. I like that. Let me fetch you a bottle. Please relax, take the couch, and I'll be back," he said before disappearing through the double doors at the far end of the room.

She walked around the room, taking in the architecture, but her mind was elsewhere. She couldn't be certain what Bernie said, but she was sure he said the doctor wasn't a person. It made no sense to her. But it would be the first question to leave her lips when he returned.

She sat on the tan leather sofa and removed her jacket. The large, open brick fireplace was hypnotic and relaxing. Flames reached for the vast width of the chimney. She sat forward, twisting her rings around her finger, waiting for her host to reappear. He seemed pleasant, polite, and distinguished. She had him around his early sixties, well-groomed and with almost ageless skin. She wondered who else would be joining her for the evening, expecting Peter to return any moment with more guests.

Steven entered and stood at the doorway. "Your wine's on the table in the dining room. Please go through and take a seat by your name at the table. I'll be joining you once the other guests have arrived. A menu is supplied for tonight's dinner, and the grand finale is taking place just before midnight." He smiled, nodded, and waited for her to enter the dining room before disappearing once again through the double doors.

Except this time, his exit was followed by a loud click. She approached the door and pulled the handle. It was locked.

What's going on?

She tried a second time, but again, no luck. She knocked loudly on the two thick, wooden panelled doors. "Steven?" she yelled.

The evening was already beginning to feel unsettling. Maybe there was a very good reason for this.

Maybe this is part of the games?

She'd never been to a murder mystery evening before. But why would it start before the other guests had arrived?

She put the locked-door mystery to the back of her mind and instead focused her attention on the dining room. It was a long, narrow room. Vast oak panelling lined the walls, with several pictures hung symmetrically. A large, deep-set leaded window sat high on one wall, the exterior light revealing glimpses of snow as it passed. The deep-red-coloured carpet beneath her feet reminded her of a pool of blood. She'd never liked red carpet. It belonged in low-rent brothels along with the seedy red lighting. She looked at the patterned ceiling. Two smaller chandeliers, less prominent than the one in the lounge, hung low from the high ceiling. But her focus was drawn to the long table in front of her, dressed in a white cotton cloth and a gold runner with fine pearl beads running along the edge of each end. In the middle sat a large glass bowl with several vibrant purple orchids on a bed of green moss.

She edged her way around the table, her hand skating the soft, white cloth and laying on the etched silver cutlery. It was pleasantly weighted. She then caressed the tall, crystal wine glasses that sparkled under the lights. She flicked the rim and smiled at its ringing.

She moved to the head of the table and looked at the cream- coloured place card, with *"Host"* printed in gold copperplate lettering rather than handwritten.

Marcia frowned at the lack of personal touch and put it down to yet another oddity in a mountain of others, all piling up to make one confusing mystery.

She moved to the next place setting, *"Austin."* And next to that, *"Rebecca."*

She went to the place setting next to Rebecca, where her open bottle of Pinot Noir was corked and breathing at room temperature, and read "Marcia."

She worked her way to the other side of the table, where she came across another place setting opposite her, simply named *"Surprise Guest."*

Next to that was another place name, again in gold printed letters, saying, *"Special Guest."*

"You're kidding me," she muttered to herself. Once again, the name Dr Arthur Toe eluded her. Why was the one person she'd had correspondence with not assigned a place at the table?

Maybe he was the special guest?

She recalled her phone call with Bernie. The line was intermittent at best, but she could have sworn he said something about him not being a person. But that didn't make sense—another thought she dismissed.

She reached for the bottle of red and poured half a glass before continuing to wander around the room, glass in hand. There was a single-panelled wood door at the far end of the room. She tried the handle. It was also locked.

Why am I locked in?

She sat on one of the tall, carved oak chairs, covered with gold-coloured brushed velvet and gold studs pressed around its edges. It was somehow flamboyant and gaudy against the red carpet.

She had seen this level of décor in many of her client's houses, mainly older, turn-of-the-century homes where aged and intricate furnishings felt better placed and in keeping with the period in which they were intended. Even a clash of colours felt acceptable in the correct period. But here in this renovated farm cottage, they seemed almost misplaced, like the house was trying to disguise its modern bones. But then maybe it just reflected the eccentric nature of the host. And, after checking her watch, a very absent one at that.

She felt the warm red wine soothe her stomach and make her head somewhat unsteady. Even so, she poured another half glass before pulling her phone from her bag. No signal.

Damn.

She picked up one of the menus that were laid out at each place setting.

Starter
Smoked salmon crayfish & dill mousse
Main
Braised lamb shank in rosemary & red wine with rustic mash
Dessert
Chocolate brownie with red cherries and cream

She nodded at the appealing courses, most of which she'd tasted when dining with some of her clients. This could well turn out to be quite an interesting evening after all.

After finishing another glass, her cheeks were flushed, and her head slightly floaty as she wandered back to the double doors and tried once again to open them.

"Hello, Doctor?" she yelled. "Steven?"

The fact that she'd been locked in the room was unsettling

in itself, and was starting to gnaw at her patience. A few seconds later, the lock clicked, and her host appeared, closing the door behind him.

"Apologies for the wait. I see you've already started to enjoy the wine."

Marcia butted in. "What exactly is happening this evening, and where's Doctor Toe?"

Steven gestured for her to sit down. "Please, take a seat. The other guests are arriving now and will be joining you. All your questions will be answered soon." Steven pulled out her chair and seated her.

"I just want to know what's happening tonight. I'm not usually kept in the dark by my clients, and I'm certainly not used to being strung along with cryptic clues and evasive answers. Even your driver was secretive. Something I don't usually tolerate." There was frustration in her voice.

Steven leaned over her chair from behind, and she could feel his warm breath on the back of her neck as he whispered. "On the contrary, Molly, you're just one big secret."

Marcia's heart leapt, and she stood up quickly, her eyes full of panic. "What did you just call me?" she snapped as he walked away, unlocking the door at the other end.

He turned to her with a smile. "As I said, this evening is full of mystery." He disappeared through the door before she had the chance to fire any more questions at him.

Maybe it was in my head. Maybe I misheard him.

Marcia hadn't used that name for over twenty years, and only a handful of people had ever known her as Molly. Something felt very wrong. She reached for her phone again.

Emergency calls only.

She had a text message flash up, presumably from when she had a signal. It was from Bernie. She opened the message.

Before she had a chance to read it, the double doors opened, and two people appeared. A man and a woman.

She closed her phone and took her seat. She put on a smile in their direction.

She eyed the couple as they stood, taking in the features of the room. She guessed they were in their mid-forties. He was quite handsome with raven-black hair swept to one side, wearing jeans, a grey check shirt, and a grey jacket. Even his dark-rimmed glasses suited him. She was thin with blonde hair, bleached, Marcia decided, and a flowing, red dress, which she carried off well apart from the surly expression on her face.

Marcia had anticipated there'd be more people for a murder mystery evening. Three seemed rather lame. But then, she wasn't here for that. She was anxious to meet this mystery doctor whose name had been engraved onto her brain for so long. She hoped this wasn't some kinky orgy her client had misled her into. Marcia always made it very clear that threesomes were never on the cards, no matter the price. She'd been invited a few times by wealthy clients seeking to indulge their fantasy with more than one participant. She left the seedy side of this to the others.

She knew from the woman's body language and the way she held herself that she was no high-class escort. But she couldn't work out yet how they were involved in the evening's event. Maybe the doctor would explain. If he ever made an appearance.

BECKY & AUSTIN
CHAPTER SIXTEEN

Becky stared at the baby-blue travel case on the hotel bed. She had little enthusiasm to pack. A day's notice wasn't enough.

The last time she'd packed in a rush was over twenty years ago. But those circumstances were far more pressing.

This hadn't been a normal day for her. It all started a little more than twenty-four hours previously when she was sitting in the staff car park waiting for her cleaning shift in the local school to start. As she was watching the pupils spilling out of the school gates, her phone buzzed on the passenger seat. That was when everything changed.

It was a call from a nursing home. She'd forgotten the name of it because the rest of the call was a blur because it concerned the one person she'd consigned to the shadows of her memory. Her mother.

Twenty-four hours later, she was here, sitting on the end of the bed in a hotel room, staring at a suitcase and wondering how one short phone call could drag her more than two hundred miles from her home in Brighton.

To make things even more complicated, she was given no reason from the woman whose voice was both sharp and direct.

"Miss Monroe, it's imperative that you come as soon as possible. It's your mother. I'm afraid time is of the essence," was all she

remembered the woman saying—along those lines, anyway.

An unsettling thought occurred to her. How did the nursing home get her number? For the last twenty-plus years, she'd been estranged from her mother.

Anxiety simmered. She placed that thought to the back of her mind for now.

Worse was being back in Cornwall. A place she escaped from and vowed never to return to. A place she associated with her unsettled childhood. And the one person she held responsible was her mother, Catherine Monroe.

Becky would freely admit that she was a difficult child. She had always considered sympathetic parenting should have been a basic qualification for all parents. All she felt from her own mother was disappointment.

But that wasn't the main reason Becky left Cornwall. She couldn't decide if morbid curiosity or greed had brought her back to Cornwall, along with her partner Austin.

I wonder if my mother still has the cottage.

So here she was in a shabby hotel room in the middle of January.

The guest house stood on the edge of Bodmin Moor. A world away from the bright lights and bustling streets of Brighton. Bodmin was as intriguing as it was lonely in the depth of winter. A bleak and lonely place. A place she once knew only too well.

Her attention drifted sideways to the window and beyond. The distant scenery was calming and unbroken compared to the view of a jungle of concrete that she was familiar with from her third-floor flat in Brighton.

A sea of undulating blonde and faded wild grass was accompanied by slate-grey rocks sprouting out from the ground like a huge, grey shark breaking through the surface, all smothered in a blanket of January snow.

As she watched the light fade and the bleak sky spill onto the window, she returned her attention to unpacking her case —another distraction from the visit the next day.

Her partner Austin fumbled around with the room key in

the door and entered the room. He stood for a moment and observed her impatiently trying to unpack before she surrendered to the single seat by the desk with a very audible sigh.

She wasn't the only person who had a past to face back here. Some would say their journey from teenage friends to a twenty- plus-year partnership was charming. But nothing was charming about it. Especially the circumstances that had brought them together. Something they both spoke very little about.

It was the early days in Cornwall that Austin most enjoyed. The outdoor life and the freedom to do a job with little pressure or direction from interfering hands. It was the upkeep that satisfied him. Maintaining the gardens and the everchanging array of colours that the plants brought. But that all changed in the summer of '96.

Fast forward twenty-plus years, and here he was. He was a middle-aged man with a failing career as a writer, but he felt lucky. This slim, attractive woman in skinny jeans with animated eyes was still with him despite a turbulent patch in his life. Writing was a very solitary career. His relationship split between his laptop and his partner was bound to drive a wedge. That, and of course, the drink. But that was now five years, three months, and sixteen days ago, a number that kept growing and a stark reminder of how far he'd travelled from self-destruction. Sadly, this was his second attempt at sobriety. The first was over fifteen years ago.

Austin was struggling in this competitive world and barely treading water. Publishing three books in five years only dripfed him a mediocre income. But like all authors, he dreamt big, hanging all his hopes on the next big story. Deep down, his writing had become a distraction from real life. Losing himself in a creative world only served to mask past events that still haunted him to this day.

Unfortunately, a last-minute meeting with his publisher back in 2017 saw him at a pivotal moment in his self-destructive days. He arrived in one piece, despite vague memories of loud-sounding horns and flashing lights from other drivers, only to be fired by his publisher on the spot. It seemed being intoxicated wasn't a good marketing move. That was the moment he reached rock bottom. The constant demons gnawing away at his conscience was a battle that he found too difficult to win.

"Grabbed you a coffee; well, it's from the vending machine, so don't judge too harshly," he smiled, placing the paper cups on the desk.

"Thanks."

He slid back his white shirt sleeves and pressed on his glasses. He picked up his coffee, sipping it as he watched the weather rolling in from the moor.

"You know, it's quite something, looking out and not seeing any buildings. I'd forgotten how peaceful this place could be. I could get used to this, and it might help me work in an environment like this. Good for inspiration and the soul," he said, taking another slurp of his coffee. "I do miss Cornwall sometimes, but not the awful things we did."

Becky ignored him and pulled more items from her travel bag before hanging them up in the rickety wardrobe. Like most of the dated furniture, it showed an obvious lack of care and attention with an abundance of battle scars.

"Well, don't get too used to it. We're only here for a couple of days."

Austin placed a caring hand on her back as she hung up the clothes. "Maybe you should have pressed harder on why they wanted to see you rather than carting us over two hundred miles from home."

Becky stopped what she was doing and shot him a look. "I know what it's about. It's about my mother. Someone I thought I'd never hear from again, and to be frank, I never wanted to, either." She continued to hang up her clothes.

"Maybe you're being a bit harsh. I mean, what if she's ill? I get why you two never saw eye to eye, but she was always good to me, even after Jack, you know, left."

Becky stopped in her tracks and frowned. "Harsh? You've

got no idea about harsh. She's in a nursing home, so I'm going out on a limb here in saying she's probably dying. If she does, there's a cottage here with my name on it."

Austin glared at her. "Wow, that's cold, even for you. So, you're not even concerned that this could be the last time you might ever see her?"

"Concerned? Are you shitting me? Why the hell would my mother want to see me after all these years? She doesn't even bother to reach out—not even on Christmas. She never does! I'll tell you something else that sly fuck Jack tried to do one time. He wanted my mother to put the house in *his* daughter's name in a trust for me until I was over twenty-five, or married, or whatever the fucking reason was that he gave her." Becky threw the rest of the clothes in the top drawer and slammed it shut.

"You never mentioned that. How'd you know that's what your mother wanted to do?"

"Because I overheard them talking about it one evening after I sneaked downstairs. That bastard had her wrapped around his little finger, and she didn't have the balls to stand up to him. He just kept spouting out about how unstable I was and how amazing his bitch of a daughter was. That's when I decided to do something about him. Then, one evening after Jack had disappeared, I had it out with her in the orangery, and she still couldn't see what he was trying to do. So, fuck her. And yes. I'm having the cottage. See? One phone call about my mother, and it's already causing problems."

Austin perched on the edge of the bed. "I thought it was all because Jack sent you away."

"That too."

"You ever think about, you know, the girl that …"

Becky snapped before he could finish. "Don't even say it, don't ever say her name again."

Austin put his hands up. "Ok. But I lost years of my life buried in a bottle because of what we did."

"And you moved on."

"You mean, you moved on," he replied quickly.

"I think we should leave it there before we both say something we can't come back from."

"But here we are, back in Cornwall. How is that not a kick-in-the-teeth reminder?"

Becky kicked off her shoes and massaged her toes. "I'm here because I was asked to be here. I'm also here because I'm not giving up what's mine."

Austin let the silence linger for a second. It was clear to him that she was able to detach herself from that awful night twenty-six years ago. Something he still struggled to do.

"What if your mother wants a reconciliation? I mean, people do change towards the end. It may be important for her that you at least give her some peace."

"You're kidding, right? She is not that kind of a woman. I doubt she knows what remorse even feels like."

Austin crouched in front of her, taking her hands in his, wearing his usual crooked smile. She always thought he had a lame smile for such a handsome man. He reminded her of Clark Kent from Superman: the sweeping, raven-black hair, rugged jaw, and, of course, the larger-than-life black frame glasses which he constantly fiddled with.

"You know, we've been together for twenty-six years. I know you didn't see eye to eye with your mother, but she was always good to me. I've never really heard you talk about your early childhood with your mother. I mean, it can't have always been like that, surely?"

Becky glared, and her furrowed brows brought a change of mood.

"Maybe because your attention was focused more on the bottle than me." Her reply came with a sting.

Austin recoiled from her. "Isn't that a bit unfair? You still don't get it. Do you? I'm the one who has to live with what I did but don't think for one minute that you weren't part of it, you and that so-called friend of yours. So yes, I may have buried my head in the bottle, but at least I've learnt to deal with what happened now, away from the alcohol."

Austin removed his glasses, pinching the bridge of his nose before replacing them. He switched his gaze to the sleet, zigzagging down the window.

Becky's face softened. "Ignore me. I'm just tired and lashing out. I need to learn to judge you on your achievements, not the past. And yes, I do still think about what happened, but I'm not going to let it ruin my life. We can't change it now, so we need to leave it in the past. I'm also not going to sit here and pretend that I care about my mother, so can we not have that conversation again? I've never really wanted to talk about my mother; she's just part of a period in my life that I had no emotional connection to, or not a positive one anyway. You know, I never really knew my father, something else she took delight in. All I got from her was, 'he's long gone.' That was it. I never even had a picture of him, so I wouldn't even know him if I ran into him on the streets. She was never really a mother. She felt more like a guardian like she didn't possess a single maternal bone in her body, just someone to look over me. Okay, so I was a mixed-up kid back then, I know that, but she always made me feel like I was damaged goods. She even let Jack decide my future. He poisoned her against me, and you know what? I have zero regrets about what we did back then. Getting him off the scene was the best thing I ever did."

"What about the school you were sent away to? You never did tell me about it, just that you'd rather forget it," he pressed.

"Look, I know you want an insight into my life, but there's
a reason I don't talk about it. I did explain in the beginning, but you were otherwise incapacitated at the time."

Austin fiddled with his frames again before sipping the now-lukewarm coffee. "Okay, I'm sorry."

She stroked the side of his face. "I told you before. I went to a special school, and we were all drugged up on Ritalin like sheep in the hope that, somehow, we'd all suddenly have a personality change. I had no say, and I hated it. I'd plead with

Mum to bring me home when I was allowed to use the phone, that was."

She turned to the window, watching the sleet drift across the car park under the lights. "I remember Mrs Stark, the head, a middle-aged spinster who thrived on last-century authoritarian principles. Discipline was very much the theme there. 'Instilling respect,' she'd say, but it had nothing to do with respect. It was just bullying. Even the dorms were run on the anticipation of fear. Lights out at nine, and if we spoke any louder than a whisper, the head of the house would make us do all the dishes for our house for a whole week. For all seventeen of us. Every time I came home, I'd beg my mother not to send me back, but all she'd say was, 'Jack says it'll do you some good.'

Becky watched a passing car disappear into the curtain of mist. The twin red taillights faded away like the dying eyes of a demon.

"Not that home was much better; my mother was as warm as a slab of meat. Stern and matter-of-fact parenting, the actions were there, just without any feeling," she continued.

"I'm sorry, that sucks. I never realised it was like that. I knew back then you and your mother had your differences. Hell, you were a stroppy teenager, but you never spoke about school."

She turned to him with watery eyes and pulled a half-hearted smile. "But hey, here I am, running halfway across the country because someone told me I need to see my mother."

Austin pulled her into his arms and reflected on the pain he'd subjected her to during his darker days of booze and distance. This wasn't a time for condemnation. Something only his sober mind now knew.

"Let's just see what tomorrow brings," she said, raising the paper cup to her lips.

A phone buzzed on the wooden bedside table. She reached for the receiver.

"Hello?"

There was a faint clicking sound on the line, followed by a grainy and distant noise, barely audible, like someone was waiting to speak, but no words came—just deep and slow breathing.

She pressed the receiver hard against her ear. "Hello?"

There was no response. Just the presence of someone on the other end. A few moments passed. Still no voice. Only the muffled sound of movement. She continued to listen.

"Hello?" she repeated. This time with a much louder and a little more impatient voice.

"Who is it?" Austin asked, pushing his frames back up to the bridge of his nose.

Becky shrugged.

Austin remained standing, swilling the last dregs of coffee around in his cup. He watched her wind the white phone lead around her fingers nervously before replacing the receiver.

"Who was that?"

Becky shook her head. "It was strange. They didn't say anything. But I could hear someone breathing."

"Who knows we're here?"

"No one. Only the nursing home. They suggested this place as it's close. And cheap."

Austin snatched the key from the desk and made his way to the door. "I'll go down to reception. Maybe they'll know."

Austin approached the front desk in the small reception area. A tall, slender man with a narrow face and poorly groomed grey hair acknowledged his presence with a less-than- convincing smile. An impression of a man whose daily duties came with a huge serving of reluctance and little enthusiasm. It was a theme that reflected the décor of this large, tired Victorian guest house.

"My partner in room seven just received a call. I think there may have been a bad line because she couldn't hear them. Can you tell me who called our room, please?"

The hotel clerk momentarily disengaged his attention beyond Austin and then back, spurring him to look behind.

An elderly gentleman with white hair and well-dressed in a dark blue pinstripe suit sat in the brown leather armchair, with his attention focused on *The Financial Times*.

Austin turned back to the clerk, who shrugged off his question with a small gesture and a confused look. "I'm sorry, I haven't put any calls through to guests this evening."

Austin frowned. "So, what about the call we received just now?"

"Sorry."

"What? So, that's it?"

He shrugged his shoulders. "Maybe another guest called your room by mistake."

"Oh really? So, that's your answer then, is it?" Austin replied, his frustration seeping into his tone.

"How many guests are here right now, then?"

The clerk raised his eyebrows and twitched his eyes once more beyond Austin and back again. "I'm afraid I can't divulge that, Sir, confidentiality, you understand."

"Maybe I'll find out myself, then. You can't have many rooms here."

Austin pushed on his frames and turned back to the elderly man whose eyes were now locked back on his paper. He made his way back to the room and went in to find Becky replacing the receiver on the phone.

"Another call?"

She nodded. "Nothing again, just a breathing sound, almost like a wheezing. Gave me the shivers. It did—bit like this place."

"Well, reception was no help. He said that no calls had been put through to any guests tonight, but I got the feeling he was being cagey."

Austin crossed the narrow room to the window. He stood gazing out at the night, feeling the cold snap seeping through the tired Victorian sash windows, another sign of neglect.

"He suggested that it could have been another guest accidentally calling our room. But I don't buy it."

She got to her feet. "What do you mean, cagey?"

Austin sat for a second on the solitary chair. "There was an elderly man at reception behind me. I didn't see him at first, but I got the feeling he and the clerk were engaged in something before I went down."

"I don't follow," she said, finally finishing the less-than-pleasant-flavoured coffee, her face reacting to its bitter hit.

"He kept looking across at the man in the chair every time I asked a question like he was waiting for an acknowledgement before he answered."

Becky smiled over her cup. "I think your imagination is running a little bit too wild tonight. Leave that for your stories," she replied, her grin growing.

Austin's attention was drawn to the window. A tall, yellow lamp hung from the entrance and bathed a small section of the car park in a dismal yellow tinge. He caught sight of a figure hurrying from the entrance to a vehicle parked opposite.

Becky joined him at the window. Austin pushed his face against the glass through cupped hands, straining to see through the watery haze of fine sleet.

"That's him. That's the guy I saw at reception."

"You sure?"

"Well, that's a sight I never expected to see outside this ancient place."

"What are you looking at?" she asked.

"The car."

"And?"

"It's a Rolls Royce, silver, I think. But it could be white. Difficult to tell in this light."

"So, the man's got money. What's your point?"

Austin pulled back from the window. "Not sure, it just seemed odd how he was staring at the clerk over his paper. Why would you stay in this dump if you had money?"

"Maybe he was visiting someone here. Does it matter?" she asked, raising her eyebrows.

Austin turned away from the window. "Guess not. It just seems a bit strange."

Becky tilted her head the way she always did when he came up with fanciful ideas. But usually, these were expressed as a verbal prompt when he was mid-flow in one of his stories. He used to sound out his ideas to her, a glass of wine in one hand and manuscript in the other until the balance tipped, and the wine became less of an inspiration for a relaxed mind and more of a catalyst for the destruction of his writing career. Three books were never going to be enough to provide financial freedom and security. Blinded by his imagination and creative personality, their hot and cold romance was already on the edge before the bottle took over. It was Becky who pulled him through. She got her Superman back.

"Well, I've got enough to think about for now, so I'm going to brave the bath." She planted a kiss on his cheek.

Austin paced the room briefly before heading for the door, shouting, "Be back in a few minutes." He stood on the narrow landing. There were two white doors on the opposite side and one next to their room.

He knocked gently on the first door. A middle-aged man in a light grey suit and a slackened bronze tie opened the door with the sound of a TV flickering in the background.

"Sorry to bother you, but did you happen to call another room about half an hour ago?" Austin asked sheepishly.

The man shook his head. "No, sorry, is there a problem?"

"No, it's ok. Sorry to have bothered you."

Austin continued with his inquisitive behaviour, knocking on doors, two with no answer and one with the same reaction. Austin was no closer to solving this. He knew he should let it go. Chalk it up to just one of those stupid mysteries. But a phone doesn't just ring on its own. The actions of the clerk downstairs and the elderly gentleman who got into the Rolls Royce continued to stir his imaginative juices.

He proceeded to the ground floor. The last two doors. Once again, one no-show, but the last door in the corner was ajar. The slither of vertical light urged him to explore after several attempts to call someone to the door.

He looked towards reception at the end of the corridor, spotting the clerk on his mobile through the glass fire exit door. His stomach tightened. He gently pushed the open door. Enough to peek in. But nervously aware he'd have some explaining to do if he was caught snooping around, especially if Becky knew what he'd been up to. A bedside lamp illuminated a range of paperwork on the single bed. A thin, green folder and a mix of paperwork and black-and-white photographs were strewn across the white sheets.

He leaned on the door frame, knocking again. His eyes were fixed on the items, but he wasn't bold enough to step beyond the threshold. That would be an intrusion.

No, I won't go in.

The bathroom door was open, suggesting there was no one in there either. A worn, leather satchel bag with brass fittings was hung on the back of the chair.

"Hello?" Austin knocked again. No response.

He checked the hallway. The clerk was still on his phone. He knocked harder. He wanted to be sure no one was in there before he committed to entering. He wiped his palms off on his black jeans and felt his face bleeding—nervous perspiration. He glanced again at the clerk and then entered. A wave of scented perfume struck him, suggesting a female guest. Austin's focus was no longer on the phone call but on the scattered photos and paperwork on the bed. He knew that it was none of his business, and being a few feet inside the room made him a trespasser. His pulse raced fiercely, his face now a full mask of sweat. He leaned over the bed, staring at the photos. Several fuzzy pictures were visible. He shifted the photos out the way, exposing a couple of handwritten, folded letters. An unintelligible signature was scribbled at the end of one of the documents.

Several other photos were scattered over the bed. Some were similar images, some of a large house.

He dropped the photos and realised he'd been in the room longer than he had intended. He exited swiftly, pulling the door to the same gap that he'd found it in. He returned to his room, filled with even more curiosity than he'd left with.

As he entered, he could smell the scent of bath salts and the sound of running taps.

"I'm back," he yelled.

He paused at the bathroom door, ready to enter and suggest some romantic bathing together.

The bedside phone rang again. He considered just letting it ring and dismissing the whole thing. But his curiosity caved.

He lifted the receiver. "Hello," he said hesitantly.

This time, there was a voice. "Hello, is that Greer?" Austin's heart skipped to his throat, and he stuttered.

"How, how do you know that I'm Greer? Who is this, please?"

"It's Jake from reception. There's an envelope here addressed to Becky & Greer in room 7."

"Sorry, what do you mean? From who?" Austin quizzed.

"I'm not sure. It's just addressed to you."

"Who gave it to you?"

"It must have been dropped off; I went on a short break, and it was here on the desk when I returned."

"Have you got CCTV in the reception area?"

"No, Sir, we don't, sorry."

Austin dropped the receiver and paced the room. He knew there was something odd going on, and it wasn't just his imagination like Becky had suggested.

She emerged from the bathroom in a white towelling robe, engulfed in a plume of steam. She caught the bemused look on his face as he removed his glasses, wiped them on his shirt, and put them back on. Her eyes followed him as he continued to pace the small room, occasionally peering out of the window.

"What's with the pacing?"

"Didn't you hear the phone ring again?" Becky shook her head.

"It rang again?"

"Yeah, it was from reception. They've got an envelope for

us."

Becky frowned. "I don't understand, from who?"

He shrugged. "Dunno, guess I'll find out in a minute." He grabbed the door handle and turned to her. "I told you something's going on tonight." He marched downstairs to reception.

"Looks like we're in for quite an evening. You seen the weather?" asked the hotel clerk, pointing to the small TV on the wall.

Austin approached the desk and nodded politely. "You've got an envelope for me? He said, drumming his fingers on the counter nervously.

The hotel clerk handed him a large, brown A4 envelope from a pigeonhole. Austin's overzealous curiosity wouldn't allow him to wait until he returned to the room. He sat in the leather armchair opposite.

The hotel clerk smiled across the room at him.

He tore open the envelope and removed a small, cream-coloured card with gold lettering and a cheque made out to cash for one thousand pounds.

Austin raised his head. The room was empty. He half-expected to suddenly be accosted by some reality TV show presenter hiding in the shadows of the hotel.

It made no sense. The name on the cheque made no sense. Certainly, not a name he recognised from either the past or present. *Dr Arthur Toe.*

Nothing but teasing confusion. He looked towards the hotel clerk, who was still glancing at the small TV on low volume, seemingly oblivious to anything beyond his desk.

Austin removed his glasses, wiped them on his shirt, and replaced them. He read the gold-lettered card, printed on high- quality paper with a fine gold border.

INVITATION

You are both condignly invited to join me this Saturday evening for a private affair. Accommodation and a 3-course evening meal will be provided.

Please accept this payment as an advance for any inconvenience. Further rewards will be provided upon completion of the evening. I look very much forward to meeting you.
Please be ready for my driver to pick you up tomorrow at 7:30 p.m.
Dr Arthur Toe

Austin leapt up from the chair and dashed up the two flights of stairs to his room, fiddling his key nervously in the door.

Becky was lying on the bed in her white robe with one hand submerged in a large bag of cheese and onion crisps and the other flicking through the TV channels with the remote.

He tried to catch his breath. "Read this! Something very weird is going on here. You can't tell me that it doesn't make you suspicious."

Becky shook her head. "Why do you always have to dramatize things? Chill out."

"Just read it." He held the envelope up to her face.

She read the card. Then again. "Practical joke, if you ask me, probably someone who knows what you're like and knows that we're staying here. Cheque's probably a dud, anyway," she said, flicking it over and back.

He perched on the edge of the bed. "Don't you think this whole thing, us being here, the phone calls, and then this weird invitation, is even a little bit strange?"

"I think you're just looking for stuff that ain't there. Look at that time when you were in college studying creative writing and reckoned your roommate had murdered someone because you found a knife covered in blood under the wardrobe. And what did it turn out to be? Used for stirring red paint for an art class. And don't get me started on the old guy you thought was growing weed at that garden centre you worked at."

Austin butted in. "C'mon, that was an easy mistake to make…"

"Yeah, and you nearly got him fired. All because you got your plants mixed up. Or was it because you were pissed up at work? Again?" she scorned.

"You can be so callous sometimes, hitting me with that again. And I showed you the pictures of the Japanese maple plant, and even *you* thought it looked like weed," he spat.

"Well, I'm not the one who's supposed to be the gardener," she snapped back, diving her hand back into the crisp packet. He snatched the envelope from her and pointed to the name on the front. "And what about that name, Greer? No one calls me that now. Not since I was in my twenties, and certainly no one in this life. It scares me a bit. Especially given its connection to the time at the lake."

"Maybe this doctor knows you from way back. I mean, it is your surname."

"Then why not put 'Austin Greer' or 'Austin and Becky' or even 'Mr Greer'? But just 'Greer'?"

Becky pressed her hand over her forehead. "Honestly, Austin, just drop it." She then grabbed the remote off the bed and flicked through the channels again to cut the conversation short.

Austin stood in despair, shaking his head. "You can be a right cow sometimes. Surely, you can see this is starting to feel like someone's playing games, and maybe, just maybe, the past is finally knocking on our door. Do you ever stop to think about that?" Austin glared at her on the bed.

Becky dropped the crisp packet and sat up quickly. "We agreed never to talk about that summer, remember?" Her question was delivered with a patronising tone. One that Austin had been subjected to for most of their time together.

He had no illusions about the nature of their relationship over the past twenty-six years. They'd never admit it to each other, but the enormity of what they did back then in the summer of '96 left a scar they were both afraid of. Keep your friends close and your enemies closer. In this case, keep your secrets closer.

The only time they'd spoken about that night was a few days after when they fled to stay with Austin's Uncle Blake. He was a man who was cut off from his own family and an ideal candidate to gravitate towards, given he owned a small B&B on the south coast of Worthing. He wanted nothing to do with the rest of Austin's family, so it was ideal. No one except his uncle knew where they were.

It was more of a pact. In the single room of his uncle's B&B, it was an elephant in the room so large that it had to be spoken about.

It was Becky who led the discussion. It was always Becky who led him. But she was very good at making him think he had choices in their relationship. She had a way of making everything seem purposeful and valid. The events of '96 were no exception.

One hour. That's how long he had to talk about what happened. That's all she allowed him. She made him promise that he'd never talk about it again. But no good could ever come from repressing strong emotions like guilt and anger. And a few years later, he turned to alcohol.

Within a few weeks, Becky found a cleaning job in local hotels up and down the seafront, while Austin got a job at a local garden centre and signed up at the local college to pursue his passion for writing. He even had some of his short stories published on the college website, some of which made it to a local community magazine. For him, it was the kickstart he needed. But for Becky, it was the publicity she wanted to avoid at all costs.

"You can't use your surname anymore," she'd say.

So, Austin Greer became Austin Bletchley. On the face of it, he rather fancied the idea of being a ghostwriter, and so he adapted.

However, he was always disturbed about how Becky never showed any remorse for what happened all those years ago.

It was very much a relationship of convenience. Sure, he'd grown to love her in his own way. To him, it was a long-standing friendship that just adapted to suit them. A habit even.

He watched the snow continuing to fall and gather on the narrow windowsill. After a few moments of reflective silence, he restarted the conversation.

"I'm just looking at the obvious here. Think about it. No one knows we're here. The envelope had Greer on it. No one's called me that since we left Cornwall, so explain that. I've just got a bad feeling, that's all."

She looked at him with a blank expression. Austin climbed into bed and cupped his hands behind his head as he stared at the flaky ceiling, pondering a head full of thoughts.

Becky reached for the lamp.

1996

CHAPTER SEVENTEEN

Laura woke up with a pain in her back and the sobering realisation that she'd slept on a discarded sofa. Diseased with stains and colours she could only imagine with gritty concrete dust embedded in her face. Sleeping on a musty, damp sofa was a really bad idea. But wandering around in the dark, lost and disorientated, would have been a worse one.

She felt the cold moisture against her skin. The sodden sofa was positioned under a gaping hole in the ceiling. The elements had seeped in from the less-than-watertight roof above.

She checked her watch, 6:50 a.m. She wandered into the other room. Her skin was damp. Her joints were stiff. Greer was still slumped against a stone pillar, just as they'd left him the night before. Becky was lying on the concrete floor in a foetal position, surrounded by several empty bottles. She didn't bother checking on Molly upstairs. She was supposed to be preparing breakfast for her and Mrs Monroe in ten minutes. And with no lift, she estimated it was at least an hour's walk.

She left the others and stepped out into the morning sun. The light was blinding, and the warm air was welcoming. She was in desperate need of a hot shower. The sour taste in her mouth was unpleasant. Mrs Monroe's tea and toast would be very welcome right now, more than they had ever been.

The trek back to the lake seemed to go on forever. Eventually, she made it to the edge of the lake and untied the boat.

She took the oars in her hand and paused. If she took the boat, how would the others get back?

Sod it. She didn't care at this point. She felt annoyed at herself for playing stupid games with childish teenagers. A huge apology to Mrs Monroe was in order. She couldn't afford to jeopardise her job—not at the expense of childish pranks and partying.

She reached into her pocket and felt for the two batteries. Anticipation surfaced. Perhaps it was just glorious pictures of wild birds, kingfishers, cormorants, goldeneyes, and other birds of beauty. If that was the case, why had it been buried? Who buried the camera and why?

If Mrs Monroe's account was right, Jack took the camera with him into the woods. So, how did the camera end up buried in the back garden? She felt a chill run down her spine.

Laura arrived at the cottage to a not-very-pleasant Mrs Monroe. She made her apologies and set about putting things right. A full English breakfast—pot of tea and a huge serving of humble pie. Laura gave no excuses other than being out with Becky and her friends, camping out overnight.

"I'd keep your distance if I were you. My Becky can be very misleading. That girl don't know rules or boundaries. Been a right struggle, she has, and boarding school hasn't helped much either, thought it may whip her into shape."

Laura needed a shower. Last night's stint on the sofa was making her skin crawl. Her skin was itchy, and her hair had attracted all manner of debris. She combed her fingers through her tangled blonde strands, despairing at the fine grit and other foreign objects that were present. But right now, her duties to Mrs Monroe took priority. It also seemed like a good opportunity to talk to Mrs Monroe and try to fill in some of the blanks.

Laura plated up the huge English breakfast, complete with a full rack of toast and a fresh brew.

"Looks lovely, dear. Think you may have redeemed yourself."

"Becky told me that Jack was her stepdad. Is that right?"

Mrs Monroe laid down her knife and fork. "Jack *was* her dad in the sense that he brought her up from the age of six. Becky was a difficult girl. She still is. But Jack had trouble understanding her behaviour; even dragging her off into the woods with him and threatening to leave her there didn't work," she joked. "She was expelled from two schools, so for a while, we mostly home-schooled her, but she just ended up walking out and disappearing down to the lake. Doctors said she had some attention, something or other, some fancy letters, prescribed her drugs, but Jack found out she'd stashed the tablets in her pencil case and wouldn't take them. He suggested we send her to a special school. I weren't none too keen, be honest, but the next thing I knew, he'd carted her off to some special boarding school. Couldn't get me head around it, be honest, but Jack insisted it were for the best."

Laura frowned at Mrs Monroe. "Did you not even have a discussion with Jack about it?"

"Be honest, I thought it may have helped the poor girl. He convinced me as such, but each time she came home in the holidays, she was moodier and had nothing to do with Jack in the end. Don't think he were none too bothered either, come the end."

Laura stared at her plate. Her thoughts about Becky were mixed. She was beginning to understand some of her behaviour now. She wasn't surprised by her lack of respect for Jack. It also appeared that Mrs Monroe didn't want to accept any responsibility for her daughter—naivety, maybe. Or just ignorance.

Whatever the family dynamics were, it wasn't for her to interfere in them. Her opinions of Mrs Monroe and her daughter needed to be cast aside. Her obligation was to her job. Becky wasn't her problem. No more silly games.

Laura cleared the kitchen and then set about making herself feel human again instead of a hobo. She figured the others would be returning soon and was anticipating a frosty response. Especially when they discovered the boat wasn't where they left it. It would take them an hour to walk back from the abandoned house and around the lake. Enough time for her to discover what was on the camera.

She took a hot shower. Longer than usual, and watched the rusty-coloured water circle its way down the plughole in disgust. After, she sat wrapped up in a yellow bath towel, combing through her freshly washed hair for a few moments of self-indulgence and reflection.

She gazed out of the open window, expecting to find an angry Becky marching up to the house with fire in her eyes and a wooden stake earmarked for her heart. But it was quiet for now.

Laura got dressed in a pair of clean blue shorts and a light blue t-shirt. She felt refreshed and empowered again. She reached into the pocket of her hoodie on the floor and took out the two batteries. She pulled the camera out from under her pillow, fitted the batteries, and powered it up.

A green light blinked.

She was nervous. Her stomach gurgled. She flicked through the pictures. The first was of a squirrel camouflaged against a dense, grey bark. A selection of birds followed. Some blurred, some close, some colourful, and some difficult to identify.

The next image was a game-changer.

And the next.

And the next.

One hand cupped her mouth. The other lay on her pounding chest.

It wasn't just the acts being performed in the images that disturbed her, it was the people in them.

She wasn't surprised that Molly's sexual advances captured here on camera hadn't been ignored by a middle-aged man, who she could only imagine had little spark with Mrs Monroe—an old-fashioned and closed-off lady, old before her time.

Several images followed. All depicting Molly performing sexual acts with Jack from the camouflage of tall bushes. One image had captured the edge of a distinctive floral dress, just in the frame. Becky's dress. It only left one person to have been holding the camera.

She suddenly felt sick. *Was he dead? Did they kill him? Now what?*

She couldn't go to Mrs Monroe. Could she? She paced her room, glancing occasionally towards the woods for the other two. How could Greer be involved? He appeared to be the only one with any morality. And why were the photos taken?

Was it blackmail? It made no sense; Becky was a lot of things, but money never appeared to be of interest to her. And Molly? The flirtatious Molly, no doubt leveraged by Becky to perform for the camera. What did she get out of it?

Laura stuffed the camera back under her pillow and sat at the end of the bed, biting her bottom lip. She contemplated her next move. Her eyes flicked once again to the open window.

A knock at her door startled her, and she caught her breath. "You in there, Laura?"

"Yes, Mrs Monroe."

Mrs Monroe opened the door and stood in the doorway holding the latch. She was unusually dressed in a red and white polka dot blouse with neck frills and a red headband to match, complete with slip-on strawberry-red shoes and a splash of rouge lipstick. Laura had never seen her dressed like this. It was a welcome sight.

"You look nice, Mrs Monroe." Her heart was still pounding. "Oh, bless you." she smiled. "Mr Rawlings is taking me to Bodmin police station. I've been thinking about what you said last week. Going to see if they'll do one last search, you know,
put me mind at rest."

The timing was almost cruel. Laura could tell her. Hell, she could even show her the camera. But it would destroy her. And what about the legal implications? But what was the crime? Despite the distasteful and uncomfortable thought of a man in his late forties receiving oral sex from a seventeen-year-old, it wasn't a crime. She was torn. Here was a woman searching for her husband. All the answers lay a few feet away, under her

pillow. Mrs Monroe had a right to know the truth. It would however sever any relationship she had left with her daughter, but Laura wasn't concerned about Becky's feelings. Just the ones of this kind woman about to pin all her hopes on another search.

Somehow, Laura would get the truth.

She had an idea. She jumped off the bed, practically pushing Mrs Monroe out the doorway.

"Is it okay if I take the afternoon off? I can do Saturday instead to make up the time," she asked, following her down the stairs.

"Can't see why not. I'll be a while anyway. Hopefully, with some good news. Maybe they'll do another search," she said, with hope in her eyes.

The timing seemed almost surreal. Somehow, she'd sparked Mrs Monroe into rethinking Jack's disappearance, and despite her unconvincing explanation of being at peace with the thought of him in the wilderness, there would always be that inner voice of doubt, chipping away each time she cast her eyes out towards the vast landscape.

"Tell me about Jack," Laura said spontaneously. "While you're waiting for Mr Rawlings."

Mrs Monroe pulled herself away from the doorway and sat with Laura, fiddling with the clasp on her red handbag, her eyes drawn again to the faded picture on the fridge.

"Jack was a complicated man, be honest, but he provided for us. Used to own a farm, he did, but when his first wife died, he found it really hard. See, me and Jack met at a local fete. He sold the farm, helped his daughter out, and ..."

Laura's eyes grew wider. "Hold on, so Becky has a half-sister, then?"

"She do. But Heather found Becky difficult. See, Heather

was quite well educated, private school, then Plymouth University. I've not seen her for years; she stopped coming here after Becky was rude to her. Jack had little patience for Becky. He caught her once, going through his private drawers."

"For what?"

"Couldn't tell you, not sure what she hoped to find."

"So, how old is Heather? Is she local?"

Mrs Monroe cocked her head. "Think she were a few years older than Becky. She lives in North Devon now."

"Does she know what's happened to her dad?"

"The police notified her; I gave them her number."

Laura's mouth dropped. "Hasn't she contacted you at all?"

"She rang once, soon after, but nothing since. But we were never that close. See, Jack used to go visit her all the time after she and Becky fell out."

Things were beginning to unfold in the Monroe family, and it seemed that this rose-coloured cottage life was turning out to be a far cry from the fairy tale she'd perceived it to be. Mrs Monroe and Jack's daughter deserved the truth. She possessed some of that truth upstairs on a camera. But what was most unsettling was what happened to Jack after.

"I would have thought an event like that would bring you closer, especially since Heather lost her mum too."

Mrs Monroe shrugged. "She made it clear last time she didn't want to visit while Becky was here. I don't know what they argued about, but I can tell you, it were quite the falling out. Jack tried to square things up, bless him. Week later, he disappeared. Reckon it was the stress on his heart, bless him. I love Becky dearly, but God help me if that girl ain't caused enough trouble."

"I'm sorry to hear things have been difficult for you. You're a good sort, Laura Myers."

"Would you like to know the truth, Mrs Monroe, even if it was a difficult pill to swallow?"

"I'm hoping this visit can do just that. As you said, it's the 'not knowing'. I tried to convince myself it were all okay. But isn't really."

Ten minutes later, Mr Rawlings turned up in his Land Rover. He got out, tipped his cap to Laura, and escorted Mrs Monroe into the passenger seat like a true gent.

Laura stood in the kitchen, full of thoughts. She formed her plan. This time, she had something to fish with. She also had the perfect game to fish in. Truth or Dare!

She set about gathering some food together from the larder and filled a wicker basket. She marched into the lounge and opened the glass-fronted oak cabinet in the corner, removing two bottles of Gordon's gin and a bottle of red wine. This time, she had a very good reason to take Mrs Monroe's alcohol.

Tonight, she'd be in control. One last game of Truth or Dare.

And she knew just the right questions to ask.

BECKY & AUSTIN
CHAPTER EIGHTEEN

The morning snow lay thinly around the moor. The narrow, winding Cornish roads required an extra level of vigilance, especially this morning. So, Austin drove with caution.

His mind was still occupied with the previous evening's events circulating repeatedly around his head.

There was no doubt that his imagination ran at an unusual pace. But the life of a writer requires every inch of imagination, weaving a web of interesting and elaborate stories. It was a skill or a gift, he never quite knew which, but he thought he had it. He was sure the clerk in reception had something to hide.

The way his eyes leapt to the elderly man in the corner. He hadn't imagined that. And why would a man who seemed to exude class and style, with a Rolls Royce to boot, be interested in the guest house? But more tantalising was the phone calls to the room. A thought that troubled him more. Then there was the lavish invitation, not to mention the cheque. It all seemed very strange.

"If I was writing about last night, the phone call, I would have turned that into a plot; the reception clerk working undercover. Maybe he called us to check we were in the room before he sent up a hitman. Yes, yes, that works. A case of mistaken identity," he exclaimed with a cheesy smile.

Becky rolled her eyes at him. "Your imagination is worse than a six-year-old's."

"It's my toolbox."

She leant across and kissed him gently on the cheek, leaving behind a scarlet-red lip print.

Austin raised his eyebrows, glancing at her form in the passenger seat. Her pencil-thin skinny jeans and red, figure-hugging jumper. He winked at her as seductively as he knew how.

"Keep your eyes on the road, Clark Kent," she said.

Becky had two sides. A playful and enticing woman whose affections were either on or off and very much on her terms. And then there was the silent and controlling side, giving subtle nudges to steer their relationship.

"You know, last night, while you were in the bath, I couldn't get the phone call out of my head or the strange behaviour of the hotel clerk, so I asked some of the guests, the ones that answered the door that is, if they made a room-to-room call."

Becky dropped her smile.

"Why are you still obsessed with the phone calls? I would have thought after we spoke last night that you'd understand that I've more worrying things on my mind," she replied.

"It's just bugging me, that's all."

Becky crossed her arms and turned to him in her seat with furrowed brows. "What the hell for? You can't go around bothering guests like that over a misplaced phone call."

"There's something else," he said gingerly.

"What?"

"There was one room on the ground floor. I noticed the door was slightly open. I knocked, but there was no reply."

"Please tell me you didn't go in," she angered.

"You know what I'm like, I'm curious. I can't help it."

She tutted loudly. "There's curious, and then there's trespassing. What's wrong with you? Why would you go into someone's room?" Her voice rose. "What if you got caught, Austin?"

"Something drew me in. There was no one in there, but they'd left the door open, and pictures scattered everywhere, all over the bed, including old letters, something to do with a contract."

"Austin, you can't go snooping around in people's rooms. It's not right. This curiosity of yours is going to get you in trouble. The last thing we need is attention with the law. How many times have I said that?" She slid the heater control on full.

"I know, but there were two pictures I looked at on the bed, one of a man in a wheelchair who looked vaguely familiar, but I'm not sure why, and the other of a middle-aged woman."

"So, it's just pictures and letters, so what? Here you go again. I suggest you stop all this and just concentrate on why we're here."

Austin shook his head in a way that signaled his frustration to communicate exactly what he'd seen. For now, at least, he'd have to leave that one.

Becky turned to the passing scenery outside. Her troubled mind now centered on her mother and the uncertainty of her expectations. There was nothing her mother could say that would alter any feelings of animosity she held against her. She was still unsure what had prompted her to drop everything and come running. Blind curiosity wasn't the single driving force. She had to admit to herself that if her mother was about to croak, then she wanted what she was entitled to. Three generations of entitlement.

Becky threw a question in the air. "Would you move back to the cottage with me?"

Austin took his eyes off the road momentarily. "You know what you're suggesting, don't you? I mean, Jesus, Becky, your mother could be at death's door, and you're already planning on getting the cottage. Fuckin' 'ell, you really are something."

"How dare you judge me?" she yelled. "That cow ruined my childhood, listened to some bastard who pretended he knew what was best for me, so fuck her. If she dies, then the cottage falls to me. That's how it works."

Austin's head shifted between her and the road. "You're such a hypocrite. You want to avoid anything to do with what happened around here, including not talking about it, but you're happy to move into the one place that holds all those memories, and I'm going to say this. Not far from that fucking lake. Jesus, Becky."

He grabbed a cloth from the pocket on the door and wiped the inside of the windscreen vigorously.

"Just until it's sold, then we can buy a place of our own rather than renting a stinking two-bed flat. Think about it, we'd be quids in, you can write without worrying about money and not have to subsidise it with gardening, and I can give up cleaning, maybe find a better job I actually like."

"Are you allowed to sell it? You're supposed to hand it down. Isn't that how it works?"

Becky laughed. "And leave it to who, our imaginary kids? And since I don't want kids, it's the end of the line."

He turned his head to her. "And what if she just wants to talk? You know, make things better."

"Then it's a waste of our time coming here," she replied coldly.

He wiped the screen again. "So, why did you come then?"

"Good question. Maybe I *was* curious about the cottage."

A few miles later, he pulled into a gravel car park that fronted the large, red-brick Victorian double-fronted nursing home, switched the engine off, and turned to Becky, his arm slouched over the steering wheel, picking at the worn rubber.

"What if your mother has sold the cottage? I mean, anything could have happened in the last twenty-odd years. It might have even been sold to pay for her care. Would you still have made the journey?"

"It's not sold."

He frowned. "How can you know that?"

Becky's eyes fell to her lap. "I just do."

Concern rose on his face. "What are you not telling me, Becky? I know you."

She slipped a strand of hair behind her ear.

"Because I've been calling the house every few months, and my mother always answers the phone, 'Hello, Mrs Monroe speaking.' Then I'd put the phone down. Except she stopped answering six months ago. But it's still been ringing, so I know it's still connected."

Austin punched the steering wheel. "Jesus, Becky, haven't we got enough secrets already? Why the hell didn't you tell me?"

"I was just curious, and I wanted to make sure Jack hadn't returned."

He removed his glasses and pinched his eyes. "All this time, I was supposed to keep what we did buried, and what, for all these years, you've just gone and delved straight back into the past." Austin curled his lip tight. "And what if Jack *had* answered the phone, then what?"

She yelled back. "I had to be sure, okay? I had to be sure we didn't have to look over our shoulder every day. I did it to protect us."

"You serious? You're worried about Jack coming back on the scene, and yet you haven't once considered the repercussions of the police finding a damn body in the lake. Jesus, Becky, why do I feel like I'm being dragged down a bloody rabbit hole now?"

"They haven't," she replied instantly.

He watched the flakes of snow settling on the windscreen. "Dare I ask how you know this, too?" he snapped.

"Because I've done nothing except try to protect us all these years. I've googled the shit out of police cases in Cornwall for years. I even went to the local library and scanned through the archives for shit that happened way before the internet, starting with the mid-nineties. Nothing. And you're welcome," she huffed.

He threw out his hands in a show of dismay. "I'm lost for words. I mean, all these years, I've had to live with what happened and wonder if we were going to get a call or a knock at the door one day and be dragged off in handcuffs.

And all along, you knew?"

Becky shrugged and gazed out towards the large house. "I guess I didn't want to talk about it. I'm sorry."

Austin felt betrayed. All these years, she'd had the answer to his anxiety. The guilt he'd had to live with. That was his alone to digest, lament on, and manage. But the anxiety that spiked each time there was a knock at the door could have been avoided. If only she'd told him. He still thought about the girl in the lake. She still visited him in his dreams.

Now, all he saw in Becky was greed. And it was ugly.

1996

CHAPTER NINETEEN

It wasn't long before Becky came marching in the front door, slamming it behind her and rattling the copper pots hanging up in the kitchen. She stomped into the kitchen, where Laura was packing the last of the items into the wicker basket on the table.

Becky was both unkempt and short on patience. Laura didn't expect anything less and true to form, Becky fired the first shot.

"What the fuck, Laura?" she spat.

"Sorry I took the boat, but I needed to get back to my job." "It's not even your boat, it's Greer's. Why didn't *you* walk around?" she snapped.

"I was hoping you'd understand."

Becky stood with her arms firmly folded across her chest and a killer scowl.

"I work for your mother, remember? I had to be back at seven a.m. I was late as it was, but fortunately, she was understanding."

"Shame she didn't sack you." Laura recoiled, shaking her head. "So, where's the old cow?"

"She's out with Rawlings. She's gone to the police station, see if they can put together another search."

Becky muttered under her breath. "Yeah, well, that's pointless."

Laura caught the last of her comment but chose to ignore it. As much as it pained her to resist the temptation to rise to Becky's selfish attitude, she needed her on side to deliver a plateful of doubt and a pinch of "does she, or doesn't she know?"

"I get you're not interested in what happened to Jack, but your mother deserves some answers, don't you think?"

Becky shrugged and grunted a response, her eyes not landing on Laura. Laura was hoping for a slither of compassion from her, but knowing what devious act she'd been part of, Laura was surprised that she even expected it. Laura thought about her own mother and the pain and hurt she caused her growing up. A similar situation, maybe. Her dad was better off without her mother. Laura meant her mother no malice. Not even in her darkest moment, surrounded by the feeling of total abandonment, could she wish her mother gone. Mrs Monroe wasn't a bad person. Ignorant about her daughter's struggles, but never anything other than a parent trying to understand her child.

Mrs Monroe deserved the truth. No matter the pain it caused. Today, Laura was going to get it, even if it meant losing her job.

"Think you need to take a shower," said Laura, moving on. "Is Greer around?" she added.

"Gone home to get changed."

Laura nodded. "Can we move on?"

"Guess so," Becky shrugged as she picked the debris from under her nails.

"I figured another picnic was on the cards. I don't get much chance to socialise, and last night made me realise what a laugh I had." Laura pulled a bottle of red wine from the basket and cocked a wink at Becky.

Becky gave her a wide grin. "Well, ain't you full of surprises?" she beamed.

If only you knew about the surprise that I've got in store for you.

"Figured if your mother was out, why not take the opportunity?"

Becky's eyes were wide and aroused. "The cat's away, so the mice will play. But you better not sneak off before us in the morning and nick the boat again."

"Of course."

"I need a shower," Becky said, bouncing up the stairs.

Laura pulled up a chair and sat at the kitchen table, perched on her clenched hands. She stared at the sun-scorched picture of Mrs Monroe and Jack. It had been an intense week so far. In all her time spent in the busy hub of London's West End, she'd never once felt the touch of crime on her shoulders. Crooks, criminals, and a multitude of rowdy misfits passed through her bar. But not once did she feel unsafe. But only a seasoned gambler would take the odds on this sleepy country cottage being the centre point of a twisted family plot of blackmail or murder.

You couldn't write this.

The kitchen clock struck three. Becky descended, two steps at a time. This time, she was in jeans and a purple t-shirt, her hair up, and a splash of glitter makeup that Molly had given her.

Laura left with her, traipsing across the fields to the lakeside.

This time, she had the sense to wear trainers.

Laura sat on the edge of the boardwalk, casting her eyes on a ballet of darting insects gathered around the sprouting water grasses and the swans gracefully propelling themselves across the lake.

"Do you think you'll return to the city at the end of the summer to visit your dad?" asked Becky, scanning the lake for Greer.

This was the first question Becky had asked her that lacked a condescending tone, and it was a welcome surprise to the usual vicious tongue Laura had been the recipient of. Maybe there was a sprinkle of wonder sparked by Laura's earlier questions about her real father. Maybe there was a hidden heart mixed in with all the resentment for him. For a second, Laura almost felt sorry for her. But the images from the camera crushed any sympathy she might have had. Whatever the reasoning or motive behind the pictures was, it would never be an acceptable act and had to be raised, no matter how much of a U-turn their friendship might take. Laura focused on one goal but replied in the same tone.

"Depends if he's back from Australia. I may take some time away. I'm sure your mother would be okay with that. But at the end of the day, Becky, I chose to move here, and for now, it suits me fine. I can't imagine moving back to the city now, and I think every city person needs to spend a week in a place like this. You really are quite lucky. You should try and appreciate what you've got around you."

Becky dropped her rucksack between her feet and placed a hand over her eyes to shield the glare from the lake. "I think I can see him."

Becky didn't respond. For a moment, Laura hoped a slither of any non-judgemental conversation would have been progress. But it was just plain rudeness again that shone through. Still, this time, trying to gain any favourable friendship wasn't on Laura's agenda. In fact, after this evening, Laura would become a sworn enemy. The only part she'd feel bad about would be when she had to deliver the crushing truth to Mrs Monroe. She could just take the camera to Mrs Monroe, show her the pictures, and leave Becky to face the music. But there was just a slither of deviousness inside her that wanted to play this out in a game, watching to see if the subtlety of the questions would be enough to push Becky to a full confession. Molly, on the other hand, was an inconsequential cog despite being the leading character in this lewd act. It was the puppet master who should pay the price.

Becky waved her arms at Greer like an aircraft marshal docking a 747 as he approached the boardwalk from a hundred yards out. Laura remained seated, watching him maneuver the boat to the end of the jetty with fine precision.

He wasn't dressed to impress this time either, instead reverting to his old faithful dungarees, pinstripe shirt, and flat cap, no doubt in protest to the previous bombardment of ridicule.

"What's going on tonight, then?" he asked, tying off the boat.

Becky turned and gestured to Laura. "Laura's idea, another party at the old farmhouse. You game?"

"I ain't got any drink if that's what you want."

Laura held up the basket. "Good job, I brought plenty, then," she smiled.

"And Molly?" he asked.

"Can you call her?" Laura added.

"I have to call her care home. Sometimes the staff gets a bit funny, especially if she's on restricted free time."

Laura looked puzzled.

"Staff are wankers. They only let her have so much free time. If she breaks the curfew, they restrict her. When she stayed out last night, they probably reported her missing, so she may not be able to come. They're pathetic. Fucked if anyone tried to tell me what to do," Becky spat.

Laura felt a streak of disappointment. She needed Molly there as well. Already, her plan was sinking. She'd just have to work with what she had.

Becky threw her rucksack in the boat and parked herself on the seat.

"We going then, or what, Greer? Don't just stand there. Get your arse in the boat."

Greer pulled out his Nokia to call Molly. "Worth a shot."

Laura had a sudden brainwave and snatched the phone from him. "Let me call."

"Why you?" Becky quizzed.

"Have you spoken to the staff before?"

"Course I have, loads of times, what about it?"

Laura sighed. "And how many times have they known that you two are trouble and Molly's then broken her curfew?"

"So?"

"So, they're likely to make an excuse why she can't come to the phone. I'm guessing your name spells trouble."

"Laura's right, she's our best shot," said Greer, lifting his cap and raking his hair.

"They won't let her out. You're just wasting your time," Becky said.

Laura placed a finger on her lips. "Shush." She dialled. "Good afternoon, Briary House, Mike speaking."

"Oh, good afternoon. My name is Mrs Evens. I live just across the lake in Tregellan." Becky and Greer sniggered simultaneously. "I had a young girl called Molly here with my daughter Jessica. She was ever so helpful on my farm, you know, stacking bales in the old barn. She was here until late, so apologies, but would it be possible to speak to her? I'd like to thank her, such a polite young girl."

"You are talking about Molly, right?"

Becky and Greer were still sniggering in the boat, Becky gesturing a Pinocchio nose to mock Laura's lies. Laura turned away, instead focusing on the swans a few meters away.

"Hold on a second."

Molly came to the phone. "Hello?"

"It's me, Mrs Evens, wink-wink, don't say any ..."

"Is that you, Laura?"

Laura shook her head in frustration. It seemed even dropping a hint larger than an atomic bomb still didn't deter Molly from putting her foot in her mouth. Why was she not surprised? She was more tits and attitude as opposed to brains and brawn.

"Forget it. Can you to come out tonight with us, to the old farmhouse again?"

"Fuckers grounded me for forty-eight hours, but yeah, I'll leg it out, what time?"

"Make it a couple of hours, say five p.m.?" "You got any booze? I can't call Aaron."

"Of course, see you then." Laura hung up and passed the phone back to Greer.

"Fucking crushed it." Becky raised her hand for a high five.

This time, Laura obliged, relief slipping from her chest.

Molly was now on board. The game was afoot.

BECKY & AUSTIN
CHAPTER TWENTY

Tollgate Nursing Home was just a few miles from their guest house, surrounded by boundless acreage of rolling moor. It was a tranquil and peaceful setting.

They exited the car and pulled their coats around them.

The large, double-fronted Victorian house was grand in its appearance, maintained to a high standard, with all the original exterior features sympathetically restored, including a pair of stone carved eagles on either side of the entrance.

To the side, there were well-tendered gardens, sparse of vivid colour during the winter months, but it wasn't difficult to imagine them in full bloom during the summer months and the spectacle of colour.

Austin surrendered himself once more to Becky's selfish ways. Another blot he had to endure living with her. She had two settings. Hot and cold. As usual, he dealt with the awkward silence by way of humour.

"This looks like a lovely place. I wonder if they take advance bookings," he joked, trying to leave his anger behind.

Becky remained quiet, rolling her blonde locks around her finger and gazing at the house.

"You sure you want to do this? We can just turn back."

"No, it's fine. Let's just see what the old cow wants. We've driven over two hundred miles; it better be good."

They made their way to the entrance under the dim winter

sky with the morning larks in full voice.

The original Victorian stained-glass front door was open and spilt a kaleidoscope of azure blue and sunflower yellow across the terracotta-tiled entrance.

He glanced upwards to the large stone arch lintel above the doorway, intrigued by the inscription carved into it.

"Wish I could read Latin," he said to Becky, pointing up.

"It's French, not Latin. I'm not sure what it says, though. I guess La Monte is the person who quoted it."

"Well, you're full of surprises, didn't know you spoke French. Looked like Latin to me," he said, pushing his glasses back up.

"My mother made me learn it when I was home-schooled, something else I hated."

Becky stopped at the entrance.

"I remember this woman who came to visit my mum occasionally, a French teacher. She'd talk to me in French sometimes, for no apparent reason, like I understood her. I was only ten and never understood a word she said, mind you. She was very stern. One day, I heard her explaining to my mother what a waste of time it was. She was right, of course. After that, she never came back." Becky shrugged her shoulders. "I guess some French words got ingrained in me subconsciously."

A larger-than-life nursing assistant in a stretched pale blue uniform with blotchy skin, short, greying hair, and an unfriendly face answered the door. A waft of antiseptic followed.

"Can I help you?" asked the assistant, with an absence of any kind of smile.

"I'm here to see Catherine Monroe."

The assistant looked at her through half-rim gold-framed glasses.

"Sorry, but we don't have anyone here by that name anymore."

Becky's mouth fell open. "Are you kidding me? We've driven over two hundred miles because I got a call from someone here to say my mother wanted to see me. Hold on. What do you mean anymore?" she quizzed.

The woman frowned. "No one here has contacted you. I would know, I'm the matron here, and all family contact goes through me," she replied.

Austin stepped forward. "Well, we did have a call, and we're here. It's been a long and anxious trip for me and my partner," he said, slipping his arm around Becky's waist.

The matron grunted, suggesting her authority had been challenged, and shifted looks between them like she was eyeing up some prime meat on a butcher's hook.

Austin immediately took a dislike to her and caught a young assistant hovering in an arched doorway behind her, with a similar look to the hotel clerk, shifty and suspicious.

"So, you don't know?"

"Know what?" asked Becky.

"Wait here a moment." The matron went over to another young assistant, wheeling a trolley full of multi-coloured drugs along the corridor. Her conversation with the young assistant was conducted in a mere whisper, like some covert operation, before they both disappeared.

Becky shuffled about impatiently, eyeing the artistic features of the surroundings while she waited. The close weave of the cornice, deep and well-crafted. The floral plaster ceiling rose, which a delicate crystal chandelier hung from, throwing a prism of colour onto the fern green walls.

She spied the open guest book perched on a white-washed French ornate sideboard with large cabriole legs and, above it, an oval-shaped gilded mirror. It all seemed far too opulent for a care home.

"I can see why they charge a fortune for these places. All this restoration and turn-of-the-century furniture don't come cheap."

"Turn-of-the-century furniture?" he replied, raising his eyebrows.

"My mother's fault. Her house was crammed full of the stuff. She paid more attention to her damned furniture than she did to me. I wouldn't be surprised if half this stuff came from her as payment. Some of it even looks vaguely familiar."

Austin glanced at the large silver clock on the wall. "It's been ten minutes now. What the hell is she doing, dressing her?"

He stepped towards the sideboard and swung the guest book around, flicking back through the pages. "No one's been here for nearly a week. That's odd."

"Or the signing-in routine is as overlooked as the communication," she replied.

As Austin slid the book back around, he caught a glimpse of something in the mirror above it. A picture hung on the opposite wall, hidden behind a square pillar, prompting him to look.

"Becky, come look at this."

He ushered with his hand, pointing to a black-and-white photo of a large house in a slim black frame. A very grand house. "This is like the one I saw on the bed in the hotel room. Except it looks different, somehow."

Becky rolled her eyes. "Really Austin. It's just a picture of a house."

"You have to admit it's a strange coincidence. The pictures I found in that room and now this one, here." He pointed to the picture again.

Before she had time to respond, a young assistant in the same light blue uniform, slimmer and with a face better suited for greeting people, ushered them down the corridor and into a room.

Becky noticed the matron hovering at the end of the corridor, like some overzealous security guard. The young assistant escorted them down the corridor to a room at the end.

She stood by the door. "Please have a seat," she said, gesturing at the chairs.

The small waiting room contained a red double sofa and two wooden chairs. A tall coffee machine sat at the far end on a small wooden table.

The young assistant fiddled with her keys and opened the conversation. "When was the last time you saw your mother?" she asked nervously.

Austin jumped in. "Can someone tell us what's happening because we've been waiting for the last fifteen minutes for someone to explain this to us?"

The young assistant blushed and fiddled even more with her keys. "I'm not sure why someone would have called you from here. But I'm really sorry to say that Catherine Monroe passed away a month ago."

Becky's face was vacant.

"That doesn't make sense," quizzed Austin.

Becky stared at the young assistant. "Why was I not told until now? Why was I called to come all the way down here after she died and not before? I don't understand."

The young assistant looked sheepishly towards the matron who had entered the room.

"As I said, no one here called you. I know because your mother had no next of kin on her records, only ..." she flicked through a small, blue file in her hand, "A 'Dr Arthur Toe'. Her trustee."

Becky and Austin exchanged glances. Both shared the same thought. The invitation they received was starting to make sense.

"And secondly," the matron added, "We don't have a number for you."

Austin stepped forward towards the matron. "Can you describe this doctor?"

"Yes, he was a kind man, always very chatty with our staff. Tall, well-built, black hair, and a beard. I'm sorry you were never contacted; Mrs Monroe never talked about a daughter, I'm afraid. Maybe it was the dementia in the end."

The matron dismissed the young girl, who made a fleeting apology and hurried off in the opposite direction. Probably glad to be away from the awkward situation.

Austin reached over to comfort Becky, but she dismissed

him. She grabbed the keys from his hand and stormed off to the car park.

Austin was compelled to ask more questions —questions he felt any daughter would want an answer to. The matron hovered in the doorway, trying to look compassionate. But it wasn't working. Austin sensed only an irritating air of impatience from her, like she had a million things to do, and spending time discussing a woman who passed away a month ago wasn't one of them. But he wanted answers even if Becky didn't.

He slipped his hands into his pockets and leaned against the wall, signaling that he wasn't ready to be fobbed off just yet.

The matron's description of the doctor seemed at odds with the elderly gentleman he spotted in the hotel reception the evening before, which spurred a question.

"Do you happen to know what car the doctor drove?" he asked.

"Yes. It was a silver Rolls Royce. Why?" she asked.

Austin remained silent for a few seconds, trying to fit all the pieces together, but nothing was making sense. "Oh, no reason," he said, smiling. "How long was Mrs Monroe here for?"

The matron looked to the ceiling, teasing her memory. "Probably a few months, maybe four or five. Unfortunately, she came to us with aggressive dementia."

He shook his head, trying to make sense of something. "Hold on. You said this doctor was a trustee. You mean he had power of attorney?"

The matron crossed her arms. "Mrs Monroe was quite clear when she came to us that the doctor was to handle all her affairs and had a vested interest in her care. He visited regularly. Rest assured, Sir, if we'd known she had a daughter, we would have certainly made contact. We can only go on the information we receive, and none of my staff ever heard her mention a daughter. Her admission paperwork asks for details of any family or next of kin, and both Mrs Monroe and Doctor Toe clearly said she had no family."

"Do you know anything about Mrs Monroe's estate?"

The matron shook her head. "You'd have to ask the doctor that."

"So, what happened to her body then? Was she buried around here?" he asked.

"As far as I remember, Doctor Toe made the arrangements, and she was collected by a local funeral director. Our responsibility ended after that point. We followed Mrs Monroe's wishes as recorded. I'm sorry your girlfriend wasn't informed, but I can only assume that Mrs Monroe had her reasons for not notifying her. That's your business." The matron checked her watch. Another signal of rudeness, he thought.

"Do you have a contact number for this doctor? I'd like to talk to him, please."

The matron pulled a face. "I'm afraid not—not to hand anyway. If that's all for now, I have duties to attend to."

"So, who the hell called us then?" he asked, standing firm.

"I'm sorry, but it wasn't anyone here."

He leaned against the doorway. "But my partner received a call. Why else would we drag ourselves all the way down here? And they specifically recommended the guest house up the road. Maybe one of your staff called without you knowing. That's possible, right?"

"Not possible, Mr …?"

"Bletchley. Why?"

"Because we don't have any numbers for you."

Austin slipped away from the doorway and removed his glasses, massaging his eyes. It was obvious now. Of course, they didn't have his number.

What the hell is going on?

And there it was. The courtesy smile before being dismissed.

Austin hurried back to the car to find Becky sitting quietly with the radio on low and the engine ticking over to power the heater.

"The person who called you from here. Was it a male or female voice?" he asked quickly.

"Female, why?"

"Okay. It definitely wasn't anyone in there. I thought maybe her doctor friend called you."

Austin took her hand. It was pale and cold. He wasn't going to mention the doctor not being the same person he saw the night before in reception. She'd only accuse him of more fanciful ideas. He'd leave that until he felt the time was right.

"I asked where your mother's body was taken, thought you might like to know, but the doctor took care of it all, so we can ask him later."

"I really don't care," she said quickly. "But I think it's beginning to make sense now. He must be the executor of her will. That's why we got the invite." Her smile was broad and cold.

He was more than a little crushed by her callous disregard for her own mother's final resting place and her only concern being her inheritance. He'd not seen his parents for many years now. He'd call them once a month, lie about where he and Becky lived, and make arrangements to see them, which he would then consistently break. After twenty-six years, his life was beginning to feel like a cage, and the boundaries beyond it were the forbidden lands. Coming back to Cornwall only served as a stabbing reminder.

Becky took his hand. "I need to go to my mother's cottage.
I want to know how she left it."

Austin glared at her and shook his head. "No, I'm not going anywhere near that place. How can you want to do that? You wanted to bury what we did for all these years, and now just go back like it's some casual visit."

She caressed his face. "I get this is difficult for you, and it's not easy for me either, but all my mother's things are in there, and I want to know what condition they're in."

His expression was savage. "You didn't even give a toss

where she was buried two minutes ago, but now you're interested in her cottage. Do you have any idea how that looks?" he raged.

"I don't care how it looks, and I'm not apologising for how I feel about her, but I'm not about to give up the one thing I deserve. What we deserve. Aren't you fed up of living in a poxy two-bed, third-floor flat while that bitch got to rattle about in that cottage with him making all the decisions about my life? That woman had no fucking backbone." Becky held out her hand. "Give me the keys, I'll go on my own. I'll drop you off at the hotel."

He turned to the window, watching the crows fighting over roadkill half-buried in the snow. It seemed quite ironic that they were all desperate to get what they could from the corpse. It was even more ironic that they had no sense of morality or empathy.

"I give up with you. I'll take you, but I'm not going any further than the gate. I don't want anything to do with that place."

Becky's attitude switched in an instant. A smile grew. "Thanks, love."

Austin drove the precarious roads in silence. It was only the radio that made it feel less uncomfortable.

They arrived at the bottom gate to the cottage. Austin felt the weight of what this place had cost him. He turned the engine off. "This is as far as I'm going. The rest is up to you. I'll wait here," he said.

"Fine," she spat, slamming the car door.

Becky walked up the narrow lane to the cottage. The bare skeleton shrubs lining the lane had grown unattended and were starting to impose themselves across the lane. She rounded the corner to the cottage where she'd spent her agonising childhood in.

The exterior was how she remembered it. Apart from the flaking paint and unloved garden that surrounded it. Overgrown and drowned in a blanket of white.

She shuffled through the powdery snow to the front

window and peered in. The lounge was partially empty. Just a built-in cabinet remained where the TV once stood. She hurried to the kitchen window. Nothing. No long wooden table or chairs, and no white goods. Just space with discarded paper on the floor. She remembered her mother used to keep a front door key under a loose doorstep tile, but they'd all been replaced. She went around the side to the orangery. The windows were foggy and framed by droplets of condensation. She tried the door. It was locked. She returned to the front and stood facing the white horizon. The Christmas card picturesque view of the lake did nothing to remove the tainted memory she'd tried so hard to evade.

Was she still in there?

Becky should have felt something, but she didn't. She just felt cheated. She looked at the cottage and finally realised this was her ticket to a new life with Austin. A life she'd been waiting to have for a long time. The invitation from the doctor appealed to her even more now, and her imagination conjured up all manner of possibilities.

She turned from the lake and eyed the ageing cottage one last time, her eyes following the crumbling render snaking its way across the front and making mental notes of how and where improvements would need to be made. The thatched roof was no longer its original blonde colour but had now aged to a dark and greying thatch infected with legions of moss like an all-consuming cancer. She liked the cottage. She just didn't like the memories that were made there.

"Can I help you, Miss?" came a voice from behind, causing her to flinch.

She turned to see a rounded man, advanced in years, in a green, well-filled-out overall and a chequered flat cap, which he removed to scratch his bald head.

Becky placed a hand on her chest. "You made me jump. I wasn't expecting anyone to be here."

"Well, this is private land, Miss. And seeing as you came from the driveway, you'd know that," he said, returning his cap.

She removed her hood and offered him her hand. "I'm Becky, Becky Monroe. I used to live here with my mother."

The man's eyes narrowed, and his silver moustache changed shape with his bemused expression. "Mrs Monroe, you say. Hmm," he said, making all kinds of shapes with his mouth like he was chewing something.

"Never mentioned a daughter to me, Miss, and I've known her a few years now. See, I look after the place. Have done since she was in that home up the road. 'Tis a lovely cottage. I come by every week and make sure it ain't got no squatters in and such like. Daughter, you say? Hmm."

She felt even more betrayed by her mother now. First, the nursing home, and now this piggish man, all oblivious to her existence. Had her mother so much hatred for her that she denied all knowledge of her daughter to the world? Becky felt slightly annoyed that her mother was dead, as there was no opportunity to have her say now.

"Yes, I'm her daughter." She pointed to the driveway. "My partner is in the car at the entrance. I can get my driving licence if that'd satisfy you, but I can assure you that I am," she replied sharply.

She had a sudden realisation. "You do know my mother is dead, don't you?" she asked matter-of-factly.

"I'm sorry, Miss, no, I didn't. Oh, I'm Les, Les Northwick."He removed his cap and stroked the edges. See, I was asked by the Doctor to keep an eye on the place after your mother, well, you know, became unaware of herself, if you get my drift."

"I was told it was dementia, but then again, I had nothing to do with my mother until I was dragged back down here. Seems we were both in the dark about her death, but that's another story." Becky felt the weak sun penetrating through a gap in the clouds and reflecting off the snow, forcing her to squint.

Les moved to the entrance of the cottage and pulled a key from his overall pocket. "You want to look around? Not much in there now, I'm afraid, but if you want to, I got a few minutes."

She looked at the door and shook her head. "You say you knew my mother. How long for exactly?"

Les dropped the key back in his pocket and nestled his hands on his hips. "Must be about three years now. I did some gardening for her, and such like until one day, an ambulance came. All a bit sudden. A stroke, I believe, poor woman. See, I presumed my services would be cut short, but I got a call from a gentleman, some doctor, a few weeks later asking me to keep an eye on the place."

She stepped closer to him, her eyes wide. "A doctor, you say? You mean Doctor Arthur Toe?"

"Yes, that's him. You know him?"

She sighed and kicked some snow from the doorway. "Another long story, but no, not really." She locked eyes with him. "You met him? What's he like?"

Les scratched his head and replaced his cap. "Nope, never met the chap, only ever spoken on the phone. The place was cleared out shortly after Mrs Monroe was taken in. Told me he'd continue paying me from Mrs Monroe's account, left a key for me, and told me to pop by each week." He brushed the snow from the window frame by the door, then patted his gloves off. "How long has she been gone, then? Because I still get money paid into me bank."

"A month. Or so the nursing home tells me."

"So, am I assuming you'll be taking over the place? That's why you here?"

Becky huffed and rolled her eyes. "Well, it's not quite decided yet, but yeah, I'm hoping to do the place up, but we won't be living here, I'm afraid. I think the doctor is taking care of her estate. We're seeing him tonight, actually, at his place.

Les reached into his pocket and handed her the key. "Guess I won't be needing this then."

She stopped his arm. "Keep it for now until everything's finalised."

"If you wish, Miss."

Becky smiled.

Les pulled his cap off again and scratched his head. "You know, you're not the only person I've seen snooping round the place."

Becky looked startled. "What? Who else has been here?" she asked, touching his arm.

"A woman. Similar age, I reckon, said she was just looking and then strolled off."

"And this was when?"

"Oh, recently, probably a couple of weeks back."

Becky watched the birds digging in the snow, her eyes following them as they took flight into a nearby tree.

"Can I ask, do you know anyone called Jack? I mean, did Mrs Monroe mention anyone by that name?"

Les dropped his head, his mouth moving like a grazing cow. "Nope, don't ring any bells, I'm afraid. Why?"

"No reason. Thanks for your time, Mr Northwick. I'll get the doctor to get in touch."

Les tipped his cap like a gentleman as she turned towards the drive. There was one other question which she felt compelled to ask.

"Excuse me, Mr Northwick?" He turned on the spot and shuffled back through the snow.

"Miss?"

"Have you heard any gossip about this lake, either a while ago or recently?"

Confusion crossed his face. "How'd ya mean, Miss?"

"Oh, I heard something about a girl accidentally drowning in the lake. Just wondered if it was an actual thing. I mean, a story, you know, in the papers, and did the police ever, I mean, you know, if it did happen." She felt the blood rush to her cheeks. She'd never been so nervous, and it was the closest she'd ever come to talking about it. She'd also just unwittingly confessed to knowing about it. She tried to deflect. "Just something my mother told me a long time ago. But I was at boarding school," she added quickly.

"Nope, can't say I have. Not something you'd ever forget.

You mean this lake?" he asked, pointing to the white landscape beyond.

"Maybe it was just a rumour. You know, my mother liked to gossip. I'll leave you to get on."

Becky headed back down the lane to Austin waiting in the car and fell into the seat with a huge sigh.

"Well?" he asked.

Becky was beaming. She planted a kiss on his lips; hers were as cold as ice.

He looked suspiciously at her. "You took your time. Anyone living there?"

She explained the conversation with Les.

His thoughts turned to the doctor. The man appeared to be like a ghost. For someone who had a vested interest in the late Mrs Monroe's affairs, it appeared his presence was very much absent. He'd even eluded the Mr Northwick. The name kept coming up more and more frequently, but his identity still seemed to remain a mystery.

Austin compared the last twenty-four hours to an episode of *The Twilight Zone*. A series he favoured a lot growing up. He could explain his thoughts to Becky. But she'd just revert to default and ridicule his logic. Her naivety to piece together the missing parts or at least consider the strangeness of the past events bugged him. She was only fixated on what benefitted her. Nothing beyond that.

Austin sped off, his concentration switching between Becky and his tangled mind.

"You know, all her furniture has gone. There's nothing in there, completely empty, but the cottage looked bigger than I remembered."

"Maybe it's all in storage. Maybe the doctor friend might know. I take it we're going tonight now?"

"Of course," she beamed. "I'm intrigued, aren't you?"

He felt the car take leave of its grip for a second on the icy road, and he fought the wheel momentarily, his heart spiking. He expressed a thought. "You know what I think. Too many strange occurrences. I mean, who sends a cheque to someone they haven't met, and why did the envelope have 'Greer' on it? That's the one thing out of all this that's troubling me most."

Becky side-glanced at him. "Don't be dumb. Obviously, Mrs Monroe told him about you. I keep telling you you're trying to see things that aren't there. Must be exhausting being in your head."

Austin grunted, unconvinced by her explanation. Why would Mrs Monroe mention a gardener she employed over twenty years ago?

Becky quickly changed the subject. "I know. Let's go for lunch. Somewhere posh. I'm going to buy something nice for this evening, and you need a new shirt. That blue one's too old. I've got the cheque with me, so let's cash it in and start spending my inheritance. This is turning out to be quite the trip now," she said, beaming.

Austin didn't share her excitement. How could he? This place was his kryptonite, and the further he could get away from here, the better. Her enthusiasm for her mother's property was a cold contrast to her concern about where she was buried. He found this part of her very difficult to understand. Selling her mother's cottage and spending her money to make their lives better wasn't the answer for him. It was just another slice of guilt. Exploiting a dead woman's misery, which he'd had a hand in. It left nothing but an uncomfortable taste in his mouth.

There was a part of him that wanted justice to intervene. But after so many years, that idea was nothing more than a faded thought. There was no value in trying to convince Becky to tread cautiously or explore any other idea except the one she'd already planted in her head. Maybe he *was* overthinking everything. Maybe it was all just as simple as an invite to a reading of the will by her doctor friend who wished to remain private. For now, he'd concede to Becky's notions and just ride the train.

1996

CHAPTER TWENTY-ONE

Greer rowed them across the lake and docked the boat as usual. It never became mundane, boring, or anything other than tranquillity personified for Laura. But what she would be giving up would be justified. A decision which she could live with as a decent human being. Something her father had instilled in her. "Morals should always be top of the agenda when making difficult choices," he'd say.

As crushing as it would be for Mrs Monroe, she deserved the truth. "Better an honest devil than a deceptive angel." Another Myers family saying. But her father was right.

And Becky? Laura wasn't doing this for revenge. That heavily weighted emotion, which most lean on as an excuse to avenge something. This would be more a case of actions having consequences, and somewhere in that would sit justice. Trekking the moor to the abandoned farmhouse was a painstaking affair and one that Laura found particularly difficult given the additional weight of three full bottles of alcohol.

Even though Becky had persuaded Greer to carry her rucksack after whining longer than a toddler who'd been denied sweets, his pace was swift, much to Laura's annoyance. The afternoon sun didn't wane in its efforts to cook her alive either.

"Can you slow down a bit, Greer?" asked Laura. "You're

the one not carrying ten kilos of alcohol."

Becky turned around. "This was *your* idea, remember?"

Hold your tongue, Laura Myers.

"Hold up, Greer, can you chuck a couple of bottles in the rucksack? My arms are killing me."

"He's already carrying mine. Besides, it's not far now."

Since Laura's brain was moving far quicker than her legs, she figured something out. All along, she'd credited Greer as being a strong character, especially when it was just him and her present. But Becky's presence seemed to alter him. Like the first time, Laura went across the lake with him, and they returned to find Becky less than happy. Greer never defended his actions of taking Laura; instead, he scurried off to fetch a wheelbarrow and left Laura to face Becky on her own. Carrying Becky's rucksack without question but not blinking an eye when Laura asked for help.

Did Greer know where the camera was buried? She figured not. If he was the cameraman in all of this, then it made sense for Becky to have a hold over him. This was blackmail in its coldest form.

Becky was going to answer for this.

It wasn't long before they came upon the old farmhouse. Unlike last time, the damp concrete floors concealed in the shadows provided the only relief from the muggy air. But the relief was just replaced with the pungent scent that most abandoned buildings have. The previous night's candles and crushed beer cans were still there.

Laura would play this cool. Give just enough hints to inflict doubt in their minds.

She set the basket down. The relief came quickly, and she rotated her arm like a windmill, her shoulder clicking.

Becky ran upstairs to explore the other rooms again, filling sunbeams with dancing clouds of dust in her wake. The house appeared less intimidating in the daylight, apart from the creeping ivy engulfing the half-rendered walls like sprouting triffids.

Laura ventured from the large hallway through the lounge

and into the dining room. She recognised the blue velvet sofa she'd slept on. Except this time, a fanning beam of light revealed a canvas of forensic assortments.

Her stomach turned.

"Check this out," bellowed Greer from the kitchen.

Laura moved to the kitchen to find him holding a blue camping stove in his left hand and a saucepan of beans in the other.

"Looks like the beans are still fresh. Anyone got a lighter?"

Laura fetched a box of matches from the basket and handed them to him.

"Hey Becky, down here," he shouted.

Becky bounced down the stairs in her size five Dr. Martens. "We got hot food," he said, holding up the saucepan.

"That's gross. You don't know who's been here. I'm not touching that shit," she said.

"Yeah, don't bother lighting it," added Laura.

"Someone's been here recently. Even the bed upstairs has a new sleeping bag on it, sure it wasn't there last night," said Becky.

"How would you know? You were pissed," he replied, laughing.

Becky retaliated. "Fuck off, you were stoned out of your head."

Laura left them to banter and headed upstairs. The long landing was clad in a tattered red carpet with a latticework of hessian patches worn from the heavy traffic. She imagined this being a grand house in its day with generous rooms and spacious quarters to entertain downstairs. All the rooms had ample views of the moor, which spanned the horizon in every direction. Not a single structure, other than rock tors breaking up the ground.

She explored the other rooms. Most were graveyards of discarded furniture, some in better condition than others. Even family pictures still hung from the cracked walls, evoking a sense of pity for the previous family that used to

live here. She stared at them in wonder. Their content faces captured in a
single moment of happiness.

She thought about the images of Jack and the dreadful secret they shared. Disgust stabbed her in the gut. Carrying on like nothing happened. She felt sickened, wondering if they'd committed the ultimate sin. She was sure that Becky had plotted the whole thing, manipulating the other two like pawns.

Laura wanted answers.

BECKY & AUSTIN
CHAPTER TWENTY-TWO

Dusk fell early, as it usually did in January, and they returned to the hotel with full bellies and new purchases. Austin had almost forgotten how he felt about the whole affair earlier, and Becky's more jovial spirit bled into him. They even shared some intimate time in the shower, rekindling earlier days, and now, with a newfound future on the cusp, dreams of making a new start were already taking shape in their minds.

Becky sat at the small dressing table, applying a splash of makeup, not something she usually did. She was more of a natural-appearance type of girl. Another small significant thing she was deprived of by her mother, who saw makeup as a waste of time or some provocative act to entice the boys. But it was okay for her mother to wear it occasionally when venturing into town. Once, when she was fourteen, she snuck into her mother's bedroom and tried it on. Red lipstick, dark eyeliner, and blusher, all badly applied, of course, and much to the horror of her mother, who whisked her straight off to the bathroom and made her wipe it all off.

"Pink or red?" she asked, holding up two bottles of coloured nail polish.

Austin was trying his new shirt on. A black and grey checked cheesecloth. "I don't know, red, I guess," he said, staring at himself in the mirror.

"The car will be here in an hour. I wonder where we're going. Just seems odd that there's no address on the card," he said, making a small parting in his hairline. "I'm hungry now as well, seems a rather lavish event for a will reading, don't you think?"

"I guess. Not really thought about it," she replied, painting her nails.

Austin parked himself on the end of the bed and picked up the invitation. "What if it's not what you think?"

"Austin, don't start that again. It was obvious after this morning. She's gone, so it makes sense that her estate is in probate. I expect we'll have a nice meal with her doctor friend, get to know him, pretend I miss her, fake tears, boohoo, and reminisce about how she was such a good mother, blah blah, and then sign some paperwork and leave."

He sat forward, his left leg twitching up and down like a sewing machine, and flicking the invitation in his hands. "What if it's more complicated than that? It's been over twenty years since you saw your mother. What if she's sold it to someone else already? It could be empty because it's waiting for the new owners to move in."

She turned to him from the dressing table and delivered a look. He was used to that.

"Les would have told me. Just for once, can you stop dissecting every conversation we have around my fucking mother? The cottage hasn't been sold, it's been in the family for three generations, and she was a stickler for tradition. That place hasn't been lived in for a very long time, trust me."

"What about the woman Les saw? You said he'd seen someone else there. A female, didn't you say?"

She stopped painting for a second. "Maybe it was an estate agent doing a valuation for probate or something. Can you forget your conspiracy theories just for one night and enjoy the evening? Please."

Austin remained silent.

She stood up and twirled in her new bright red dress. "How do I look?" she asked with a broad, red-lipped smile.

He nodded. "Yeah, nice."

He wasn't sharing her enthusiasm inside. Instead, he was plagued with irrational thoughts of how the evening could go. He wouldn't be surprised if Mrs Monroe had left the cottage to some obscure charity. He felt a sense of pity for her; a woman who'd done no wrong by him. Becky was no easy child, he remembered that. And he could only imagine what went through Mrs Monroe's mind when they both just upped sticks and left. No goodbyes, no explanation. Not even a note. As far as she was concerned, she'd already lost Jack, so first she'd lost her husband, then a daughter.

I wonder what happened to him?

Austin never shared his shame with Becky. It was just another emotion he learnt to bottle up. What they did to Jack made him ashamed for a long time. Another reason why the bottle took over. He'd now spent more time thinking about the god-awful things they did in the last couple of days than he'd ever done in the last twenty-plus years.

Being back in Cornwall and the thought of stepping back into that cottage again haunted him. Twenty-six years of Becky's coldness had never been so prevalent as it had in these last few days. A dark side of her he couldn't live with for much longer.

Maybe it was time to re-evaluate his life.

For now, he'd just humour her and banish any other thoughts about what the night might hold. Maybe this *was* nothing more than a reading of the will. Everything certainly pointed that way, except he couldn't shake this feeling like he was venturing into a deep, dark cave with no certainty of ever coming back out.

"Make sure you let the doctor know how much you enjoyed working for my mother, you know, and how sorry you are about her passing," she said, making last-minute adjustments to her hair, which she'd spent the last half-hour curling. "I want to give him a good impression."

"I'm pretty sure the doctor knows we've been absent from your mother's life for the last two decades."

She turned from the dressing table. "Because we made our own life away from Cornwall. Just because we never visited doesn't mean we didn't care about her. That's all he needs to know."

Austin closed his eyes, shaking his head. But she didn't notice. Her eyes were glued to her reflection in the mirror.

He got up from the small chair. The snow looked heavier under the entrance light below, and he had doubts if their lift would make it. Then, through the blanket of falling white snow, a dark-coloured Mercedes emerged, pulling up outside the entrance below. He pressed his face against the cold glass, watching the driver dash to the entrance.

He turned from the window. "Think our lift's here."

Becky picked up her black and white herringbone coat and slung it over her arm. She faced him and adjusted his jacket lapels before pecking him on the cheek. "This could be a new start for us. Tomorrow will be the beginning of the rest of our lives."

He smiled. But it was nothing more than mechanical. The bedside phone rang. He lifted the receiver.

"Lift's waiting. Better go, I suppose."

They made their way down to the reception area to be greeted by an elderly man in a light grey suit and black gloves with paper-white receding hair. Apart from confirming their names with them, he said little else.

Austin instantly recognised him from earlier. It was the gentleman he saw in reception. Except last time he was driving a Rolls Royce.

He opened the rear doors and gestured for them to get in, taking their overnight bag and placing it in the boot. Becky jumped in the back, and Austin followed.

Austin whispered to her. "That's the guy in reception I was telling you about. The one driving the Rolls."

Becky rolled her eyes and said nothing as they drove away from the hotel.

She took Austin's hand and squeezed it nervously. "How long has the doctor known my mother?" she asked the driver.

"I'm sure he can answer that when we get there, Miss."

Austin pulled himself forward on the seat. "So, who else will be there? What about Mrs Monroe's solicitor?"

"Everything will be made clear when we arrive, Sir."

He fell back in the seat and leaned towards Becky. "It's all a bit evasive, don't you think? A bit overdramatic for a will reading."

She whispered back. "Maybe the doctor wanted to make it a memorable event, you know, reminisce about Mother over dinner. Just play along."

"Do you even remember your mother having a Doctor Toe?"

"Maybe she knew him after we left. It was a long time ago." "Like I said earlier, he'll know we've not had any contact with her for all this time. How are you going to explain our absence? I mean, not even a phone call. Doesn't look very caring," he whispered.

"Doesn't matter. He's legally bound to contact me as the next of kin. I don't have to make excuses. And I'm not going to. It's not like we're ever going to see her doctor friend again." Austin glanced at the scenery outside, but it was hard to make out anything other than a carpet of whites and greys bleeding across the landscape. There were no streetlights or passing vehicles. The ride was twisting and laborious, the car occasionally breaking grip.

"Is it far?" he found himself asking.

"Just a few miles," the driver replied.

Austin knew the area well. The hotel was just a stone's throw from the lake. Uncomfortably close. His sense of direction was usually pretty good, and he was sure they were heading onto Bodmin Moor. It was all a bit too coincidental. Becky couldn't see it, though. She was single-minded about the whole affair. Even though there were no obvious indications that this was anything other than what they anticipated, Austin couldn't help but have a prickly feeling about it. He looked ahead to what might be possible for his life without Becky. The last couple of days had revealed her true colours. She really did have a heart of stone.

Tonight would certainly be the beginning of the rest of their lives. But not in the way Becky wanted it to be.

He noticed the car ascending a steep, narrow road, and the grip was once again compromised. Eventually, it made the difficult climb and levelled out. Once over the crest, a large house emerged in the headlight beams.

Becky craned her neck forward to see the house. The car stopped briefly at a set of black wrought iron gates, which opened electronically and allowed them into the graveled area to the front.

The snow-capped roof and white exterior appeared fresh. The front door was a large slab of oak, scarred with a history of use and lit up by a Victorian-style lantern. It was a grand and imposing place.

The driver exited the car and opened their doors.

"Please go straight in and wait in the hallway," he said.

They dashed to the porch, entered, and stood in the large hallway, dwarfed on either side by two large oak sideboards and a wooden coat rack. A jade green runner underfoot ran from the front door with exposed oak flooring on either side. In front were the large funnel-shaped stairs which wound around to the left. Large wooden double doors lay to the right side of the hallway, and on the opposite side, there was a red leather sofa and a tall lamp with oak panelling on the walls.

"Looks kind of creepy, don't you think?" said Austin, scanning the room.

"This furniture looks weirdly familiar," Becky said, stroking the wooden sideboard.

She caressed the carved columns on either end of the sideboard. "I know this. It was my mother's from the dining room. He's got my mother's furniture. What the fuck?"

Austin ignored her. "Are you nervous? I am. Nice house, though." He checked his watch and shuffled around the hallway, picking up and putting down various ornaments. A nervous impulse.

She scouted the dimly lit hallway for other recognisable furniture. But there wasn't any.

Austin continued to shuffle about, touching and feeling just about every wooden surface.

"Sit down, you're making me nervous."

"I am nervous. Just looking around, that's all."

A few minutes later, the driver appeared again at the front door, brushing the snow off his jacket, and apologised for keeping them waiting. It was the most words he'd spoken so far.

"One question before we begin the evening," the driver started. "Do you know where we are?" he asked, raising his white eyebrows.

Austin pulled his hands from his pockets. "No, not really, somewhere near Bodmin. Why?" Austin found this an odd question to ask.

Becky dismissed his question in favour of her own. "Why has my mother's doctor friend got her furniture?" she asked sharply.

Austin squeezed her hand. "Not now, Becky, leave it," he whispered from the corner of his mouth.

"Becky doesn't know where we are either," he replied, trying to cover his embarrassment.

"You'll figure it out as the evening unfolds, I'm sure," he said.

"Please go through to the sitting room," he said, ushering them through the double doors.

They stood at a set of three small steps that led into a grand room with two large, brown leather sofas facing each other and a glass coffee table in the middle. On the left wall glowed a large, open stone fireplace crackling away, so fierce they could feel the heat radiating around them from a good twenty feet away. The opposite wall housed two large bookcases, a drinks cabinet, and a wall-mounted TV on the other side with another two doors to the side. A large, silver chandelier reflected prisms of colour around the room like a disco ball, with three further wall-mounted upturned lights that were dimmed.

"I know this room," Austin mumbled, but Becky didn't hear him. She was busy exploring the room for more recognisable furniture, convinced the doctor had cleaned the cottage out.

"Help yourself to a drink. Your host will be along shortly. Oh, and you'll be joined by one other person," he said before disappearing through a set of doors.

Becky frowned, turning from the tall bookcase. "Another person? What, another person in the will?"

Her question came too late. The room was theirs.

Austin headed to the cabinet and picked up a bottle of coke.

"You want some wine?"

Becky removed her coat and threw it over the arm of the sofa. "Nah." She wandered around the room, checking all the furniture. She caressed the bookcase. "What an asshole. This bookcase was in my mother's spare room. She used to keep spare towels and linen on it. It's even got the brass bracket at the top where Jack screwed it to the wall. "Don't you think he's taking the piss now?"

Austin raised his hands. "Look, it doesn't matter, maybe she gave it to him, you can't go around accusing him. Let's just see what happens tonight at the …" Austin stopped himself mid- sentence.

"What?" she asked, noting the strange expression on his face.

He placed a hand on her shoulder. "Don't you recognise this room? Look at it and think."

Becky shrugged. "No, why would I?"

His heart skipped momentarily at a past memory.

"Remember that old, abandoned house we used to mess about in? Me, you, and that friend of yours, Molly, was it?"

"C'mon, Austin, are you really suggesting that this is that house?" Becky replied with a dismissive look.

He pointed to the double doors. "I remember the steps

into the lounge and the fireplace. Admittedly, the doors were missing, but those steps just seem familiar, the way they curve into the corner of the room."

"I think you're just stretching your imagination, and you're beginning to piss me off. And don't start with your stupid stories and stuff. I'm sure the doctor won't be interested."

He undid his top button. "Don't be such a cow then, and stop banging on about your mother's furniture. It's probably quite hard for him if he's just lost a friend."

Becky poured herself a Coke and slouched on the sofa. "Whatever, Austin."

He perched himself on the steps. It was the furthest point from the fire, and he was beginning to feel sleepy. "Anyway, doesn't the will have to be read by a solicitor or something?" he asked.

She shrugged. "Dunno, guess not."

He made his way to the drinks cabinet and pulled out another Coke. He stood briefly, staring at the bottles of wine. Even after all this time of being sober, the urge for a full-bodied red was still strong. If ever there was a moment to slip off the wagon, it was here, tonight. He closed the cabinet door quickly before temptation took over.

He checked his watch again. "It's been fifteen minutes. If no one comes through that door in a minute, I'm going out to get some fresh air."

"Sit down, for God's sake. Just chill."

Austin fell onto the end of the sofa. He watched the fire licking the air, mesmerised by the soothing flames.

"Where's this doctor then, the one who invited us?" he asked.

"How do I know? Maybe he'll be along in a minute."

He removed his jacket. "I'm heading back to the hallway for now. Get some cooler air."

Austin reached for the wrought iron handles. "They're locked," he said, turning to Becky with a confused expression.

She stood up. "Don't be stupid. You're probably not

178

pulling the handle down far enough."

She went to the door.

"You're fucking kidding me. Try the double doors at the other end."

He hurried to the other doors at the far end.

"Nope, they're locked too. Hold on, I think I can hear someone." He pushed his ear to the door. "Sounds like someone shouting for the doctor."

Becky frowned. "What? Shout back."

"No, let's just wait. We're guests, remember."

"No, we're clients, remember. He's already got half my mother's stuff, and I am going to ask him about it once he's read the will."

"Just be nice about it, Becky, okay?"

She rolled her eyes. "If it was up to you, you'd say nothing." Austin shook his head and fell onto the sofa again. He'd never noticed Becky's attitude as much as he had recently. It was during these last few days that her demeaning tone and disregard for anything but herself had truly come to the forefront. If he was honest, he wasn't bothered about the will. He imagined it would only drive a bigger wedge once she had what she wanted. The past was his anchor. A heavy weight he carried around with him and one that Becky never wanted to
face or let him talk about.

He threw a question at her. He knew it was like poking a hornet's nest, but he was bored of waiting, and she was getting on his nerves.

"What are you going to do if you don't get the cottage? I mean, what if it's been sold already to pay for your mother's care?"

Becky stood at the edge of the sofa with her arms crossed and a scorned look.

"Are you shitting me? My mother was loaded; she never went anywhere or spent anything except on fucking furniture, oh, and my miserable home-schooling. Even if it did get sold with all the land, there'd still be more than enough left over.

Don't forget Jack sold his properties when he moved in with her, and I expect she's collected his life insurance since the police thought he was dead."

Austin stared at her. "How can you be so cold about it all? I mean, what if Jack returned one …"

Becky interrupted. "We don't talk about it, remember? How many times do I have to tell you?"

She stomped off to the drinks cabinet, pulled out a bottle of red wine and a corkscrew, and handed it to him. "Open this, please. I need it," she said, thrusting it at him.

He took the bottle and corked it. "Better get two glasses," he said.

"Like hell I will. There's no way you're drinking." She poured a glass.

He looked at her with a slither of contempt. "You know what, I'm sick of being told what I can and can't talk about and what I can and can't do."

Becky approached him. Face to face. "If you want to fuck up your life again, then go ahead and drink the whole fucking bottle. Except this time, I won't be sticking around to pick the pieces up again. And for the record, I'm the one who, for the last twenty-odd years, has been trying to keep us from being caught, and that means knowing when to open your mouth and when to keep it shut. What happened, happened, so just forget it, enjoy the evening, and then we can celebrate the spoils later. Okay, love?" she said, kissing him hurriedly.

There it was again. Hot and cold. He wondered how many times he was going to ride this rollercoaster with her. He swallowed hard and resisted responding for now. Because they'd been invited to the doctor's home, he thought it more respectful to put his grievances to one side and just play along with the evening.

He meandered around the room again. This time, gazing at the large, framed pictures. At the far end lay a photo, lit by a downturned silver wall light. It didn't take him long to recognise the picture in the frame.

"Becky, come look at this."

She stood with him, gazing at the picture. "That's the old house we used to muck about in, isn't it?"

He nodded. "Sure is, must have been taken a fair few years ago. You can see how the roof's caved in."

His face froze.

"What?" she quizzed.

"Hasn't it sunk in yet?" He opened his arms like an eagle and turned to the room.

Becky felt her gut tighten. "You're saying that this is that house?"

"We're on Bodmin, that I know, but it was too dark to tell where we were heading. I told you that I recognised the steps into the lounge."

Austin slid his palms over his face and sighed.

Becky necked her wine and paced around the room. "It's just a coincidence, right? I mean, there can't be many large houses on the moor, and it stands to reason that someone eventually bought it and saved it." She paused, staring at the fire. "Do you think we should be worried?" she asked, watching the embers dancing in the flames.

Austin shrugged. "Yes, it is just a house, but with everything else that's gone on since we've been here, I'm beginning to think that there are too many coincidences. The phone calls, the invitation, and the fact that your mother's nursing home has no record of anyone there calling us. And yet, here we are."

Becky put on another unconvincing smile and reached for some more wine. "You're right, it's just a house. And that matron can't really know if anyone called me. It could've been any of the staff. They probably didn't even tell her."

Austin finished his drink. "That may be the case, but you're forgetting one thing."

She frowned. "Which is?"

"How did they get your number? Think about it. You're the one who kept spouting on about changing our numbers every time we got a new phone, like some CIA paranoid spy shit."

Becky walked off towards the double doors and tried the handle again.

Austin shook his head. *That's right, walk off when you don't like a question.* As he watched her pulling on the handles, the door at the other end opened, and a voice startled them.

"Please, come through to the dining hall," the driver said, gesturing as he held the door open.

Becky swung around. "Is Dr Toe in there?"

The driver ignored her. "I'm Peter. I'm here to show you to your seats for this evening's meal. Please come through."

Austin smiled and took Becky's hand as they entered the dining hall. Their eyes drifted around the room for a moment before falling on the lavish table in front of them. Austin noticed the attractive woman at the table, but not before Becky caught him staring and tugged his hand.

Peter disappeared just as quickly as he'd entered, followed by the unmistakable sound of a locking door.

1996

CHAPTER TWENTY-THREE

From downstairs came cheery voices with the addition of Molly's usual coarse and vulgar tones. Laura headed downstairs to find a distasteful Molly trying her best to pole-dance around a fallen beam in denim hot-pants and a skimpy top. Greer's eyes were glued to her every movement.

Laura had always been a pretty girl growing up. Her father had to assume the role of her mother due to her frenzied bouts of drinking, rendering her incapable of even functioning like a human being, let alone a responsible one. Laura was never allowed to wear short skirts or heavy makeup like some of her friends. Everything she wore had to have the seal of approval from her conservative father, who knew the world and all the ulterior motives of the teenage boys within it. But she was glad of it all despite the father-daughter differences of opinion. She knew he was protecting her. Instilling morals that made her who she was today. At twenty-three, even though Laura hid her slender figure in baggy t-shirts and favoured virgin skin, free from all that makeup, she was still far more attractive than Molly. Molly was the epitome of everything Laura's father didn't want her to become.

For the sake of this evening, though, she laughed along with Molly and Greer acting out and playing the fools.

As the burnt orange clouds signalled the departure of the

sun over the moor and daylight drew to a close, Becky pulled some more candles from her bag and then scouted the room for suitable places to put them.

Molly pulled a bottle opener from Laura's basket, along with a bottle of red Bordeaux. "Here you go, Greer, pop the cork on this, will you?"

"Bet she'll pop your cork any day now," laughed Becky.

"Can't say I didn't see that coming," said Molly, beaming a smile.

Becky brought down an old blanket from upstairs and laid it on the concrete floor. Greer found an old wooden chair in the kitchen and parked himself down on it.

"Are you going to fill the air with that crap again?" asked Laura, watching him take a small bag of weed out of his dungaree pocket.

"Got to be done, Laura, you should try it, might chill you out."

"No thanks."

Molly sat on Greer's legs like a child, with one arm around his shoulder. "How about me then, handsome? I fancy some."

Greer blushed.

Becky looked annoyed. "He don't need any encouragement, leave him be."

Laura sat on the blanket observing the playful drama between them, Molly flirting with Greer and Becky doing her best to keep her jealousy under control.

Becky poured some wine into a plastic picnic cup, sinking it like lemonade. Molly pulled the joint from Greer's lips and took a drag.

It was as though Laura had suddenly vanished into thin air. An inconsequential fourth person looking in from the outside at the carefree and childish lives of three unscrupulous people. As the wine flowed from mouth to mouth and they sunk slowly into semi-awareness, the time came to put the suggestion into the mix. With the loosening of inhibitions, Laura loaded the gun.

"Truth or Dare, anyone?"

But the suggestion fell on deaf ears.

"You're not drinking. You need to catch up, girl," said Molly.

Laura raised her plastic cup. "I've already got some, but you're too drunk to notice."

But she'd poured herself cherryade. She needed to keep a clear head.

Becky stepped into the other room. "Hey, Greer, come help me with this."

Greer rolled his eyes and got up reluctantly, muttering small objections to himself. Even in the shadows, the distinct shape of the blue velvet sofa was striking. Moments later, amid deep groans echoing from the adjacent room, Greer emerged carrying the blue velvet sofa, followed by Becky with gritted teeth pushing hard against the other end.

"Bagsy the sofa," hollered Molly, leaping onto the end cushion before the other two could catch their breath. Laura was in no rush to get acquainted with the sofa again, especially having seen it in the light. One drunken night on it was more than enough.

Becky sank into the middle cushion. Greer felt more comfortable on the wooden chair away from their teasing hands.

Laura stayed on the blanket, leaning against the fallen beam.

Molly pulled a bottle of Bordeaux from the basket, passing it to Greer to open.

Darkness descended, and only the flickering candles hinted at the muted colours in the room. Laura caught the scent of cannabis sticking in her throat again. It was enough to spur her to go outside, an excuse to pee and get some air.

On her return, she squeezed on the end of the sofa, avoiding Greer's obnoxious habit a few feet away. The sofa seemed to be the lesser of the two evils.

Becky nudged Laura. "Drink up."

"Still got half a cup. No rush."

Molly topped her cup up for the third time.

Laura picked another moment. "Come on then, Truth or Dare, who wants to start?"

Greer rolled his head back. "Ah, not again. Bet I'm going to get stitched up by you three."

Becky squealed. "I'll get this party started." She landed a look on Greer. "Truth or dare?"

Greer was slumped on the chair with a large grin and wide eyes. "Told you! What a bitch. Go on then, I'll take a dare."

"Dare you to eat the beans from the saucepan. Cold," she laughed.

Greer fetched the saucepan from the kitchen and gazed at the beans in the bottom before tipping the contents into his mouth. "Not bad, actually." His expression said otherwise.

"That's rank," said Molly.

He wiped his mouth on his sleeve and dropped the saucepan. "My turn then. I'll pick Laura. She's a much safer bet than you two."

Molly teased him. "What a cop-out, you pussy."

Molly's laugh was raucous, possessing the entire room each time, just like her voice, gritty but sexy. It wasn't a stretch to imagine her on the end of some phone sex line. Laura despised her.

"Truth or dare?"

"Truth," answered Laura.

Greer removed his hat and played with his hair. It was clear that all that weed had messed with his brain. "Give me a moment. I ain't that good with questions."

Molly leaned forward on the sofa. "Come on, Greer, get on with it. I'll be sober by the time you think of something. Just ask her a question, like do you spit or swallow." Her laugh drowned out Becky's giggles.

Greer looked awkwardly at them on the sofa, his leg twitching like a jackhammer.

"When was the last time you had sex?" he asked awkwardly.

Laura wasn't surprised his question was influenced by the

other two. But she could at least credit him for airing on the right side of coarseness.

"About six months ago," she answered with a little hesitation.

Another raucous laugh cracked the air. "Jesus, girl, you need to sort that out. I've got some mates I can hook you up with." Laura laughed with them. But it was false. *I'm not a slut like you.* That was what she wanted to say. There were lots of things she wanted to say as she sat next to them. All of it was hiding behind this facade of teenage humour and carefree attitude. *What have you done with Jack?* It was probably the one question she wanted an answer to most. But that would come eventually. Delivered with intelligence and a hint of suggestion.

Molly topped up their cups. She leaned across to Laura with the bottle. "Come on, girl, keep up."

Laura allowed Molly to pour her some wine, but she sipped it slowly.

Greer raised his cup. "Cheers, Laura. Your go."

Laura turned to Becky. The perfect opportunity had just presented itself. She was about to poke the lion.

"Truth or dare."

Becky tapped her lips. "Dare I reckon, least she won't have me eating woodlice or shit."

Molly tapped cups with Becky, red wine spilling on her shorts. "I'll drink to that one."

Laura was hoping Becky would choose truth. But she could work with dare. She made deliberate eye contact with Becky and revealed her first question. "I dare you to share a secret that only you three know."

Let that one fester in your evil head.

Becky's expression was of disdain for Laura. Laura wanted to wear the same smirk Becky gave her at the kitchen table when she'd asked her about her stepfather. But she'd save that for later.

Becky frowned. "What the fuck does that even mean?"

"A secret you might have with everyone in the room

except me."

Laura watched Molly's eyes connect with Greer. Both were stone-faced for a second. Their jovial facade was on pause.

"So, I'm supposed to have a secret with these two, but not you?"

"I don't know, that's the dare, do you?"

"Why the fuck would you ask that anyway? A dare is something you do; that's a question, dumb ass."

Laura held her cool. "Not always."

Greer and Molly remained silent.

"It's just a game, Becky. It just popped into my head," Laura replied calmly.

Got you wondering now.

Becky slouched back into the velvet sofa, her arms across her chest and her eyes full of fire.

The silence in the room was deafening. Laura's question was a huge bomb of exploding doubt. It filled the room. The first seed had been planted. All she needed now was to grow that seed.

Molly broke the silence. "More wine, anyone?"

Becky snatched the wine from her and drank straight from the bottle.

"Fucks sake, Becky. Use your cup."

Greer relit his spliff despite its length being insignificant.

"I nicked twenty quid from my mum's purse. Happy now?" Laura doubted it was a secret she'd shared with the others,
but it didn't matter.

Becky high-fived Molly. "My turn then."

Laura braced herself for the repercussions. To her surprise, she was spared. At least this time, anyway.

Becky threw her arm around Molly. "Truth or dare, sister, truth or dare?"

"Dare," replied Molly with excited eyes.

Greer buried his head in his hands, anticipating the ridiculousness of Molly's dare.

"I dare you to give Greer a lap dance."

"Oh, here we go, fucks sake, Becky."

Greer downed his wine to drown out the forthcoming embarrassment.

Molly wandered over to him. She parked herself backwards between his legs. One hand on each knee, her short hot pants
exposing most of her bottom, which she waved from side to side like a pendulum in front of him. He was frozen. There was a mixture of awkward embarrassment and eager pleasure in his mind. Molly picked up his hands and placed them on her breasts as she continued. Even Laura felt his embarrassment.

She watched Becky. The way she watched them. Awkward jealousy grew in her expression. She couldn't decide if Becky genuinely had a thing for Greer or if it was more of a friendship attachment with a twist of possessiveness. Either way, she wasn't surprised when Becky interrupted it.

"Ok, Molly, think he's had enough," she said. Her smile carried no sign of enjoyment.

Molly returned to the sofa full of giggles.

"I need a piss," said Greer getting up from the chair and staggering around the sofa.

"Hope you ain't got a stiffy. Could be awkward," Molly teased, followed by another raucous laugh.

Laura despised Molly's coarse behaviour. She expected nothing less, though. The more she thought about the images on the camera, the more she realised how dangerous Molly's behaviour could be. But it was all choreographed by Becky. She was the dangerous one. And it would appear that Greer was just swept along, manipulated by Becky. Maybe she promised him all manner of sexual gratification from Molly. Whatever the reason, it was a dark triangle of friendship.

Laura felt sick to her stomach.

But something didn't fit right. Greer had already revealed that he was embarrassed by Molly's sexualised behaviour. So why would he stand there in the bushes, taking pictures while watching the sexual advances of Molly degrading herself with a man in his forties?

What was Greer getting out of this?

The dynamics between them all were odd at best.

Greer returned to his chair and proceeded to roll another spliff.

Molly piped up. "Guess it's my go now, then."

"Leave me out of this one," said Greer.

Molly huffed. "Well, you're no fun. Guess I'm going with Becky," she said, facing her. "Truth or dare?"

"Fuck it, I'll go with a dare," Becky grinned. "But no kinky shit."

"I dare you to snog Laura."

Laura shuffled about on the sofa. Dread followed.

"I said no kinky shit, you bitch."

Molly shrugged. "Got to do it. Rules are rules, girl."

Greer dragged on his spliff. "This should be fun."

"Perv," said Becky.

Laura needed a moment to prepare for this. But before she could even comprehend the depth of distastefulness that she might feel, Becky had turned in her seat, grabbed Laura's chin, and planted a kiss on her lips. Laura could taste the alcohol on her. She was just grateful it wasn't a deep, lingering one.

"You're quite pretty, Laura, if you made a bit of an effort." Becky then turned, high-fiving Molly.

Becky's condescending remark didn't rile her this time. She was beyond all that now.

The summer warmth, which had been so comforting earlier, had fizzled out. Laura reached for the blanket off the floor and put it across her legs. The candles were now burning low. Laura still had some questions, and the game was taking longer than she wanted. She wondered how Mrs Monroe had got on at the police station—if another search was authorised. And even if it was, would they find his body this time? But it was strange, sitting here, knowing that all the answers Mrs Monroe wanted were right here in this room.

"Looks like it's my turn now," said Becky.
Pick me. Laura wished.
Her wish was granted. Becky turned to her. "Truth or dare." Laura wasn't in the mood to be exploited for any more
spontaneous sexual requests, so she worked out the odds, knowing it would be her turn next. "Truth," replied Laura.

This time, it was Becky who let the silence linger on. Maybe she was delving into her devious mind to find a question that
would somehow feel like a comeback for earlier. But what she delivered was the perfect opening.

"What do you think happened to Jack?"
Are you fishing? Did my last question raise your suspicions?
Was this the wine freeing up Becky's conscience, or was this a fishing expedition? If it was the latter, then Laura had the perfect answer. She broke eye contact with Becky and locked on Molly, who was unusually quiet and fiddling with her cup. Greer was stoned and gave no discernible expression other than being completely disengaged.

Laura decided to go with humour, cleverly disguised as a Trojan horse. "Honestly? I think you killed him with Molly's help." Laura delivered the line with a straight face, just for a couple of seconds. It was long enough for it to land doubt in their mind. But those two seconds told her everything. She then let out a bellowing laugh. Her laugh was enough to camouflage her answer.

Sit on that one, Becky Monroe.

Molly gave the best reply. It was silence. Not a raging rant full of defence, or even in support of Becky. Just silence.

"Is that supposed to be funny? What the fuck, Laura? Why would you say that? Molly, you going to say something?"

Molly giggled into her cup.

"I'm just kidding, lighten up. Unless you did kill him, I mean, you didn't like him anyway," Laura replied. She stroked her hair. "Must be my turn now."

Becky grabbed the bottle of wine— if looks could kill.

Greer was fidgety.

Laura wanted distance. Not friendship. She didn't care about upsetting them. Her responsibility rested with Mrs Monroe. A woman who'd fallen under the spell of disillusion about her daughter and whose efforts to seek closure now lay in Laura's hands.

Laura thought about her father. Trapped in a tug of war between instilling right from wrong with just enough discipline to keep her centred, and enough slack to allow her freedom to grow, coupled with the love she lacked from her absent

mother. It was this fine balance of single parenting that had brought her to want to do the right thing. But this game allowed her to enjoy it on the way.

"Truth or dare?" Laura asked Becky.

Becky's expression didn't waver. It was still sour. Laura could almost hear the resentment and anger rattling around her head. Another push, that was all she needed.

Becky shrugged. "Truth, I guess."

The cards had fallen into place. She would poke the lion once more and see if it bit.

"What was the last thing you buried?" she asked. Delivered with the smirk she'd been saving. *Touché*.

Becky leapt up from the sofa and stood over her. "What are you playing at? What kind of question is that? What did I bury? Why don't you just ask me? Go on," she shouted angrily. Becky's fists were clenched, her words spitting in Laura's face.

Molly grabbed Becky, pulling her back. "Sit down. She's not worth it. She don't know anything, anyway."

Laura sat forward, raising her eyebrows. "What don't I know, Molly? Tell me," she replied with a calm delivery. But she wasn't calm. Not inside. Adrenalin coursed through her veins.

Greer dragged on his spliff. "I reckon she knows."

"Shut up, Greer," snapped Becky.

Laura teased again. "What do I know, Greer?"

Greer removed his hat and ruffled his hair, his leg twitching. "Shit, Becky. I knew this was a bad idea. What did you do with the camera?"

And there it was. The concoction of weed and alcohol had clouded his mind and devoured it of all rational thought.

Becky launched her empty cup at Greer, striking him in the head. "Shut the fuck up."

Laura remained seated, watching Becky trying to manage an already-failed situation. Molly did what she always did when things got ugly. She remained quiet. Head to the ground.

Greer picked up an empty bottle and tossed it against an adjacent wall. The bottle exploded with a pop.

Tension grew.

Greer paced the floor. "What do you know then, Laura? Tell us now," he yelled as he marched back and forth. She'd never seen him raise his voice in anger before.

Becky shrieked. "Shut the fuck up, Greer, before you get us all into trouble."

Laura watched from the shadows. A drama she'd orchestrated. She watched Greer pacing back and forth and Becky trying to keep a lid on a boiling pot. It was almost humorous.

Molly was an enigma. Only predictable in mildly influential situations, but what was she like when she was cornered? Laura didn't hold back any longer. If the truth was ever to come to a head, it would be now.

Amongst the chaos and bewildered exchanges of desperate conversation, Laura delivered her final blow.

"You mean the camera you buried."

Silence prevailed in an instant, and all eyes fell on her.

Molly leapt up from the sofa. Face-to-face with Laura. Eyes narrowed. "You sly bitch, you knew the whole time. You were just playing games with us."

Molly shoved Laura in the chest, and she stumbled backwards. Heart racing. Molly held her hand out in front of Laura. "Hand it over. Now."

Becky leaned on Molly's shoulder. "Don't matter, there were no batteries in it. I took them out."

Laura was trembling. She could feel the pulse in her neck. Maybe this wasn't the place to have confronted them. In an abandoned house. Miles from anyone. How far would they go to protect their secret?

Becky grabbed Laura's top and twisted it around her fist. "Where did you find it?"

"Cabbages," she uttered, her voice strained. Becky released her. Laura straightened her top.

Greer whined. Close to tears. "I told you, Becky. I told you this would backfire."

Now the cat was out of the bag. There was little point in subtle questions and innuendoes.

"What the hell were you thinking Becky? And deceiving your mum like that. I mean, that's just plain cruel. Jack didn't deserve that. And Molly, what the hell did you get out of this? I mean …"

A second later, Laura felt her head recoiling and a sharp pain searing across her face. It took a moment for her to realise Becky had struck her hard.

"You bitch. So, you know what's on the camera. How? I made sure there were no batteries in the house. It was my safeguard."

"Oh Jesus, Becky."

"Shut up, Greer, you're in this too."

"Only because you promised me …"

"I said shut up, let me think."

"What did she promise you?" asked Laura, holding her nose with trembling hands and feeling the warm, sticky blood oozing from her nostrils.

Molly pointed at Greer. "Don't even think about it."

"I got the batteries from the torch," said Laura. "I took the batteries out last night. Then, when I got back, I loaded them into the camera. Point is, what you all did was degrading. Why? Where's Jack, Becky? Tell me. What happened to him?"

Laura felt her heart pounding and the blood streaming down her face. She tilted her head back slightly, hoping to stop the bleeding.

Molly spoke first. "Jack won't be bothering her again. We made sure of that."

Laura shuffled backwards, putting some distance between them. She turned and saw the front door was slightly ajar, and the silvery glow of the moonlight was creeping in across the floor. Her chest was tight, and the pain in her face was a throbbing ache. But at least her nose had stopped bleeding. The candles in the room were nearly spent, flickering violently in the last throws before darkness fell. Laura had more questions. But the evening was already ugly enough, and it was time for her to leave.

Laura stepped towards the door, grabbing the handle. But Greer's size ten foot anchored to the floor in a split second and stopped it.

"I want to know what you're going to do. Are you going to say anything?" he asked, looking to Becky for affirmation.

Molly moved towards Laura, her face up in hers. Laura could smell the alcohol on her breath. "Yeah, bitch, so what now? You come here from the big, bad city and interfere in our lives like some fucking do-gooding hero. You know nothing, girl, the shit that arsehole put Becky through."

Laura was shaking. Her escape was blocked.

"So, where's Jack? I mean, I'm guessing you didn't kill him." Her words came with a tremor.

Becky and Molly shared a laugh. "Nah, better than that," spouted Becky. "I hope he's a million miles from here. He won't be showing his face round here again after we threatened to show Mum the pictures and post them to his bitch of a daughter, Heather." Becky picked up the remaining bottle of wine, swigged it, and passed it to Molly. "You know what that bastard was going to do?"

Laura shook her head nervously.

"He was going to persuade my mother to change her will, leaving the house to Heather in a trust for me. Well, fuck him," she raged.

Molly nudged Becky. "Tell her about putting the pictures up. That was class," she said, laughing.

"Yeah, we were going to put the pictures up all around the village on every lamppost and wall. Ain't no way he'd come within a million miles of this place. The old cow believes he's dead, and to be fair, he may as well be because she ain't casting eyes on him again. And that," Becky said, poking Laura in the chest, "Is how you take care of things the Monroe way."

Molly pipped in. "Ain't that the truth."

"And Greer, how did he end up in all this?" asked Laura.

"Becky told me she ..."

"Shut up, Greer."

Greer looked to Becky. "I want to know what she's going to do. Rawlings knows my family. They'll kill me if this gets out."

I need the camera back," demanded Becky. "You need to leave and fuck off back to the city."

Laura's mouth was dry. Her adrenaline peaked. She felt the one emotion she never thought she'd let off the lead. Anger.

Until now, she'd held her cool, every move calculated with an agenda to reveal the truth. Becky raised the stakes, showing her true colours, and struck her again, hard. Laura could feel the bridge of her nose swelling and bloody snot filling her sinuses.

Greer closed the door and stood beside her.

Laura let rip. "You really think you're going to keep this to yourselves? There are more people involved than just Jack. What about the police? What if Jack decides to tell the truth? What about your poor mum? And no matter how much you may hate your half-sister, she deserves the truth, too. She's out there thinking her father's dead, just like your mother. Your mum was right about you. You don't care about anything unless it benefits you. And as for you, Molly, you have zero morals and even less sense to let her talk you into that vile act. I mean, what do you get out of this, huh?"

Amidst the heavy breathing and nervous jostling, Molly grabbed an empty bottle and smashed it on the concrete floor before raising the jagged neck to Laura's throat. "We haven't finished playing yet, have we, Becky? I believe it's your turn."

Laura froze in fear, the jagged bottle just a few inches from her throat.

"Go on, Becky, ask her."

Becky spoke softly into Laura's ear. "Truth or dare, Laura? Actually, we'll pick. We'll go with dare. Well, ain't that a bitch."

"What's wrong with you? Why are you carrying on this charade? You've been exposed, your lies are out, you can't seriously think you're going to get away with this." Laura's words came with fear. She was scared.

"Greer, we're going. Make sure she don't run off. Leave everything here, we'll collect it tomorrow," said Becky.

Greer continued pacing around randomly. "What are we going to do with her? She's going to grass us up. I know she is."

Becky squeezed Laura's face. "Dare you to swim the lake with your hands and feet tied."

"Yes, Becky, love it! Bitch is going down, girl."

"Greer, grab her arm, make sure she don't run off."

Greer pushed Laura out the door, his hands wrapped tightly around her skinny arms. Molly and Becky followed with the flashlight, trekking the moor with the bright moon assisting.

They're only bluffing about the dare. Just hold your cool.

Laura said nothing. The three inebriated people full of anger needed no further provoking. She'd said her piece. In the morning, she would pack her bag, take the camera, and set about exposing the lies.

She could hear the exchange behind her. The whispering voices. The sniggering. She wasn't playing their games anymore; in fact, she couldn't wait to leave now.

At the jetty, Greer prepared the boat, fixing the torch to

the bow while Becky and Molly stood over Laura.

Becky held Laura's arm; her grip was strong. Molly sidestepped, taking her other arm. "Greer, use the baler twine, tie her hands and her feet up," instructed Becky.

He paused and looked at Becky. "You're joking, right? We're just going to frighten her, right? But she'll ..."

"Exactly. You don't want this shit coming out, do you?"

"Course I don't, but ..."

"Then just do it."

Laura struggled, trying desperately to lose their grip, but to no avail.

"We're just going to scare her, right?" Greer asked again, fetching the twine from the boat.

"Don't be a pussy, Greer, just tie her hands and feet up."

Laura bellowed in defiance, her voice filling the night. She was no longer calm and compliant. This was escalating into something far more serious.

Molly wrapped her arms around Laura, her torso twisting.

"See how you swim now, bitch."

Greer bound her wrists with orange twine.

"And her feet, Greer. Go on."

He shook his head. "I can't."

Becky snatched the twine from him and wrapped it tightly around her ankles.

Laura was petrified.

"Take her to the end and drop her in."

"For real?" he said struggling with her.

Laura yelled. Her lungs felt like they were bursting, and bloody snot flowed from her nose.

"Yeah, for real, unless you want to explain to the whole village why you were taking pervy pictures. She ain't gonna ruin our lives, not now," spat Becky.

Once Laura's shrieking had subsided to paralysed fear and the realisation that her slender frame was powerless against Greer's brute strength, there was little fight left. Laura tried frantically to anchor her feet on the space between the rough planks as she was led onto the narrow boardwalk.

As Greer dragged her closer to the end, the boardwalk seemed much shorter at that moment. Shorter than it did at the beginning of the summer when she sat at the end, dangling her feet in the icy waters of the lake, watching the cormorants diving for fish and occasionally throwing a handful of seeds and fruit to the goldeneyes as they gracefully propelled themselves towards her. All battling for her spoils.

But it was Greer who had control. He propelled a fear in her she'd never experienced before.

Trying to appeal to his better side had proven futile. Given the amount of booze and weed circulating around in his brainwashed mind and the two overpowering personalities controlling him, Laura's odds of evading this were looking slim to none.

Becky and Molly watched on in hypnotic jubilation, chanting, "Truth or dare, truth or dare," seemingly oblivious of just how far they were taking the game. A simple game that had turned dark.

Greer was battling against Laura's thrashing limbs in a last-ditch effort to avoid the lake. If only she'd seen this coming, she could have run. She should have run. How had she not seen this coming?

The intense moonlight gave moments of clarity as it appeared from behind the rolling clouds, casting an occasional reflection across the water.

As Laura reached the edge of the boardwalk, the two girls were relishing in her fear. This was no longer a game.

Greer looked to the other two for one last moment.

"Just do it," yelled Becky.

Greer released his grip, and Laura hit the water screaming. Then, silence as she disappeared below the surface, along with their secret.

DR ARTHUR TOE
CHAPTER TWENTY-FOUR

Austin's eyes lay on the woman at the table revolving the wine glass between her fingers. He approached the table, nodding politely. He adjusted his glasses, more out of habit than necessity.

'Hi, I'm Austin, and this is my partner Becky," he said, pulling out a chair for her.

Becky sat at the table, ignoring her place setting next to Marcia, and levelled out the cutlery in front of her. Austin pulled out a chair and sat next to her, smiling across the table at the woman opposite. The air in the room was warm and comforting. The chandeliers sprinkled dancing light across the table and made the silverware sparkle.

"I'm Marcia," she started. "Are you expecting anyone else this evening?" she asked, hoping to fill in some of the blanks.

Becky continued fiddling with the cutlery and tucking the curls of blonde hair behind her ear, so Austin replied. "I don't think so. Only the host and some of his guests, I believe, by the looks of things," he said in a tone that suggested some confusion.

Becky questioned Marcia. "Did you get an invite from a Doctor Arthur Toe?"

Marcia's eyes widened. "Yes, I did."

"So, are you here for the reading of the will?"

Marcia perched her elbows on the table. "I'm sorry, I

don't follow. The reading of the will, did you say?"

"That's the hope." Becky reached for the open bottle and poured a large glass of red wine. "So, why do you think you're here?" she quizzed.

Marcia reached into her Prada bag and took out her invite, placing it in front of Becky. "Well, I did think before that we were all here for the murder mystery evening, though if you say you're here for the reading of a will, something doesn't seem to add up." Marcia sipped her wine. "I was invited on a personal level. Look, I don't mean to be rude, but I was expecting to be greeted by this elusive doctor. So far, I've just been herded from one room to the next with no idea about what's going on. Do you?"

Becky read Marcia's invite. "What the fuck? I'm not sure I understand." She slid the invite under Austin's face. "Two thousand six hundred pounds. Are you kidding me?" Becky's face was no longer soft and playful. She downed a mouthful of red and stamped the glass back on the table.

Marcia removed her jacket and placed it on the back of the chair. Austin eyed her curves under her tight-fitting, white top over the top of the invite. There were just enough buttons undone to hint at the cleavage that lay buried, but it was buttoned high enough to remain elegant. He watched her delicate hand playing with the glass stem.

He cleared his throat and returned the invite. "Well, we only had a thousand pounds. But, I mean, we're a bit confused about this evening as well."

"You said a reading of a will. Is that why you're here?" asked Marcia.

"That's not what our invite said exactly, but everything seems to point that way. The doctor knew my mother, who recently passed away, and since I'm the only surviving relative, we presumed it was to sort out my mother's will."

Marcia leaned forward. "So, you know Dr Toe?"

"No. Not really. It was my mother who knew him, apparently. I've never met him. Things were very complicated between me and my mother. It's a long and very miserable story. We never really got on." Becky necked the rest of her wine, and her cheeks flushed. "Truth is, I hated the old cow."

Marcia gave a sympathetic nod.

Austin left the conversation, and his attention fell to the room and all the beauty it had to offer in the way of the use of wood and its finish. He looked at the pictures opposite, set against the wood panelling; all lit up by individual silver lighting.

Suddenly, their noses were filled with a rich aroma entering the room.

"Someone's cooking, it seems. I'm starving," said Austin.

Marcia ignored him, instead observing Becky, whose drinking etiquette was as unrefined as her language. She'd already made a judgement about how she appeared to be a woman with some class, but underneath the red dress and over-indulgent makeup lay someone who failed in that role the second she opened her mouth.

"It's a full red," Marcia found herself saying. "It should be savoured. I also corked it earlier, so it's been sitting at room temperature. Unfortunately, not long enough." Marcia shifted her gaze to Austin, who was fixated on the pictures. "Do you not drink wine? It's rather good," said Marcia, trying to distract him from the pictures.

"Sorry?" he said, his attention snatched away.

"No, he doesn't, he's tee-total," interrupted Becky. "You say you're here for a murder mystery evening. I don't mean to pry, but why were you paid? Usually, at those kinds of events, you have to pay them."

Marcia raised her eyebrows and lifted her glass to her soft lips. "Why were you paid then if you think you're here for a will reading?"

"As an advance on my inheritance," she said, swilling the dregs around the glass. "So, how do you know the doctor?" Becky asked.

Marcia rolled her head back and gazed at the patterned ceiling before engaging with Becky's question. "I don't.

Hence, the *elusive* Doctor Toe. It's a long and, quite frankly, complicated story. Never met the man, and to be honest, the way things are going so far, I'm under the impression that might still be the case, even after tonight." Marcia got up from the table. "Excuse me, but I need to make a phone call."

She went to the far end of the room, but there was no signal. She then remembered that she'd been interrupted before she'd had a chance to read the text that came through earlier from Bernie.

Becky nudged Austin. "Can you make it any more obvious?" she asked sharply.

"What?"

"Staring at that Marcia," she scorned.

"She looks kind of familiar, but I don't know why," he replied, with his eyes still engaged on her.

"You're kidding, right? That's just an excuse to ogle some attractive woman. Thanks, Austin, you really know how to make a girl feel special." Becky folded her arms, throwing them heavily on her chest. He knew when she did this, it was a signal that her mood was going to change.

Becky poured another glass of red, leaving half the bottle.

Austin was momentarily vacant, like a switch had suddenly flipped in his head. "Something doesn't feel quite right."

Marcia returned to the table with her attention very much focused on her phone.

"Everything ok?" pried Becky.

Marcia didn't respond. Austin gathered from the look on Marcia's face that something was wrong. A short silence fell.

"Will someone tell me what's going on, please?" asked Becky.

Marcia must have read the message from Bernie a hundred times, or at least that was what it felt like.

Hi Marcia, hope your journey was pleasant, given the weather. I've been researching that doctor's name extensively and placed the task with a few of my contacts, who came up with nothing. I did have one

interesting conversation with a rather eccentric gentleman on my books who suggested it wasn't a real name but a pseudonym. I'm currently looking into this, but unfortunately, without any form of reference between you and the name, it may prove a little difficult. I'll be in touch when I have something.
Regards
Bernie Goodman

DOCTOR ARTHUR TOE

CHAPTER TWENTY-FIVE

Marcia placed her phone on the table. She was aware that Austin's eyes were on her, but his thoughts were elsewhere. She felt compelled to respond.

"You know, in my line of work, I'm always aware when someone's staring at me. Either to undress me or imagine some kind of fantasy where I'm playing a part. Don't get me wrong, most of the time it's quite flattering." She tilted her head and narrowed her eyes at him. "But that's not how you're looking at me, is it?" she asked, picking up her glass.

Austin's cheeks flushed. His attention was stolen. "Sorry. I mean, no. I was just saying to Becky how you seem familiar somehow."

Marcia frowned. "Unless you've hired me, then I very much doubt it."

"Hired you?" he quizzed curiously. "For what? Are you an actress for this murder mystery night?"

Marcia threw back her head and laughed. "You could call it that, and yes, I suppose I do act." She sat upright and placed her folded arms on the table. "So, let's clear the air, shall we, and some of that confusion I can see dripping from your faces. I'm a high-class escort."

Austin tried to get his words out. But nothing came except stuttering. Becky sniggered into her wine glass, almost spitting its contents over the edge.

Marcia studied her. She could tell by her wandering eyes and distant look that she'd already consumed too much wine in too short a time. Austin had already clocked her floundering behaviour and moved the remaining wine out of her reach.

"Escort, aye," he nodded. "Interesting line of work," he said with an awkwardness in his voice. He loosened his tie and felt his cheeks glow once again.

"Now that's out of the way. Shall we move on?" Marcia replied, raising her glass to her lips.

Austin nodded. Marcia smiled subtly behind her wine glass. She could sense the questions bouncing around their heads. Most people are usually too embarrassed to ask more questions like it's too much of a taboo.

She glanced at her watch. "Okay, I'm not sitting here all night to be ignored by my host. I don't know about your circumstances, but I was hired by Dr Toe to spend the evening here with him. Now, in my line of work, that could mean anything from accompanying businessmen on trips, at parties, just plain company, or fulfilling wild sexual fantasies. It makes no difference to me what I'm here for as I've already been paid, but I get the feeling that you two have got the wrong end of a very large stick."

Becky rose from her chair with her glass in her hand. "Well, that answers that, then. I'm going to find out what the fuck is happening here."

Austin grabbed her arm. "Just sit down, Becky, will you?"

A loud click echoed around the room. The double doors at the end opened, and they were greeted by Peter wheeling in a silver trolley. This time, he was wearing a red jacket and matching tie. Austin found it almost comical, like a stage show where there are limited actors all playing multiple roles. And the fact they sat opposite a prostitute and being paid a thousand pounds to eat a gourmet meal in a luxurious home, but still had no idea why they were there. It all seemed a little bizarre to him. He was almost laughing inside. But he still couldn't ignore his gut feeling that something very sinister was going on.

Peter served them their starters and corked another bottle of red wine. He smiled politely but said nothing. Marcia took the opportunity to try and get some clarity on the situation, evidently with little patience.

"Peter, isn't it?" he nodded. "Can you tell the doctor I'd like to see him, please? I've spent the last several hours in the back of a car, and whilst I appreciate the fine wine and good food, I'd like to know exactly what's happening tonight. Like I said in the car, I'm not big on surprises."

"Same here," Becky added. "We're not here for the same reason as her; we're expecting the doctor to discuss my mother's will."

Peter stood at the head of the table, leaning on his fists. "How long have you all been in this room?" he asked.

They all looked at each other. "Half an hour, I suppose, why?" asked Austin.

"And yet none of you have made the connection. It seems time has disguised you all well. Your host will be in after the main course. Do enjoy," he said as he walked away.

"Excuse me," hollered Marcia. But he'd already slipped away.

Austin leapt up from the table and ran to the doors, but they had been locked again. He threw up his arms. "Unbelievable," he muttered and returned to the table.

Becky loaded her fork with salmon. There was little etiquette involved as she crammed a large forkful into her mouth.

Becky nudged Austin and pointed to the bottle, which was just out of her reach.

He slid the newly opened bottle towards her. She poured.

Marcia looked at Austin.

"I'm not sure she's going to be in any fit state to listen to the reading of a will tonight. It's a full-blooded Cabernet Sauvignon, and it's supposed to be paced with food, not drunk like lemonade. It's to compliment the lamb later."

Becky peered over her glass. "Excuse me! Don't tell me

how to drink. And why are you talking to him like I'm not here?" she snapped. "Advice from a fucking prostitute. Yeah, that's rich."

"Yes. And an educated one at that," she smirked. Tension was beginning to surface.

Austin moved the bottle away. He shook his head. "Jesus, Becky, can you be any ruder? Think you've had enough already. Sorry Marcia, it's been a bit of a strange two days." He loosened his tie even more. He then fetched a jug of lemon water over and placed it in front of Becky as she crammed in the last mouthful of salmon.

"It's okay, Austin, it's been pretty much the same for me. It's been a rather complicated week." Marcia leaned in closer. "Actually, can I let you into a little secret?"

"Sure," he said, pouring the lemon water.

"When I got my invitation, I hired a private detective to investigate this elusive Doctor Toe. You see, nearly all my clients are wealthy businessmen, and I like to do my homework before I commit to a contract. What I'm trying to say is that this client doesn't seem to exist. He's certainly not a doctor or even a real person, from what I can gather. The message I got just now was from Bernie, my PI confirming this. He even suggested it could be a pseudonym."

"So, why did you come here if you had doubts, then?"

Marcia sighed. "Well, that's the million-dollar question. Let's just say it's a name which has been with me for a very long time."

"Sorry, I don't understand. So, you do know him from your past, I mean?"

"No, never met him. Look, it's a rather long and personal story. I was more intrigued by the name. That's why I hired the detective. I'm not interested in the games tonight or any carnal affairs. I'm just curious about the man behind the name. That's it."

"Are you saying that this is some kind of trick? I mean, the nursing home said that ..." Austin let his last word hang mid-sentence.

"What is it?" Marcia asked.

"The nursing home said he was Becky's mother's trustee."

Becky jumped in. "The robbing bastard has most of my mother's furniture. I saw it out in the hallway."

Marcia turned to Becky. "Didn't you say the doctor was a friend of your mother's? If you're here for a will reading, then maybe it's all part of it."

Becky shrugged. "Guess I'll find out. So, you're here to entertain him, then?" she asked, grinning.

"It's probably a good idea that you sober up before you make an even bigger embarrassment of yourself, don't you think?" replied Marcia.

Becky rose to her feet, dismissing Marcia's last comment. "I need to sit on something more comfortable. These chairs are way too hard." She staggered towards a small leather corner sofa and fell into it, her head nestled in the wing.

"She can be such a bitch sometimes. Sorry."

Marcia shrugged. "Don't worry. I've had worse."

Austin swirled the lemon water around in his glass. Thoughts about the evening played on his conscience. Uncertainty coursed through his body, and he tried to piece together all the events that had led them all to be in this room. Something didn't add up. Fear simmered in his stomach. There was only one very large skeleton in his closet that could make this worse. He applied logic. It didn't fit.

He leaned across the table. "Did you hear what the driver said when he brought our starters in?"

Marcia shrugged. "Something about time. I wasn't really listening, why?"

"He said something about us making a connection. I think he was referring to us three."

"Maybe he means our connection to the doctor," she replied.

"Maybe."

"So, where are you from?" he asked her.

"London. And you two?"

"Brighton. But we're both originally from Cornwall. I used

to work as a gardener for Becky's mum, but we decided to make a fresh start. I'm a writer now. Maybe you've ..."
Marcia's face paled. She placed her hand on her chest. "You all right? You look like you've seen a ghost."
Marcia leaned forward and pushed her plate to one side. "Can I ask you a question?"
"Sure."
"What's your surname?"
Austin frowned and smiled at the same time. He was expecting a more serious question.
"My surname? It's Bletchley, why?"
"Doesn't matter. It's just what you said reminded me of a similar situation. I knew a girl once whose mother had also hired a gardener. I'm pretty sure her name was Becky. It was in another life, but the gardener had a different name. For a split second, I thought it may have been you, but your name doesn't ring any bells, which, if you knew my past, you'd know is a good thing. Kind of put my mind at rest."
Austin was plagued by a thread of curiosity. He knew the surname he gave her was a cover. He stared again at her face. He was sure she was familiar somehow. Just like old school reunions when you have an in-burnt image of a classmate from the past, and somehow their childish features still resonate despite changing hair lines and wrinkles. It's always the eyes. The eyes never age.
"So, you don't drink then," she asked as she topped up her crystal glass.
"Well, actually, I did, yes. That was the problem. So, now I don't."
"Recovering alcoholic?"
He felt a pang of awkwardness. He'd never actually used those words or had anyone use them for him. It wasn't a denial, but it was a kind of disassociation. Saying you have a problem with drink is far less patronising and embarrassing than saying you're an alcoholic. But Marcia pulled no punches, and he felt compelled to reply honestly.
"Yes. Yes, I am, but I've not had a drop for a few years

now."

"Does it bother you? Seeing us drink tonight?"

"Not really. You can't hide from temptation forever."

She smiled compassionately. "Good for you, Austin."

Becky stirred from the sofa at the far end. Her hands reached for the ceiling, and she groaned like a tormented spirit.

DR ARTHUR TOE

CHAPTER TWENTY-SIX

The double doors opened, and once again, the silver trolley with porcelain plates all steaming with fresh food was wheeled in. The aroma of scented mint wafted through, and Peter nodded towards Becky on the sofa. "Someone's had too much wine, I see."

Austin quickly dismissed his comment. "She's fine. Look, what's happening here tonight? It's all a bit too vague for us, and we're eager to get it done, the will reading, I mean."

Marcia hooked eyes with Peter. "You told us that the doctor would be joining us. It's been a good hour now, and I think a little courtesy wouldn't go amiss here, don't you?"

Peter stood to the side, his hands clasped in front of him in a waiting butler pose. "I never said anything about a doctor. I said your host would be here after your main course. He has a surprise for you all."

He broke his pose and leaned towards them. "That is unless you've managed to work it all out now." He smiled hard, but only one side of his face curved. Like he'd had a stroke. "Maybe I'll give you a push in the right direction." He threw the serving towel over his shoulder and leaned on the end of the table. "Start with your actual names. That should spark things off," he said, giving an exaggerated wink with his left eye.

Marcia rose from her chair, taking an instant dislike to his smug comments. Just as he was about to exit again, she exclaimed, "I've had enough of these games, either the doctor comes through that door in the next few minutes, or I'll be calling a taxi."

Austin followed her comment. "Can you at least confirm if we're here for a will reading or not? It's just that I'm feeling a little confused about what's going on here." He gestured a hand to Marcia. "Like she said, we're not really into playing games."

Peter turned to them and let out a raucous laugh from the doorway. "From what I gather, you all like your games, why do you think you're all here?" He returned from the doorway and approached the table. He pulled three pens out from the top of his red jacket pocket and dropped them on the table. He then followed with a small notepad. "All take a pen and write down 'DR ARTHUR TOE'. Rearrange the letters. See what you come up with. That should give you all the clues you need. Enjoy the lamb. It's quite exquisite." He then withdrew backwards through the double doors, leaving them with a teasing half-smile.

"That guy gives me the creeps," admitted Austin.

Marcia cut into the lamb. "What the hell was all that about?"

Becky waltzed back to the table, her hair taking on different directions and her lipstick smudged halfway down the side of her mouth. She sat and bellowed a yawn. "Shit, that wine was
strong."

"I did try to tell you," Marcia said.

"Looks like our host is playing games with us. And what's with the pen and paper? I didn't quite get what he meant," said Austin.

"Except he's not our host," added Marcia. I'm beginning to understand the whole Dr Arthur Toe thing now, why he's such a mystery. It's looking like this is a pseudonym. Just like Bernie said."

Becky looked bewildered. "What about the will, Austin,

did you ask?"

Austin nodded. "Yeah, he just kind of ignored me and then chucked a load of pens and paper on the table."

Marcia picked up one of the pens and started to rearrange the letters on the paper. Nothing was coming to her. "This could take all night and I haven't got the patience." She dropped the pen in favour of her wine glass. "Cheers. Here's to being messed around," she said sarcastically, raising her glass to the others.

"What did he mean about our real names?" asked Austin, poking at his food.

Becky looked at him. "What are you talking about?"

"Peter. He keeps making cryptic comments, and it's pissing me off. Something about using our real names and telling us to write 'Dr Arthur Toe' down and rearrange the letters. Something like that, wasn't it, Marcia?" His eyes flicked across the table at her.

She didn't answer. Becky attacked the lamb shank. "I'm starving."

"Did you not hear anything I just said?"

"Of course I did. He's probably just making small talk."

Austin pushed his plate out of the way and grabbed a pen, shaking his head.

Becky glared at him. "What?"

"It must be nice to be completely oblivious to the shit that's going on around you. This weekend has been more than a little bizarre, even *you* have to admit that. First, the phone call from the nursing home, which they then said they didn't even make. The calls to our hotel room, which somehow, no one there knows who made them, the strange guy in reception, who it turns out were our driver, and don't patronise me about my imagination, and then this Dr Toe bloke who no one seems to have met, but who keeps coming up in conversation like a bad smell, and now this Peter wants us to chase shadows with the letters of his name."

He got up from his chair and wiped his glasses on his napkin. "He said we like playing games. Well, I'm with Marcia on this. Getting a taxi, that is." He strode over to the doors and yanked the handle. "Still locked. Unbelievable," he said, throwing his arms up in frustration.

His inquisitive mind was then drawn towards the small picture hanging to the left of the double doors. He gently lifted it from its brass hanger and gazed closely at it.

"Told you this was the house we used to meet up in." He turned to Becky, holding up the picture. He moved to the last of the five pictures and removed it. "See? It's this place that's renovated. The pictures are all in sequence. Before, during, and after the work."

Marcia looked up from her scribblings and glanced towards the picture he was holding. She got up from the table and grabbed the picture from him. "Are you saying that this is the house we're in now?"

Austin nodded. "Yeah, why?"

"Because I also recognise this house."

They looked at each other. There was a moment of mutual panic. Austin felt afraid. He tried piecing the recent events together, and one large and very heavy penny was dropping fast.

They hadn't noticed Becky edging towards them. The look of fear painted on her face was almost animated. She looked petrified. She shared the same startled look that a rabbit in the headlights has moments before it becomes roadkill. Eyes filled with fear and panic.

He took her arm. It was trembling. "What's wrong?"

She held out her phone. Her words broke. "I put the letters you wrote down into an app. To make anagrams."

"Well, that was the quick way, I guess. Good thinking, Becky, I'll give you that," Marcia said.

"And?" he asked, rushing her.

Tears pooled in the corners of her eyes. "You were right, Austin. About everything. All of it. I'm scared."

"What's wrong? What does it say?" Marcia asked impatiently.

"Most of the words made no sense, but there was one

anagram that made my heart stop. I don't think it's a coincidence." She turned her phone towards them.

Marcia covered her mouth instantly. "Oh fuck."

Fear raged like a volcano on the verge of eruption. Austin paced the room. "Fuck. I knew it. I so knew it. I knew this whole thing was way too bizarre to make any sense." He threw up his hands. "We're fucked."

Three words were all it took to bring their realities crashing down to earth. Dr Arthur Toe was an anagram of Truth or Dare— a reference to the childhood game they were all too desperate to forget.

DR ARTHUR TOE

CHAPTER TWENTY-SEVEN

Austin turned to Marcia. "You. Who are you, and why does that shock you as well? I saw the same look on your face as I had, and yet we're here for different reasons. How do you explain that?"

He stepped back, his brows furrowed. "I know you, don't I?" he said, waving his finger.

Becky sat and put her head in her hands. "I need to leave; I can't do this."

Marcia dropped on to her chair and muttered, "It's a trap. It was always a trap. How did I not see it?"

"So, who are you, then?" he asked.

She looked up at him with empty eyes. "Marcia isn't my real name."

Becky lifted her head. "Please don't tell me you're her."

"Who?" snapped Austin.

"You're Molly, aren't you?"

Marcia nodded and dragged the bottle of wine over. She poured it quickly. She sank half a glass and then dragged the back of her hand across her mouth. Etiquette was the last thing on her mind now.

"You're Molly?" Austin exclaimed. "I knew I recognised you."

She poured again. "And your surname isn't Bletchley, is it?" He shook his head. "No. It's Greer," he said after a short pause. "Was Greer, whatever, it doesn't matter now." He sat at the table and played with his lamb dinner. "This is bad. Us here altogether." He thumped the table and stood up. "Fucking secrets, we've just been kidding ourselves all these years."

In a single flash, he reached for the bottle of wine.

"Don't you dare," cried Becky, launching herself across the table to grab the bottle and knocking over the gravy boat. A lake of brown liquid bled into her red dress.

It was too late. The deed had been done with no comprehension of the consequences. For him, the wine was too good to resist against the backdrop of an even greater curse and one in which the jaws of judgement were about to eat him whole. The bottle was now between his lips, and its contents flowed freely.

He tore off his tie and threw it across the table, pointing at Becky. "I told you something was going on, but as usual, you're too pig-headed to see it and now look. The charade's over," he hollered.

Marcia snatched the bottle from him. "You're an idiot, Greer, still the same joker you were back then."

He shrugged. "Haven't you realised that this charade we're all part of is nothing more than one big lie? Our lie. The game's over, Marcia, Molly, whatever you're called now."

Marcia paused in silence. He was right. It was one huge charade, and it had been since she was sixteen. The visitor in the dark suit and the slip of paper she was handed at the detention centre was just a long tease. If only she'd remembered the conversation, but as a spirited young girl with little patience for anyone with a hand in her future, she had no memory of it. She couldn't even remember why she carried the piece of paper around with her, and at some point, it got lost. But the name stuck. "Remember this name because one day it'll mean something to you." It seemed they were all part of some elaborate game designed to taunt them and incite fear. It was clearly working.

If this was planned all those years ago, then they were all in
for a very sobering evening, and it seemed that the games had already begun.

As Marcia wallowed in her thoughts, Becky took the bottle from her and poured the wine into her glass. She stared at the blood-red wine and swilled its contents slowly around the glass before putting it down again.

Fuck it. I need a clear head, thought Becky.

Austin looked at Marcia. "So, you're what, a prostitute now, Molly?"

She rolled her eyes. "And you're an outstanding example of the community, are you?" she replied sarcastically.

"Fuck this." Becky leapt up from the table and stormed over to the doors, banging on them hard with her fists.

"Open this door now. Show yourself. Whatever you think we've done, you're wrong," she yelled. Becky thumped again. "Did you hear me?" she continued yelling.

Marcia hurried to her and grabbed her arm, dragging her away from the doors.

Austin grabbed the bottle while Marcia was busy with Becky.

He took another mouthful. His stomach warmed.

Becky suddenly snatched the bottle from his hand and launched it at the wall. The bottle exploded, and the wine ran down the wooden panelling like bloody tears.

"You want to throw away all those sober years? We need to have a clear head. I ain't staying here."

"Becky's right," said Marcia. "Who knows what's in store for us tonight? I just had my entire life crushed. Everything I thought I knew had been nothing more than an elaborate trick to get us together in this room. How can one made-up name cause so much destruction?"

Austin felt disconnected. His head was numb.

Becky picked up a napkin and began dousing the gravy stain on her dress. "Well, this is turning out to be one fucked up reunion."

"Hold on. So, who is that guy?" Austin said, pointing to the doors. "I don't recognise him, but he knows us. Right?" he
added with a flushed face.

Marcia looked across the table to Becky, who was still distracted by the large stain.

I think that's the least of your problems, girl.

Austin pulled his phone out. "We should call the police, right? I mean, we're hostages. He can't keep us locked in here forever. We can just deny anything he says. I mean, he's got no proof, right?"

Becky dropped the napkin and marched around the table to him. "That's the last thing we want, you out of your fucking mind." She snatched the phone out of his sweaty palms and placed it on the sideboard out of direct reach.

The fragrant smell of cooked lamb and warm mint was gone. It was replaced by the ugly stench of panic hanging in the air like a thick fog.

None of that mattered now.

"We need to talk about that night at the lake," said Marcia abruptly.

The atmosphere changed. All eyes fell on her in an instant.

Austin shook his head and raised his hands. "No fucking way, that's one place I'm not going."

Becky stared at the plates of uneaten food. Half an hour ago, she was starving. Now, she was petrified and confused, trying desperately to piece together everything that had happened in the last twenty-four hours or so. Nothing in front of her was appealing now. All she could taste was the acid rising and falling in her throat.

The realisation that there was no will was sobering. Now, she had time to revisit all the events she'd so quickly dismissed earlier. Something clicked in her head. It wasn't the nursing home that called after all. It was the person behind all of this. The wizard behind the curtain. Orchestrating the whole evening. Was this all a sophisticated and well-thought-out trap? An elaborate and well-crafted plot for revenge? The

teasing phone calls to the room and the misleading invitation with the cheque. It was all a rouse.
Was the hotel involved as well?
Marcia's comment had stirred an earthquake. For the past two decades, she and Austin had been dancing around the elephant in the room, naive in their delusion that if it wasn't talked about, it didn't happen.

A huge wall was about to fall.

DR ARTHUR TOE

CHAPTER TWENTY-EIGHT

Austin ran to the lounge doors, grabbing the handles hard. He kicked the doors repeatedly in desperation. However, they just rattled in the frames. Becky jumped straight to him, pulling him away just like Marcia had done with her.

"Austin. We can't run from this. We need to talk about what we're going to do," yelled Marcia.

"Leave me alone," he raged. He shrugged off Becky's hand and yanked the handles again, harder this time. Marcia leapt in. She struck his face with an open hand. He stopped and turned as disoriented as he had become. It was enough to break him from his spiralling panic.

She picked up his glasses from the floor, wiped them on a napkin, and passed them back to him.

Nothing was said for a minute or so. Austin's breathing was laboured, and tears began to fall from his chin. He shuffled over to the steps by the doors and sat down. Marcia and Becky joined him. Becky put a comforting arm around his shoulder.

"You're right, Marcia. We need to talk about this," Becky said, pulling Austin in tight.

Marcia nodded. "It's been a while, and while I'd love to hear about you both, I think we need to talk about what we did. Because any moment now, someone's going to be coming through that door who probably knows more than

we can possibly imagine. We need to figure out who that could be and
why."

"I fucking knew this day would come," said Becky.

"I never imagined you two would get together," said Marcia.

Becky's eyes fell to her lap. "It was because of what we did. Figured since we were best friends and we carried this secret together, we could hide it together. But here we are."

Austin raised his head and rubbed the side of his cheek. "Sorry, Marcia. I lost my shit."

"I'm not sorry for slapping you; you'd lost it, and panic is dangerous. It wasn't personal, you understand."

Austin smiled, but it was short-lived.

"This could be Jack," said Becky.

"Did he ever return to your mum's place?" asked Marcia.

She shook her head. "Nope, but then we left a couple of days later. He wouldn't have known what we did, anyway."

"True." Marcia twisted her rings around her finger. "You ever think about what we did back then?"

"All the time," said Austin. "It's always in my head. No matter how much I try and forget, it's always there. But it's not what we did with Jack that worries me. I mean, it was pretty spiteful, but nothing compared to the other thing."

Marcia raised her pencil-thin eyebrows at him. "What we did to her, you mean, not what happened to her. We can't keep pretending anymore. Someone behind those doors knows the truth. I've no idea how, but denial isn't going to cut it tonight, I'm afraid."

Austin raised a hand. "Wait. What if the rooms are bugged, or they've got hidden cameras in here?"

Becky frowned at him. But unlike other times when his ideas seemed fanciful, this time, here in this house tonight, it all seemed more than reasonable to her.

"I'm serious."

Marcia cut in. "He could be right."

Austin turned to the back wall, feeling the wooden panels

for any wires or microphones. He pulled the carved drinks cabinet out from the wall, but there was nothing behind it except evidence of poor cleaning. Becky and Marcia watched him remove the pictures and inspect the back of each one before replacing them. He gazed up to the ceiling and cast his eyes to the plaster architrave which bordered the room. Nothing unusual. His attention then turned to the table, and immediately, he was on his hands and knees under it.

A short moment passed before he reappeared. He pointed under the table, his finger over his lips. "Shush."

They peered under the long, flowing tablecloth. A small, round, black device was stuck to one of the inside legs.

Marcia grabbed the pen and paper she'd been using earlier to try and decipher the anagram. She wrote on the paper and held it up to them.

We can't talk about that night.

Becky pulled out a chair and sat down. She scooped up a fork full of mash and stuffed it in her mouth.

Austin picked up the pen and scribbled a message back.

They know we talked about her.

Marcia took the pen from him. *But not what we did.*

Becky dashed under the table and emerged with the round object. "Fuck this." She brought her heel down heavily on it. Pieces of plastic crumbled under her foot. It was now destroyed. "We can say what we like now," she said, looking at the shock on their faces.

It took a moment for them to realise the possible repercussions. Becky's intentions were good. The repercussions, not so much. They had lost an advantage by destroying the bug. But it was done. They could speak freely for now, but they now needed a plan they could all stick to.

"Well done, Becky, that was clever. You could've at least given us some warning you were going to do that. Marcia and I were swapping notes. We'd have figured something out."

Becky picked up her wine. "Well, now we can talk about it, can't we?"

"Austin's right. We could've used it to our advantage, but

I guess you didn't stop to think about that, did you?"

Becky sank her wine and stood face to face with Marcia. Her eyes narrow and enraged.

"And where did Marcia come from? Your name's Molly. Did you hear that? It's Molly. Molly, Molly, Molly," she yelled at the top of her lungs.

Tempers rose. Marcia grabbed a handful of Becky's golden locks in her fist, dragged her across the room, and pushed her backwards onto the leather couch. "Not helpful. Sit down, sober up, and shut up unless you have something constructive to add."

Austin looked on in shock but had secretly enjoyed the moment. Someone was finally putting Becky in her place. He'd seen a different side to her tonight. A side he didn't much like—selfish. No matter how things turned out tonight, his relationship with Becky would never be the same. It was never about love with her. Just an inner fear of having their secrets exposed. It was nothing more than a relationship of mutual convenience. If his past was exposed tonight, then he no longer had a reason to be bound to her.

He watched her struggle to get up from the sofa with dignity, pulling down her ruined dress and trying to compose herself.

Marcia sat at the table and picked at the cold dinner, suddenly realising how hungry she was. Inside, she was angry. Angry at how the last twenty-plus years had been nothing but tantalising lies about the man who made her remember a name. Just like the other two in the room, she'd been played. The question now was, who else knew, and what did they know about that fateful night in the summer of '96?

Austin pulled out a chair and sat staring at his dinner. But he wasn't hungry. "We need to clear the air. I need to talk about what happened. I can't carry this secret anymore."

"As long as no one outside this room knows the truth, I'm not having my life destroyed. Not now, after all these years," said Marcia.

"So, what are you saying?" he asked.

"I'm saying we need to come up with a story that we all stick to."

DR ARTHUR TOE

CHAPTER TWENTY-NINE

Becky left the sofa and marched over to the table, leering at Marcia but saying nothing. Marcia picked up the remaining bottle of wine and poured it into the plant pot. "No more drink. Clear heads from now on."

"It's been half an hour, and nobody's been in yet," Austin said.

"So, who's going to start then?" said Becky, clearly still in a sulk.

Austin shrugged. "Start with what?"

Marcia leaned forward on her elbows. "Somebody knows we played Truth or Dare here all those years ago. Maybe they were in the house with us, and we didn't even see them. Who knows? It was a long time ago."

"What if it was Jack? It's possible," Austin suggested.

"I don't think it's Jack we need to worry about. I mean, what we did to him was awful, but we didn't commit any kind of crime, not really," Marcia replied.

Becky raised her eyes to Marcia. "You're the one that seduced him, not me."

"And you watched and took photos. Just like *you* planned, so don't even think about taking the high moral ground. I don't care what you think of me. I make very good money doing what I do, and I don't feel in the least bit guilty about it, but something tells me you're not ready to face what you did blackmailing Jack. You couldn't wait to get rid of him. You used us for your own agenda. Unfortunately, we were too dumb to realise it at the time. Young, dumb, and full of fun. So, we're not dancing around this anymore. I don't care about Jack, but I do care about the part we *all* played in Laura's death. There, I said it."

Austin stepped in front of the long window and watched the snowflakes settle on the stone lintel. It felt calming for a moment, like normality was just the other side of the glass. "How the hell did we all live with that on our conscience?" It was rather rhetorical what he said, staring hypnotically into the void.

"How can anyone know about it? There was no one there except us. It was the middle of the night, if I remember." Becky massaged her temples in small circular motions. "The police never found her. There was no body," she added.

"And you know this how?" asked Marcia.

"Because I googled the shit out of anything to do with dead bodies found in lakes in Cornwall. I even went to the library in Truro to look at the old archives. That's how paranoid I was about being caught."

Austin threw a damning look at Becky. "And you didn't ever think of telling me that?"

"I was trying to protect us."

"Did you not stop to think that I might've wanted to know that? Instead, I spent years wondering if the police would come knocking on our door one day." Austin removed his glasses and pinched the bridge of his nose as if it gave him some relief. "Every time there was a knock at the door, my heart skipped a beat. But that's just you all over. Self, self, self."

Marcia raised her hands. "This isn't helping. So, Laura was never found then?"

Becky shook her head. "But it's a huge lake."

"Okay, so that's something, I suppose."

Austin leaned against the wall, shuffling his hands in his

pockets, and stared at the floor.

Marcia poured a glass of water and handed it to Austin.

"Drink this. You look flustered."

"He doesn't need you pampering him," Becky snapped.

Marcia ignored her. It became quite apparent to her that Austin's relationship with Becky was built on nothing but fear and control. It was also clear that Becky hadn't changed one bit. She was still the obnoxious, self-centred brat she knew all those years ago.

Marcia stood and shifted the broken glass with her Jimmy Choo shoes, kicking small pieces under the table.

"We stick to the same story, keep it simple," suggested Marcia.

"Which is?" asked Austin.

Becky jumped in. "Laura fell out of the boat, drunk. Austin tried to save her but couldn't find her. That's nice and easy."

Marcia laughed. "You haven't thought that one through, have you? Jesus."

Becky shrugged. "You said to keep it simple."

"Simple? So why didn't we report it then?"

Austin stepped in between them. The last thing he wanted now was for them to be divided. He turned to Marcia. "What do you suggest?"

"That all depends on what you told your mother, Becky. Why didn't Laura show up the next day, and what happened to her belongings?"

"My mother's dead. What difference does it make now?"

"Because she could have shared her concerns with others. If you're saying that this doctor, whoever he really is, had contact with your mother at the nursing home, then it's quite possible he had your mother spouting on about the home help suddenly disappearing."

Becky responded. "I packed all her stuff up in a black plastic bag and buried it somewhere, can't remember where, but somewhere on the grounds. Aaron took her car, but I didn't tell him what we'd done. I made up some story about

Laura going away with her dad, I think, and didn't need the car. The old cow assumed she'd taken off. To be honest, I didn't hang around long, only a couple days, then me and Austin fled."

She poured herself a glass of lemon water and gulped it quickly, followed by an audible belch.

"I think I remember her asking me why she just disappeared. I probably just ignored her. I usually did. Me and Austin took off soon after to his uncle's flat in Brighton, and I never really had anything to do with her after that. She never did me any favours anyway."

THE HOST
CHAPTER THIRTY

The conversation was then stolen by the sound of a tumbling lock. The man Marcia recognised as Steven stepped into the room wearing the same dark cord trousers and black polo-neck, this time with a less-than-accommodating face. His presence instantaneously drained any feeling of calm.

They watched him pull out a chair from the head of the table and put a large, black leather A4-sized folder in front of him. He smoothed his tramline-straight hair back with one hand before opening the folder.

Anticipation brewed in equal measure to fear as they waited for him to break the silence.

"Molly," he stated in a voice like broken glass. "There's no murder mystery here this weekend. Just like there's no Doctor Arthur Toe, but you've already worked that out, haven't you? Yes, of course, you have," he remarked, watching the colour drain from her face. "And yes, I've brought you here on completely false pretences, not for fun, not for games, but for penance, which I'll come onto a bit later in the evening once you've had time to lament your actions."

Marcia felt her control evaporating inside her. The one thing she always had and the one thing she couldn't bear to lose. It all crumbled away in a second.

Steven held the room in a way a teacher does when

addressing a classroom of little ones.

Becky watched and listened, confused and mesmerised at the same time. Austin fiddled with his glasses far more than usual, wondering where all this was leading.

Steven switched his attention to Becky, and she felt the pit of her stomach tighten, which sobered her up quickly.

"Becky Monroe, whatever whimsical fantasy you conjured up about inheriting your mother's estate and everything in it, I can assure you that the only thing you'll inherit here will be justice and disappointment."

"Mr Greer," he barked. Austin felt his body tense. "It appears that running from the past is fruitless, and you can never evade the inevitable, no matter how much you try and hide. Because what you're running from is in your head, and the only way to escape it is acknowledgement and full disclosure."

Austin nodded nervously. He didn't know why he had nodded, but fear was always something that had a hold on him, and compliance was his only way of dealing with it. Unlike Becky, who faced fear with equal distaste. Head on. But he wasn't seeing that in her now as he side-glanced at her for a moment.

Steven sat bolt upright. His hands lay on the table, caressing the corners of the black leather folder in front of him. His voice was gruff and firm. Indeed, authoritarian in its delivery.

"The three of you have no idea who I am other than a man who, at first glance, appears to know your demons, the ones you've all brought here tonight. Well, I can tell you now that you're all going to face those demons."

He turned to Becky, whose attention was distracted by Austin's nervous hands tearing off small pieces of a paper serviette and rolling them into a ball.

"Let me start again and introduce myself properly this time. My name is Steven Myers." He let the silence in the room linger for a moment.

Becky spoke first. "You're Laura's father?" she said in a

calm but broken voice.

Marcia and Austin exchanged a look. They knew in that instant why they were here. They knew this was going to be a very uncomfortable evening. Austin desperately wanted a drink, and his addiction from here in would only pale into insignificance compared to the very sobering situation he was now facing. Looking at the father of the girl he'd drowned over twenty years ago in the eyes was haunting. Frightening even.

"I am indeed the man, her father."

More silence fell, with none of them wanting to take that first commitment to talk about that fateful night. If telepathy were real, they'd all be having the same thought right now. *Are we sticking to our agreed story or the truth?*

Marcia raised her hand coyly. "I don't know what you know about what happened to your daughter...."

"Laura, you mean, her name is Laura," he interrupted sharply like he knew the name would be uncomfortable for them.

"We were all together, here in this very house, but obviously, it was abandoned twenty-six years ago. We played stupid kids' games and drank. I don't remember much, but we argued, I think. Maybe the other two can remember," Marcia continued, drawing them into the tangled web of lies in the hope they'd follow her.

Becky blushed, her words stuttering from her lips. "I'm not sure what it was about," she said. "It was that stupid game. I feel so bad. We all feel bad about Laura, but after that night when she stormed out, we never saw her again."

"No, we didn't. Even Becky's mother drew a blank," Marcia added, looking to Becky for confirmation.

"That's right. My mother liked her as well, but we all felt somehow responsible; we were young and stupid back then. You know how it is with arguments."

Steven's face didn't flicker or hint at any recognition of their story.

"What about you, Austin?" he asked.

Austin remained focused on the small pieces of tissue he'd torn up nervously earlier. He avoided any eye contact with Steven.

"Same as them. I don't remember much," he replied. The fear in his voice was obvious.

"You're lying, aren't you, Mr Greer? You know exactly what happened. The fact of the matter is that you all know what happened. But I get it. You're all hoping that by sticking to the same story, your secrets will somehow diminish into the aether." Again, he let the silence in the room linger.

Marcia retorted. "I don't know what else you want us to say."

"We presumed she went home for some reason, especially when she didn't return the next day," Becky chipped in with an air of confidence. But inside, she was a coiled spring, wound tightly by the uncertainty of what Steven might know. Communicating with the other two was done through subtle cues and exchanges of micro-expressions like a secret code they all shared. What Becky wanted to say was teetering on the edge of her lips. It was a bridge between his knowledge of what she thought he might know and the sheer audacity of calling him out.

Prove it.

Becky resisted, for the time being, at least. A variety of thoughts occupied her now. How could he possibly know what happened, and what proof could he possibly have? She'd spent many an hour scouring the archives for any glimpse of a crime in the area involving a recovered body. Another thought occurred to her that was just as perplexing. How did he know they played Truth or Dare, and why was the reference to this in an anagram? Denial was her best hope, at least until she could figure out what he knew.

The sound of the double doors opening interrupted the conversation once again, this time by Peter with a trolley of stainless-steel pots and black pottery cups. Peter said nothing as he laid out the cups and beverages on the table, nodding to Steven before going back out through the double doors.

Steven gestured for them to help themselves and poured himself a cup of black coffee. The rich aroma filled the room. Austin reached for a cup and dragged the hot stainless-steel flask towards him. As well as wanting to dilute the stale taste in his mouth, he needed to do something other than sit. He didn't do well when it came to sitting still in high-stress situations, and it showed, especially with the array of discarded torn tissues in front of him.

Marcia fired a question at Steven. "So, was it you who came to visit me all those years ago in the detention centre? I don't understand why you didn't just ask me what happened. Why the teasing name? I could have saved you a lot of time and energy,"

"Ah, you mean you could have just told me the same bullshit that you've just told me now." Steven leaned forward on his elbows, holding her gaze. "For the record, that wasn't me. I had much better things to do than visit a self-centred, delinquent teenager who, as it turns out, has made no moralistic contribution to society other than providing a seedy service for high-paying businessmen." Steven lifted his cup, blew his coffee, and then sipped it gently before continuing. "Why am I not surprised that you amounted to nothing more than a hooker? Clearly, you're comfortable with being used as an object of gratification for others, so why shouldn't I take advantage of that and use you for my gratification? In this instance, gratification for me came in the form of prolonged teasing, hence the slip of paper with the name Dr Arthur Toe." He took another sip. "If I recall, I sent a dear friend of mine, a young lad who'd just joined the police force. Chap called Philip if I recall."

Steven sipped his coffee again, allowing the penny to drop. Marcia stood up quickly. "Open the doors now. I'm leaving. I've had enough of your games."

"Isn't that what my daughter said before she disappeared?" Steven turned to the other two. "Perhaps you both want to leave as well. It's minus four out there, and the snow is settling fast. We're at least three miles from a main road, but please, be my guest."

He removed a key from his pocket and tossed it on the table.

Becky snatched the key. "Come on, Marcia, let's go. He obviously doesn't believe us, so fuck him," she yelled.

Marcia turned and stared at the door. Was this real freedom he was offering? She knew deep down she was fooling herself. This wasn't something she could run from anymore, and she knew it. She also knew that he knew this, too. And now, another seed had been sown. Was this Philip the same one she'd broken all her own rules for and spilt her secrets to? Frustration and anger simmered in her gut. Was Philip all part of this elaborate game, and had he been stringing her along all this time, sent by Steven to infiltrate her life?

She didn't notice Becky dashing past her towards the door, trying to jiggle the key into the lock.

Austin was standing behind her, fiddling with his glasses and glancing back at Steven, who was just watching the chaos unfold like a soap drama and sipping his coffee like he had all the time in the world.

Becky threw open the door fiercely enough for it to crack against the wooden panelling before disappearing. Austin turned to Steven like he was waiting to be told to sit down. Becky's voice echoed from the other room. "Austin, c'mon, let's go."

Marcia returned to the table and sat down, pulling a cup from the silver platter and pouring the percolated coffee. "You've got no right to judge me on my life. You want answers. I want answers," she demanded.

Austin threw up his arms and returned to the table with Marcia. "Bollocks to her, this is all too much. I ain't running from this shit any longer."

Steven placed his cup down and dabbed his beard with a white cotton serviette. "In the words of Hannibal Lecter, quid pro quo."

"Suppose we do know what really happened that night, and hypothetically, we tell you. Then what?"

Stevens's eyes were drawn to the doorway where Becky re-emerged with a sullen face and crossed arms.

"Please sit," he gestured. He didn't feel the need to patronise her on her little drama. The other two had already done that by ignoring her and returning to the table.

Becky marched over to the drinks cabinet and cursed at the empty cupboard.

"I believe the last bottle ended up down the wall," said Steven with a condescending smirk.

Becky stood against the cabinet and rolled her lips against her teeth. She was ready to fire.

"Coffee?" asked Steven, gesturing to the tall aluminium pot.

"No, I don't want coffee. I want to know why you think we had anything to do with your daughter going missing and why you're playing these stupid mind games with us," she said
fiercely.

Steven remained composed and crossed his legs, resting his coffee cup on his lap.

Austin slurped his coffee, waiting to see where this conversation was going. He didn't want to be the one to say the wrong thing and end up incriminating everyone. He was, however, of the same ilk as Becky on this one. *You can't prove anything.* He was also unaware that his right leg was twitching like a jackhammer and occasionally catching the top of the table and vibrating the cutlery, much to Marcia's annoyance.

"I think you'd better sit down for this, Becky," said Steven. Becky pulled out a chair and sat with crossed arms.

"I'm going to tell you a story about a man I once knew," began Steven. "You all remember Mrs Monroe's husband, Jack, don't you? It was a rhetorical question. Of course, you do because you degraded the poor man into disappearing."

They couldn't hide their surprised looks from each other. Steven took this as another moment to be savoured and lifted his cup slow enough for the moment to fester in their heads.

Becky leaned forward. "What the fuck are you on about?"

Marcia shook her head in disbelief, and Austin reached for his glasses to fiddle with again.

Steven said nothing. He reached into his zip-up leather folder, pulled out a silver camera, and placed it on the table in front of them. He then sat back and folded his arms, waiting for their next move.

"How did you get that?" snapped Becky.

"Interesting. Not where did you get that?" he said, raising his dark eyebrows.

Marcia was reluctant to get drawn into this. She had a vague recollection of the camera they used all those years ago but hadn't even considered where it had ended up.

She knew Steven had this all planned out. If she'd learnt one thing over the years, it was to read people. It was a self-preservation requirement. Knowing if she was to be the next body to be pulled from the river relied on a first meeting over drinks. Watching mannerisms and body language was essential. As was the way the conversation unfolded, often driven by her in an attempt to wheedle out any red flags. She catered for most sexual fantasies but drew the line at any requests for violence or strangulation.

Steven was an intelligent man; she could tell that. He was methodical and precise in the way he directed the conversation. He'd had over twenty years' head start on tonight. Twenty-plus years to prepare for it. Truth or dare was there all along on the slip of paper. She almost admired his taunt.

The question on her mind now wasn't what he knew because she was sure as hell that he knew exactly what happened, but she had no idea how. The question was, what did he want from them?

However she spun this, the truth would always remain the same. They left his daughter to drown in a lake in the dark on her own.

Tonight, one way or another, they'd have to atone for

what they did.

Steven picked up the camera from the table and turned it on. Marcia took the initiative to intervene before Becky leapt in feet first. She had to play Steven at his own game, and this meant not insulting his intelligence.

"We don't need to see the pictures again. What we did, what I did back then, was appalling, and I feel ashamed. I was nothing more than a messed-up teenager seeking attention. Angry, destructive, and selfish."

Austin continued to avoid eye contact with Steven. Becky shot Marcia a look. "What the fuck, Molly?"

"Don't give me that disapproving look. He knows what's on the camera. He's seen the pictures, so why pretend otherwise? It was your idea. You wanted Jack off the scene. You used me. And him," she yelled, pointing to Austin, who was shaking his head.

"Because he tried to interfere in my life! He sent me to that boarding school, and my mother did fuck all to stop him."

"So, you thought you'd destroy an innocent man's life. I know what I am. I have sex for money, and you can call me all the words you like, but I have no guilt at all about my line of work. But I also have something you don't. A conscience. You just can't admit to anything. We all fucked Jack over, but I'm mature enough to accept it."

Steven placed his cup down on the table and clapped. "Bravo."

Becky got to her feet, grabbed her coat, and stormed out of the room.

Marcia played with her rings. "Maybe you and I should have an honest conversation, Steven."

"Well. I think this is an ideal time to break for dessert, don't you?"

Austin lifted his head. His eyes filled with tears, and he drew the back of his hand across them. "Let's just end this now. I can't keep this in any longer." He faced Steven. This time, there was eye contact.

"I killed Laura. Is that what you want to hear?" he blurted out.

Steven raised his eyebrows and stroked his beard, pulling it to a point a few inches below his chin and twisting the last few hairs. "Wow. That's one hell of an interesting statement, but it's factually incorrect."

Austin frowned heavily. "Okay then. *We* killed your daughter, and I'm truly sorry for it. There hasn't been a day gone by that I don't think about her. And there isn't a day that

goes by where I don't regret what we did."

He pointed to the open door at the top of the steps. "She's the one who steamrollered all this, this sordid secret like it would just disappear if we didn't talk about it. Everything I've done and everyone we've hidden from has all been about evading acceptance, running from the truth, running from the law. Did you know she even googled to see if a body had been recovered and went to a library in Cornwall and trailed through countless news archive articles all to try and find out if your daughter's body had been discovered."

Austin picked up a napkin and wiped the tears from the corners of his eyes. "And she didn't even tell me. And you know what the most disturbing thing is when I look back now? She had this huge smile on her face when she told me that a body had never been found. Like it was one big relief."

He began animating his anger, and no one in the room, particularly Steven, made any attempt to step in. "Why the hell did I put up with that selfish bitch for so long? So, call the police. I'm not running anymore." Austin's breath stuttered as his tears spilt over.

He looked Steven directly in the eyes. "I'll tell you everything that happened that night if you like. Maybe I need to relive that night myself. Feel the pain I caused because the only satisfaction I can gain out of all this is that *you* know the truth, and I can finally face what I did."

Marcia hadn't anticipated such a bold move by Austin. He

wasn't the mild, meek man she had him down for. He was right about Becky. Marcia could see the clues in the way she was with him. She was a control freak. No matter how much of the truth would be aired tonight, she had no doubt that Becky would default to denial every time. There was nothing she could add to Austin's confession that would make this evening any easier. But she could validate him.

Marcia sighed heavily. She, too, made eye contact with Steven, who was sitting unexpectedly composed for such a revelation, still balancing the coffee cup on his lap. It was almost like a therapist-patient moment where all the therapist could do was listen, unmoved by what they heard, separated from the emotions of their patient. But why was he so composed when the people responsible for his daughter's death were just a few feet away? She almost wanted him to shout. Thump the table or at least have some spark in his eyes. Nothing. Nothing but composure. Either way, she felt compelled to comment.

"You knew all this, though, didn't you?" Marcia sat up straight. Head tilted, her eyes burning into his mind, trying to figure out his next move. "Is Jack still alive? He is, isn't he? You've spoken to him."

Steven reached for his cup. "You needn't worry about Jack or the embarrassment of facing him again. But rest assured, I'm fully aware of your actions, and they won't go without consequence."

Steven remained stone-faced like he was waiting for her to piece the evening together before commenting any further.

"I'm interested to know where you got the camera from because, if I recall, it was your daughter who had it last."

Steven remained silent and continued twisting and pulling the hairs on his beard, raising his eyebrows in a taunt.

"I doubt Mrs Monroe knew of its existence, considering the content." She checked her gold Gucci watch, which struck 11:10 p.m.

Austin sat disconnected. He watched the conversation between Marcia and Steven unfold with little reaction to his

damning confession. He felt irritated and awkward. With his emotions still simmering and his cheeks stinging from his tears, he cast his eyes to the open doorway that Becky had disappeared out of. He'd made up his mind about their relationship. After tonight, it would cease to be anything other than a friendship at a push. Somewhere amongst the pain of his confession sat relief. Relief not only from the full weight of what he'd carried around all these years but also relief from not having to pretend his relationship with Becky was based on love or admiration anymore. No longer would his life be overshadowed by his past. If his remaining years were to be
behind bars, they'd at least be free from all that. It would be an ironic freedom but an inner freedom all the same, and for that thought, he felt some self-pride for once. He also wanted Becky to face the same music that they had.

 The conversation was interrupted as Austin stood up abruptly, catching the edge of the table and causing the cutlery to chime. "I'm going to find Becky. Doubt she's gone far in this weather. I want her to face this too," he said sharply, pulling his jacket from the chair.

THE HOST
CHAPTER THIRTY-ONE

As Austin made his way through the lounge and into the hallway, the bitter air swept across his face. He noticed that the large oak front door was ajar, and a few soft snowflakes had drifted their way onto the oak floor near the threshold. He pulled up his collar and ventured onto the front step. The porch light flicked on instantly, and his eyes were drawn to the footsteps in the virgin white snow leading from the porch to a double open-fronted garage to the right of the house.

He dashed across the courtyard under the falling sky to find Becky peering in through the window of a silver Rolls Royce.

"This is the car you saw the other night, isn't it?" she said as he hurried into the garage next to her.

"What are you doing out here? It's freezing," he said, drawing up his collar and massaging his hands.

Becky pointed to the house. "That's my mother's furniture he's got in there, and he's trying to fool us into telling him what happened. That's my stuff now."

Austin's breath poured out in a white cloud. "It's over. I'm not running from this anymore."

"Exactly. We need to stand up to him, and he doesn't have any evidence anyway. It was over twenty years ago, there's nothing left in that lake to find and ..."

"I confessed," he blurted out. "Stop pretending that we

weren't responsible. I'm done with it all. Sorry, but I can't live like this anymore."

Becky thumped him in the chest twice, forcing him back against the garage wall. "You fucking idiot. Jesus, Austin, what have you done? What the fuck did you say?"

She then took off across the courtyard into the house and crashed through the double doors at the top of the steps. She then stood opposite Steven, clutching the top of the chair. Her face was a flustered shade of red. Becky owned the room.

"I don't care what he said to you," she proceeded with anger in her voice. "He feels guilty because he was there like all of us before she just took off." She raised a finger to Steven. "You've got no right to draw us into this sordid game of yours. We don't know where Laura is, and you can't prove anything," she continued, prodding her finger in the air towards him. "Secondly, all this furniture you somehow conned off my mother is mine. The whole estate is mine, will or no will, so I don't need you teasing me with a cheque for money that's rightfully mine anyway."

Marcia winced. Becky's comments were a sure-fire way to poke the devil. A devil who knew their deepest secrets. She felt that she wasn't the real bad guy right now. She knew what responsibility she had for what happened to Jack and Laura. Although she never actually had a direct hand in Laura's drowning, she was there. She could have stopped it. But she didn't.

Austin appeared at the top of the steps, blowing into his hands. A sprinkling of white powdery snow was gathered around his collar.

"Have a coffee. Here, let me pour," said Steven, rising to grab the jug.

"The Rolls Royce in the garage. Is it yours?" Austin asked.

"You like it?"

"You were at our hotel. It was you who called our room, teasing us with silent phone calls, wasn't it?"

Becky redirected her glare to Austin. "Are you seriously

coming back in here to sip coffee with him like he's some family friend? Do something useful and call a taxi. We're leaving."

Austin retrieved his phone from the sideboard and chucked it on the table. He pulled out a chair next to Marcia and sugared his coffee. "You call a taxi. I'm staying here. In fact, Becky, I'm not coming back to Brighton. I told you out there. I've cleared my conscience. I told Laura's father everything."

Becky shook her head. "After everything I did trying to protect you. You deserve everything you get."

He ignored her for a second and turned his attention back to Steven, who was stirring his coffee like he had all the time in the world. "So, why all the games at the hotel? And the hotel clerk, was he in on it?"

Steven gave a delicate nod. "I put a lot of business through that hotel, and yes, the clerk was most accommodating. But then, you like games, don't you?" he exclaimed.

Marcia rolled her ring around her finger and shuffled in her seat. "You came all the way to London to spy on me. I saw your car from my apartment the other night."

Becky looked back to Steven, who appeared to be relishing in the unfolding drama as if he was watching some stage play. Intrigued and yet distanced.

"You'll be hearing from my solicitor about my mother's estate, including all this furniture that you somehow managed to con out of her."

Steven let a teasing smile appear. "It's interesting, Becky, that out of all this, you just pick up on your late mother's worth. You've not once asked about how I knew her, why I was even mentioned on her paperwork, and even more astonishingly, where she's buried so you can pay your respects. You are all so misguided in your knowledge of events from the last twenty-plus years."

He stroked his beard again. "Molly, you sit there like Lady Muck, hoping that all this distraction Becky is causing is going to lessen your part, and yet somehow, you manage to sit teetering on the precipice of morality, lecturing me and convincing yourself that how you earn your living is perfectly acceptable. Don't be naive enough to mistake my exclusion of you as someone who'll overlook what you did all those years ago. Why else would I go to all that trouble to send you that note?"

Steven leaned forward on his elbows. He lost his smile and warm eyes. "Ask yourself, Molly. How many of those businessmen funded your penthouse flat, kitted out your wardrobe, and financed your lavish lifestyle? And how many of those businessmen do you think I have connections with?" Steven sat back and watched the realisation of everything Marcia thought she knew to disappear in a flash.

Marcia's heart leapt to her throat. All of a sudden, she felt incredibly vulnerable.

Steven slipped his hand into the black leather folder and pulled out an envelope. He passed it to Marcia. "Open it."

She picked up the envelope and withdrew a piece of paper with a list of names. Her clients. One name stood out. Highlighted in red. *Gavin Mason.* The pseudonym she recognised next to it was Derrick. She hooked eyes with him over the piece of paper.

"He's a very good friend of mine, and do you know what he does for a living?" he said with an exaggerated grin.

Marcia didn't respond. She had a vague recollection that he was a financial advisor.

"He's a tax investigator."

Marcia ran her tongue across her lips. They were dry.

"I had many a conversation with Derrick regarding your income. It astounds me how you've managed to acquire such a lavish lifestyle and yet have contributed very little in terms of taxes. There are two organisations that you never want to be indebted to. One," he gestured, raising a finger, "The Mafia. And two," he raised a second finger, "The tax man. Granted, the latter won't fit you up with a size-six concrete shoe and drop you in the sea, but they do like to make an example out of those who see fit to deceive them."

Marcia ran her palms across the top of her trousers. They were warm and clammy. It suddenly occurred to her that her life had been partly puppeteered by Steven. Her loss of control
was real. And it hurt.

Becky afforded a glance in Marcia's direction and recognised the same petrified look she had. Austin kept turning his cup around in the saucer repeatedly.

It was all falling apart. Twenty-six years had finally caught up with them.

A phone vibrated. It was Marcia's.

She answered and took herself out towards the lounge next door, where the large fire had all but faded. She perched herself on the arm of the couch, staring at the remaining spitting embers glowing in the hearth.

"Hello Miss Cole, it's Bernie Goodman. Sorry for the late call. I hope your evening is going as intended."

"What is it?" she asked abruptly.

"The Rolls Royce that you asked me to trace."

"That's right, you already said it was registered to a holding company. Look, it doesn't matter now. I'm kind of with the man who owns it."

"Dr Arthur Toe, did you find him?"

"Kind of, it's a long story."

"Ah, apologies then if this is all a bit irrelevant now, but I managed to do some digging, and although the car itself is registered to a company, I pulled in a favour from one of my contacts."

"About what?"

"Who's insured to drive it."

"You're going to tell me it's a Steven Myers."

Bernie stuttered. "Ah, well, yes. And …"

The call cut off. Marcia redialled but reached the answering machine. She left a message for Bernie to call back before slipping the phone back into her bag.

247

She took a moment to gather her thoughts. The room was quiet. The wall lights were dimmed, and the remaining orange glow had faded. A wave of tiredness washed over her post-adrenaline from her body, being in a state of constant high anxiety.

She looked to the door. She felt a slither of contempt towards Steven. But given the magnitude of what they had put
him through, she had no right to feel this way. He had her. One phone call would see her standing in the dock, facing multiple counts of tax fraud. On balance, she knew that was a small price to pay. All the same, she was angry.

She pulled herself up from the arm of the sofa, straightened her shirt, and returned to the dining room. The atmosphere was frosty.

"Everything ok, Molly?" asked Steven.

"What exactly do you want from us, Steven? Let's cut to the chase. We're all guilty of what happened to your daughter. Austin even confessed, and despite Becky's protests, she knows what really happened, and you know she's just as much to blame."

Becky dropped her mouth to talk, but Marcia reacted quickly. "Shut up, Becky. Whatever you're about to say, just don't." She turned back to Steven.

"Austin's accepted he could go to prison, and you've made it quite clear that you can screw me over for tax fraud, but I'm curious, Steven. How exactly do you know we were responsible? I say this pre-Austin's confession." She stood firm. A glint of confidence emerged on her hardened expression. Inside, her nerves were buzzing.

THE SPECIAL GUEST
CHAPTER THIRTY-TWO

Steven reached into the black leather folder in front of him. He pulled out two A4-sized documents, both embossed with the name *Millard & Ross Solicitors* at the top and several paragraphs of text below. He placed a silver fountain pen alongside the documents.

He had their undivided attention now.

He slid one of the documents across the table to Becky. "This is your late mother's will. The one you were so eager to get your hands on and so naively presumed you would be entitled to. Let me introduce you to someone who will explain the beneficiary to you."

Steven rose from his chair and opened the double doors. Becky and the others watched on in silence as a tall, slender woman with soft features emerged, dressed in a black suit with an open-neck white blouse, carrying a large black leather handbag with gold trinkets suspended by a slim gold chain. She approached the table and placed her bag on the floor. The scent of the perfume followed her into the room. It was a scent that Austin found familiar to the one in the hotel room. Things were all starting to fall into place.

Steven closed the doors and returned to his seat.

"Hello, Becky. Been a long time," she said in a soft but assertive voice.

Becky looked at the smart-suited woman with perfectly

manicured hands and auburn hair. She recognised the heavily patterned freckles on her pale skin. Only one person she knew had those features, and although time had altered her appearance, her features remained the same.

"Heather?" she said with a puzzled expression.

"You remember then," she replied.

Becky snapped a look at Steven. "What the fuck is going on here? What do you mean by the beneficiary? What has she got to do with my mother's will?"

Steven smiled at Heather and stroked his beard. "I told you she was coarse."

The other two sat silently.

Heather stood and walked slowly around the table, observing the carnage of discarded food and the wine-stained white tablecloth like the aftermath of a medieval banquet by Neanderthal warriors. The sound of broken glass underfoot drew her eyes to the trail of exploded wine crawling down the oak panelling and pooled on the oak flooring. She crouched down, picked up the remaining neck of the wine bottle, and placed it on the table.

"Someone's fiery this evening. I'm guessing it's you, Becky Monroe," she said, picking up a napkin and wiping her hands. "It seems time hasn't altered your attitude one bit."

"What are you doing here?" Becky asked.

Heather diverted her attention to Marcia. "So, you're the infamous Molly my father was seduced by all those years ago." An awkward blush coloured Marcia's cheeks. "I'm not going to try and defend what I did, but your father made a choice that day. I was seventeen at the time, and he was in his forties. Some would say that was morally wrong."

Heather let out a raucous laugh. "You want to talk about morals? You coerced him into sex and then filmed the whole thing so you could blackmail him. And the worst part about it was it wasn't even for your benefit. It was for hers," she said, pointing to Becky.

Heather continued circling the table.

"Five days after your sordid prank, my father came to me.

I watched him become a broken man. Oh, don't get me wrong, he had his share of guilt and shame for allowing himself to succumb to the temptation and your advances," she said, hooking eyes with Molly.

"The shame of confessing to me was heart-breaking, but he had no one else to turn to. We were trying to work out how to save his marriage and wondering if the pictures would ever get sent to her. Then I got a call from Catherine Monroe asking if I'd seen him as he'd disappeared after going into the woods. Of course, I had to deny her the truth and watch a second person suffer. Jack stayed at mine for a few months, and I learnt from Catherine that the police assumed he'd died of a heart attack in the woods. So, my father was left to share the pain and constant guilt for letting his wife believe that he was dead because he feared coming home and destroying his wife with the awful truth coupled with the fear of the photos emerging."

She continued to circle the table. "Oh, I looked for you. But like the cowards you are, you ran."

Marcia spoke. "Do you not think I've had to live with what I did all these years ago? Wondered what became of Jack. Because I did, I still do. But the one thing here that surprises me the most is how Steven is just sitting there cool as a cucumber with a strange satisfaction on his face. Not anger, or rage, or even irrational shouting after what we all did to his daughter."

Steven nodded. "Interesting observation. And quite true. But we haven't finished yet, have we, Heather?" he said, raising his eyebrows.

Heather pulled out a chair next to Steven and poured herself a coffee.

"What's all this got to do with my mother's will?" Becky asked.

Heather blew on her coffee before replying. "If you'll allow your mouth to stay closed for more than one second, then I'm about to explain." She sipped her coffee.

"When you three first disappeared, leaving Catherine on her own, I ended up visiting quite frequently, and every time I saw her, I had to watch what I said in case I made any reference to my father, who she thought was dead, and to an extent she'd moved on. Then I had to return to my father and watch *him* suffering from not being able to see his wife, only to hear about her from my visits."

Heather sipped her coffee again. "Then, after a month, I had a very interesting phone call from someone. A call that completely turned everything on its head. I'll come onto that a bit later, but needless to say, my father made the brave decision to return to the cottage. Have you ever watched anyone pine for someone? Of course, you haven't, as none of you have a shred of decency in you. It's soul-destroying."

"So, what's all this got to do with my mother's will?" interrupted Becky impatiently.

Heather gawped at her. "You really are a piece of work, Becky Monroe. Shall I add a lack of patience and morals to your long list of failings?" Heather teased out a smile.

Steven closed his eyes. He knew what was coming.

"Fuck you, Heather, you sit there in your posh suit and pretend you know everything, but you don't. You don't know shit."

Heather flung her cup down, crashing it onto the China saucer. She reached into her black bag and took out a square, camouflage-patterned box, and put it on the table with a deliberate thump.

"Do you know what this is?"

Becky shrugged.

"It's your Pandora's box."

Austin cleared his throat and raised his hand like a timid student with first-day-at-school nerves. "I know what that is. I helped Jack put some of them up in the woods."

Heather nodded. "Good. Then you know what they do."

"They're wildlife cameras. They capture pictures whenever there's movement from wildlife. He used to place them in the trees, facing the bird's nests," Austin continued.

Marcia shuffled in her seat, feeling the pit of her stomach bite. She already had an idea of what was about to come.

"You're correct, Austin. These are camera traps triggered by infrared. My father paid a lot of money at the time for them. These cameras don't just take snapshots, they also record video using an invisible flash. My father explained it all to me; they use infrared waves to illuminate a night image without being detected by humans or wildlife. Because the waves are outside their visible light spectrum, the subject doesn't know they're being watched."

Heather picked up the box camera and studied it. "Fascinating, really. Can you just imagine how excited my father was when he eventually retrieved the cameras to find a very rare and once-in-a-lifetime recording?"

"So, that's how you know," stated Marcia with a deflated expression.

"So, Becky, to continue the story, my father returned to your mother realising none of you were probably going to return given the horrific thing you all did. Besides, he set about making amends. He confessed to your mother about everything, and she eventually forgave him after countless conversations and tears. The truth is, I think she was just glad he was alive."

Steven sat silently, watching their demeanours melt away as Heather systematically placed the evidence with subtlety and suggestion. Marcia didn't need to ask what was on the camera. It would be far worse than the images of what she did with Jack. It was all starting to make sense.

"So, my father decided to share the wildlife videos with your mother. An amazing video of a goldeneye hatchling struggling to burst through its shell and start a new life came up. And then came the once-in-a-lifetime capture starring none other than you three." She pointed to each of them. "You see, one of the cameras hadn't been secured quite as well as it should have been, and during a storm, it had swung away from the view of the nest to face … anyone care to take a guess?" she taunted with a grin.

Silence preceded the answer they already knew.

"The boardwalk that's just ten metres away."

Becky cut in. "So, you're going to blackmail us. Is that what all of this is about? Fucking hypocrites. So, instead of taking it to the police, you held onto it all these years just so you could play games with us tonight."

Austin dropped his head in shame. Marcia looked out the window opposite at the triangle of soft snow settled in the corner of the leaded glass where each snowflake was melting onto the glass. She was unable to look Heather in the eye.

Steven raised his voice. It was the first time he'd done so all evening. It was deep and powerful. "You're nothing but an obnoxious and selfish bitch," he bellowed as he thumped the table, making the cups dance and the silverware ring.

They flinched.

"As you've so rudely interrupted yet again, I'll shorten the story Heather was very patiently explaining, and I'll make things crystal clear for you, Becky." His cheeks reddened, and even the veins in his neck swelled. "Your mother's cottage now falls to a third party." Steven reached across and stamped his finger on the document in front of her. "Read it."

Becky snatched the document from the table and began to read a highlighted section.

The estate mentioned herein and its contents, not limited to but including all exterior items and machinery, along with any monetary assets will, on the death of Mrs Catherine Monroe, be distributed by the executor, Mr Steven Myers, of the above-mentioned address to a third party (undisclosed) at the request of Mrs Catherine Monroe and witnessed by Miss Heather Monroe of the above-mentioned address.

On receipt of any contest to all or part of this will, and at the request of Mrs Catherine Monroe, a box containing various undisclosed contents will be forwarded to Devon & Cornwall Police.

By signing this section, I, Becky Monroe, of Flat 3, Beachfront Way, Brighton, will receive the monetary assets pertaining to the above estate and waive all rights to any and all property mentioned herein.

Becky gazed blankly at Steven and dropped the document on the table. She started to speak, but the words failed to leave her mouth. She dragged her palms down her face. The others watched on in awe. But what price would they pay? Marcia had the threat of tax fraud over her. Austin had already confessed. Austin alternated between playing with a small silver teaspoon and fiddling with his glasses. He was sullen while his eyes were dead and his heart empty.

THE SURPRISE GUEST
CHAPTER THIRTY-THREE

Becky rose up from her chair in a flash, and her chair fell back onto the oak flooring. She marched up and down the room. Black mascara bled down her cheeks. Her red dress was a tainted canvas of gravy and red wine.

She turned to Steven. "So, you're just going to take my house. The one thing that's been in my family for generations. And I get what, a measly few quid?"

Austin caught them off guard by yelling at Becky. "Take the win, will you? Did you not understand what it said? You get to walk free. No more guilt, no more hiding. It's over for you. You're the lucky one. Personally, you don't deserve shit. You orchestrated this whole 'Let's keep it a secret'," he said, gesturing in the air with his fingers. "So, just sign the will and move on."

"Easy for you to say, you've got jack shit to lose."

"I lose my freedom. But I get to keep my morals and dignity. Something you'll never have," he spat.

Austin stood and addressed Steven. "Mr Myers, I'm sorry for everything."

"You're such a loser," muttered Becky.

Heather laid her hand on Austin's shoulder. "I've seen the footage. It's a bit grainy, but it's clear enough to identify you all in it." She squeezed his shoulder. He felt genuine comfort. For the first time this evening, he felt the touch of a sympathetic hand. "It's obvious you were coerced and bullied into what you did. Your actions were paused, not rushed or calculated. It also looked like you stopped to argue with the other two at one point. There's no sound, so I can only guess they cheered you on to do it. You've also confessed your part and not protested it at any time. You've not made excuses or been disrespectful to either of us."

Heather turned him around to face her and looked him in the eyes. "For that, we're not going to take any further action. You're free to go. But before you do, we have one last surprise."

Austin's eyes welled up, and tears spilled. He removed his glasses and drew his shirt sleeve across them. "But I was responsible for her death. I tied her hands together so she couldn't swim. I watched her disappear under the water, struggling to stay afloat. Not them. I deserve to go to prison. His eyes filled up again, and his lip quivered. He looked at Steven. "How can you let me go? I killed your daughter," he wept.

"You've lived with a guilt that you needn't have for twenty-six years. You've carried the pain and served your sentence. The other two, not so much."

Steven turned to Marcia and slid the second document to her. She feared its contents. She picked it up and read the highlighted paragraph.

I, Molly Cole of 9, The Mews, Battersea, London, hereby give my full consent to transfer the sum of fifty thousand pounds to S & L Holdings Ltd for investment. I understand my money will be invested as agreed in person and that any or all monies forwarded to the above account will be distributed at the discretion of S & L Holdings Ltd.

Marcia drew her gaze away from the document. Steven's face was expressionless. Anger surfaced. She swallowed. Her mouth was dry. She poured some lemon water and drank. "I don't have fifty thousand pounds."

Steven lurched forward, his face so close to hers she could

smell the coffee on his breath. "On the contrary, Molly, you have sixty thousand, two hundred and thirty-five pounds in an account owned by Bennie Harrison, who conveniently owns a posh wine bar you often frequent to meet your wealthy businessmen in. I'd call that money laundering. Now, the better part of me is allowing you to keep ten thousand. I'm sure you'll recoup that soon enough by opening your legs for fat businessmen with small dicks and large bank accounts."

He sat back. "Of course, the alternative is that I call Derrick, and you take your chances with the tax fraud department. The difference with my offer is that you avoid a prison sentence," he smirked. "Choice is yours." He pushed the silver fountain pen in front of her.

She picked up the pen and hesitated for a second, realising her options were limited, and then signed.

"You've got forty-eight hours to transfer the money. Otherwise, I'll presume you've accepted option number two instead."

"So, now you have my money and Becky's mother's house. So, it all boils down to blackmail, money, and revenge. That's all this is. You never wanted this to be about legal justice. Why didn't you just turn us over to the police and save yourself Twenty-six years of theatrics?"

Steven rose to his feet and checked his watch. "Close to midnight. Heather, would you mind fetching our last guest, please?" He threw open his arms and bellowed. "It's time for the grand finale," he announced like a circus ringmaster.

Heather left the room, closing the doors behind her.

"I can't tell you how much I've been waiting for this moment. You've all been excellent guests and very entertaining, to say the least."

Marcia leaned across the table to the only place setting that remained untouched and picked up the folded place setting that read, *Surprise Guest*.

"Don't you think we've had enough surprises this evening? You got what you wanted; you've made your point.

I'm calling it a night. I'm calling a taxi." Marcia took out her phone. There was a voice message which she listened to therein.

Becky stood up. Anger surfaced. She picked up the silver coffee flask and launched it at the doors. The metal sound clattered around the room, spilling the coffee like dirty water. "That cottage belongs to me, and you know it," she screamed.

Austin grabbed her arm. "It's over, Becky. Stop this now."

Becky yanked her arm away. "Leave me the fuck alone. This is all your fault, you chucked her in the fucking lake, but I'm the one losing everything."

Becky cast a look at Marcia. There was fury in her eyes, and her breathing was deep and fast. "And you, you old slag. You ain't no better. Sitting there in your fucking designer clothes, with your fake tits, pretending like you're someone else now. You still get to keep your filthy career and your posh apartment." Becky's face was a picture of rage.

She turned back to Steven, who was standing behind his chair, unfazed with the same cool composure he'd had all evening.

"And you're nothing but a thief. I bet your daughter would be fucking proud of you. She got what she deserved. My mother should never have hired her. I was never good enough for that old bitch. I was just some problem child she wanted to discard like a rotten piece of meat. And Jack. The only good thing that slut Molly ever did was to help get rid of him," she said, glaring across the table at Steven. "Jack deserved everything he got, and so did your stuck-up daughter."

Becky grabbed the will from the table, tore it into pieces, and launched it in the air. Pieces of white paper fell slowly across the table. "Shove your fucking will, I'm keeping the cottage. Nothing on that camera shows me doing anything to her. I'm getting a solicitor. And you, Austin, you can find somewhere else to live."

Becky threw on her coat and grabbed her bag from the

back of the chair. She headed to the doors at the top of the steps.

"Wait," Marcia yelled. She dropped the phone slowly away from her ear. A stunned look crossed her face. Becky turned round at the top of the steps.

Marcia held up her phone. She looked at Steven. Then Becky. "I just got a message from my private investigator. About the Rolls Royce outside."

"So what?" snapped Becky. "That's yesterday's news."

Steven slipped his hands into his pockets. "Something wrong?"

"Bernie called me earlier. Except we were cut off. He's told me who's insured to drive the Rolls Royce we've all spotted over the past week."

Becky pulled open the door. "You think that matters now?" Marcia narrowed her eyes at Steven and stood up slowly. She swallowed hard and asked him in a soft voice, "Do *you* want to explain to all of us who's insured to drive your car, other than you and Peter?"

THE STING IN THE TALE
CHAPTER THIRTY-FOUR

Becky lingered in the doorway, her hand still resting on the wrought iron handles.

Austin cleared his throat. "Am I missing something here?"

Steven clapped. "Bravo, Molly. That's right, Becky, it's the unnamed beneficiary of your mother's estate," he exclaimed coldly.

Becky let go of the handles. She dropped down a step. Curiosity beckoning.

"Tell her who's named on your insurance, Steven."

Steven rocked back and forth on his heels. His hands remained in his pockets.

"Who?" asked Austin urgently.

"His daughter, Laura."

Silence fell over the room.

"I don't understand," said Austin.

Becky dropped down another step. Makeup and tears mixed. "What?"

Like all well-timed stage plays, the final character emerged from the wings. A woman. Dark Jeans, cream polo neck with greying blonde hair clipped up and silver-rimmed glasses.

"Hello, Becky."

Bewildered silence hung in the air. Thoughts rushed, and confused expressions reigned over all their faces.

Austin shook his head. "No. No. No. Tell me this is some

sick wind-up."

Laura leaned casually against the large oak sideboard before addressing the room. "Twenty-six years ago, you all left me to drown in the lake. At no point this evening has my father once mentioned my death. You all just presumed I was still lying at the bottom of the lake. I very nearly was. Have you ever tried to swim with your limbs tied?"

Austin removed his glasses. They trembled in his hand. He rubbed his eyes and replaced them. "So, I'm not a murderer?" His voice was distorted.

Becky remained at the foot of the steps, paralysed by confusion.

Marcia gawped like a teenage boy on a nudist beach. "Is that really you, Laura? I don't understand."

"You didn't think about the consequences, did you? I felt my body plunge into the cold, dark water, desperately trying to free my hands. The breath in my lungs burned, waiting for death to absorb me. You have no idea. My limbs were thrashing about, trying to make some headway to the surface. But have you ever tried to tread water with your wrists and ankles tied? Then, amongst the darkness, by pure chance, my hands touched something solid. The wooden boardwalk support that was anchored into the lake. I had just enough movement in my hands to cling onto the wooden post. From there, I pulled myself to the surface, with just moments left before I lost consciousness. Had you rowed me out into the middle of the lake, we wouldn't be having this conversation."

"We didn't want to kill you, Laura. We just wanted to scare you," said Marcia quietly.

"But we didn't come back to check. We just left," said Austin.

Laura shook her head. "You never intended to come back and check on me. So, let's not pretend this was anything other than a convenient way of making sure I couldn't say anything." "Just a second here," said Becky. "Are you honestly going
to take my inheritance and Marcia's money in revenge for

what we did to you?"

"This has nothing to do with me, Becky. It has everything to do with Jack. The one person your mother loved apart from you, and you took that away from her. She couldn't forgive you for what you did."

Becky's mouth fell. "It was that slag, not me."

"You planned it. You wanted to hurt him so badly that you stooped to a new low. You let your mother believe he was dead." Laura stepped towards Becky and gazed into her bloodshot eyes. "Your mother's will has nothing to do with me. It's what *she* wanted when she found out what you did. I'm glad Jack died with a clear conscience and had a few more years with your mother. It destroyed her, you know. She forgave Jack, but she could never forgive you. I can forgive you for the lake. I can't forgive you for hurting your mother. You can have the furniture and her savings, which amounts to about three thousand pounds. I'll look after the cottage, and maybe, just maybe, one day, when you've lost that chip on your shoulder and stopped blaming everyone else for your mistakes and decided to do something constructive with your life, then we'll talk about it. For now, it'll receive the love and upkeep it deserves. From me. It's what your mother wanted, so just be grateful it wasn't sold."

Becky huffed. "So, you're doing this out of spite? Why not just sign the house over to me now? You've proved your point."

"You know, Becky, when I crawled out of that lake, my first thought was that I wouldn't return to your mother's house. Because if I told her what you did, what you all did, it would devastate her. So, I walked, soaking wet and cold, to the village, and the only person I knew there was Mr Rawlings. He gave me Heather's number. She picked me up in the middle of the night and took me in until my father returned from Australia. You know they say time is a healer. But I found time gave me an opportunity. I studied journalism and became a reporter."

She turned to Austin. "I've read your books. You write

from the heart. They were good. My point to all this, Becky, is that I put your mother's feelings first that night, as I said. When you can do the same, we can talk."

Laura turned to Marcia. "What can I say, Molly? You didn't recognise me that night, did you?"

Marcia frowned. "You're the woman who handed me the envelope?"

Laura nodded. "We don't want your money, Molly. You find a way to make an honest living, pay your taxes, and contribute like everyone else, and then maybe you can have it back. For now, it stays with us, along with the photos of you and Jack. I'm sure you don't want them circulating on social media."

"You spent Twenty-six years planning all this for what?" asked Marcia.

"Goodness no. Just the last year. Catherine and I remained friends. I used to visit her with my father when she ended up in the nursing home."

"What about the piece of paper I got when I was seventeen?" asked Marcia.

Steven shuffled from one foot to the other. "That. Well, that was coincidence and opportunity colliding together. You see, Philip, the man who kindly obliged to keep an eye on you, I've known him from a young age, and when he told me about a Molly Cole in a youth offenders centre, I just had this crazy idea about teasing you after Laura told me about the game you all used to play. It wasn't until I secured this house to renovate it that the whole idea of some mystery game to bring you all together came to fruition. We all wanted to see how you would interact. Personally, I think this evening was crazy exciting," he laughed.

Steven's light-hearted comment only served to raise Becky's anger further, spurring her to cross the room to where he was standing with a charismatic expression.

"You think all this is funny?" she yelled. "Taking everything we have just for your own sordid pleasure and revenge?" Her words were corrupted by angry tears.

Steven stroked his beard again, taking in a chest full of air and letting out an audible exhale.

"I'm going to respond to that as clearly and concisely as I can," he said with an undertone of sarcasm. "You took a man's dignity, in this case, it was Jack, a man just trying his best to understand his stepdaughter and do what he thought was the right thing, and then used it against him to remove him from your own disruptive life. In doing so, you then plunged your mother into a world of sadness for months, never quite knowing what happened to her husband, and worse still, not even having a body to mourn or bury. On top of that, you used Austin and Molly to facilitate all that, and from my understanding, you've spent the last Twenty-six years manipulating him to keep this whole shit show undetected, fearing what you thought was murder. And you have the audacity to accuse me of taking everything away from you!"

Steven filled the room with another booming laugh and a shake of his head, a frustrated reaction to her shallow mindset and one which he felt obliged to point out to her.

"So, my daughter's nightmares of drowning and years of counselling to overcome a fear of water hasn't affected me as a father, has it?" Steven raised a palm to her. "You know what, there's no need to answer that because I'm sure you'll just find another excuse, so here's what I'm going to do." Steven leant forward, resting his hands on the top of the chair, his eyes drilling into hers and holding a stare so fierce that the other two in the room could feel the intensity.

"I'm going to give you a choice, Becky Monroe. I'm going to give you a chance to keep the cottage and everything your mother left behind. But that choice will come with a very valuable life lesson." Steven turned to Marcia and Austin. "But before we discuss this choice, I need you both to leave the room, please." Steven gestured to the half-open door where Peter was waiting to retire them for the evening.

Becky looked to Austin for reassurance. Austin rose from the table quickly. "I'd like to stay, please," he said halfheartedly, raising a hand like an embarrassed infant in class waiting to be excused. "Whatever deal you're offering Becky,

I'd like to know what it is," he said, with a degree of assertiveness. But inside, a nervousness had him fiddling with his glasses more noticeably. Becky gave Austin a slim but appreciative smile.

Steven laughed again. "I never said anything about a deal. I said I'm offering her a simple choice. There's a difference," he said, again with an undertone of sarcasm.

Marcia watched them both trying to negotiate with a man who was quite obviously on an intellectual level well above their pay grade. Marcia wondered if Austin's performance earlier had just been a ruse to gain sympathy.

"Well, I guess since I'm not going anywhere tonight, I may as well wrap this up and go figure some shit out because, like you said, Steven, it's been a crazy evening," Marcia said.

Steven smiled. "Rest assured, Peter will drive you home first thing. Please allow him to show you to your room."

Marcia withdrew from the table, picked up her Prada bag, and gave a last glance to Becky and Austin. "Hell of a reunion, by the way, and if you want my advice, I'd take the win. Because if I've learnt something from this evening, it's that our host doesn't give up easily." Marcia winked at them. "Be seeing you both in the morning, I guess."

Austin watched Marcia disappear with Peter and was now left facing Steven. The room had sunk into an awkward silence. "You can leave now, Austin, if you would." Steven's words
were direct.

"It's okay, Austin. I'll fill you in in the morning. Get some rest, I've got this," said Becky, standing her ground.

Austin paused for a moment before realising he didn't have a choice. If Becky had a shot at keeping the cottage, then he wasn't going to stand in her way. Despite the evening casting some clarity on his life of half-truths and secrets with Becky, he felt she deserved the cottage. Even if he had no desire to live there with her, it was her one constant. He had enough to process already. He was truly a free man now. A feeling he hadn't experienced for the past 26 years.

"Good luck, Becky," he said as he sauntered out of the room and gave her one last glance.

Steven said nothing. The room was theirs, leaving Becky to his last throw of the dice.

CHAPTER THIRTY-FIVE
A LAST THROW OF THE DICE

Marcia woke to a chill that touched her shoulders. She raised her head from the pillow, forcing her sticky eyes open. The low sun picked out the delicate frost patterns on the window opposite. She forced her blurry eyes to focus on her slim watch on the bedside table; it was 8:10 a.m.

She threw back the thick, purple duvet and sat up shivering. *Why was the house so cold?* A sense of disappointment crept over her. She couldn't decide which disappointment was worse: the realisation that she'd been played all these years only to chase a name that didn't exist or the disappointment that the name didn't turn out to be her long-forgotten father. A fantasy that she kept trying to believe in despite her rational psyche telling her the odds of it becoming a reality were slim to none. Either way, she felt empty.

She pulled a pair of light blue jogging bottoms and a matching hoodie from her overnight bag and slipped them on. She craved a hot bath and the comfort of her own surroundings. At this moment, she had no intention of spending the next hour on personal care and makeup. She wanted out of this place.

She stuffed her overnight gear into her bag and made her way across the landing, stopping at the top of the stairs. A noise from the room to her right stopped her.

She knocked. "Becky? Austin? You in there?"

Austin appeared at the door looking dishevelled, tucking in his wine-stained shirt and fixing his glasses. "Molly? Thought you might have been Becky. She's not in any of the rooms," he said, with concern in his voice.

"You sleep in your clothes, jeez, Austin," she humoured. "I expect she's downstairs scoffing down some breakfast. I just want out of this place, back to London."

"Becky's got our weekend bag. Besides, I didn't sleep. I waited for her to come upstairs last night, but she didn't show." Austin dragged his palms down his face and sighed. "I looked in all the rooms, even yours, at some stupid hour, but the others were all empty. Doesn't make sense. She wouldn't just leave, would she?"

"This is Becky, remember. She's a law unto herself. You checked downstairs yet?"

Austin shook his head. "And why is this house freezing?"

"Well, I'm going to find Peter. I need outta here. I'll see you
downstairs." Marcia descended the stairs to a small hallway. She glanced left to a half-open door to the kitchen. She put down her bag and pushed open the kitchen door. "Austin! You better come look," she shouted.

Austin appeared behind her. "What the hell?" He entered the kitchen, walking around the centre island. All the cupboard doors were open and completely empty. No crockery, no food, nothing. No sign of any activity.

Marcia dashed to the dining room opposite. The table, along with all the chairs neatly tilted against the table, was covered in a large cotton cloth that met the floor on both sides. Marcia knelt by the wooden panel where Becky had smashed the wine bottle the night before. There was no visible stain anywhere on the woodwork. She ran a long nail down the panel and could feel a small indent in the wood. "Someone's gone to a great deal of trouble to clear up. Something's not right."

"Yeah, that's been my theme all frigging weekend. Explains why it's so cold in here," he said, rubbing his arms.

"It's like no one lives here."

"Did you say you checked all the other rooms upstairs?" asked Marcia.

"Yeah, nothing. Not even any furniture. My room just had a bed and a small cabinet. That was it. The other three bedrooms were completely empty. I'm getting worried about Becky now."

Marcia flicked him a look. "That's funny because last night after you'd spilled all your guts and feelings, you were ready to ditch her."

Austin pushed on his glasses. "Just because I don't want to be with her anymore doesn't mean I don't care. I can't just forget her after all these years. I'm sure you can understand that."

He stormed off through the lounge to the hallway. Marcia picked up her bag and followed. "Sorry," she yelled, hurrying after him. "It's been a pretty tense 24 hours. I just want to return to some kind of normal, as far away from here as I can."

Austin stopped at the door and turned to her. "Nothing will ever be normal again after this." He drew open the front door and was instantly met with a wave of cold air. The January snow had shrunk to an icy crust, and the sun had begun to dissolve the snow that was covering the tiled garage opposite, creating trails of rising steam. It felt like he'd been hiding from the world for an eternity as he stood under the cloudless sky. For a second, everything seemed calm and pleasant.

Marcia stood next to him on the threshold, gazing out towards the moor. She placed a hand on his shoulder. "Well, since all the cars are gone, it looks like we're not getting a lift back." Marcia shook her head. "Talk about being stitched up. Again."

Austin pulled his jacket in tight around him and tucked his hands into his pockets. "There's only one place Becky will be if she's taken off."

"Is that what you think? That she's taken off?"

Austin shrugged. "Why else wouldn't she be here?" He watched the drops of melting ice dripping from the garage roof, mesmerised by its repetitive timing and steering him from thoughts of last night.

"I know where she is," he exclaimed.

"Where?" she asked.

"The cottage. That's where she'll be. That's where I'm going."

Austin walked off across the gravelled yard to the open gates without uttering a word.

Marcia slipped on her coat and followed him through the gates and onto the rugged moor. She hadn't walked far before the slushy ground crept up through her shoes like blotting paper until it reached her knees. Austin's strides were large and brisk. She gave up trying to keep pace with any strategic plan to evade the slushy grasses. "For God's sake, Austin, will you hold up?" Marcia stopped for a second to catch her breath.

Austin stopped and turned. "You don't have to follow, you know. Thought you wanted to get back to London?"

Marcia threw open her arms. "If you hadn't noticed, we're not exactly on a bus route."

Austin pointed to the right. "Main road's that way."

Marcia laughed. "Can you not see the irony of what we're doing?"

Austin threw her a glance. "I'm trying not to think about it."

"Kind of hard not to. Do you really want to go back to the cottage? It was about an hour's walk when we were in our teens. I'm hardly dressed for hiking, my feet are freezing, and this bag's not exactly light."

Austin started walking again and asked her, "You really going to hand over fifty thousand pounds?"

"We did an awful thing back then, and like you, I spent most of my life hiding from the guilt. Today, I feel angry, angry at the fact we had to wait Twenty-six years to learn that we weren't responsible for Laura's death. I think my life would be different if we'd known that back then. Guilt is a virus, and it just eats away at you. So yes, I'm bitter, and do I think I should just hand over my money after all this time? No."

"What if he reports back to that guy, you know, the tax inspector?"

Marcia smiled. "If I've learnt one thing in my game, it's to always have a safeguard. I record all my clients; I have a mini surveillance camera in my work bag, which I always place strategically to film them. And before you even open your mouth," she jumped in, "I never watch the recordings. It's purely for my protection in case the worst was to happen."

Austin took Marcia's hand and helped her over a steep ridge. "You could make a killing from blackmail alone," he laughed.

Marcia stopped suddenly. "I'm not that kind of person. As I said, it's for protection only, except on this one occasion. Let's see how well my tax fraud investigation goes after I send a small excerpt to him. Steven has no idea that I have them, so I can play games as well."

"Ain't no flies on you, Molly or Marcia, which do you prefer?"

"I've been Marcia since I was eighteen. But I get that you know me as Molly, so either's fine between us." A few steps later, she asked, "How do you feel about all this?"

Austin took Marcia's bag after watching her stumble on the rugged terrain. "I don't know what I feel now," he said. "Yes, I'm angry at Becky, and maybe I wouldn't have been with her if I'd known I wasn't a murderer. I feel used, I guess, and I've learnt an awful lot about her in just two days. But I can't just walk away. She's been part of my life for so long that it feels a little cruel. I understand why she did it. I just can't understand why she couldn't be truthful with me. I think I'm angrier at Steven, being made to look like a fool."

"No more than me, Austin. You haven't been chasing a ghost for Twenty-six years. You think Becky just took off?"

"Maybe she had no choice. Maybe walking away from everyone was the choice he gave her to keep the cottage. Maybe that's his way of punishing her, separating her from the people she cares about so she's alone. See, Becky doesn't really have many friends, she's an acquired taste."

Marcia exaggerated a nod. "You got that right. What are you going to do now?" she asked.

"Stay with my uncle for a while, I guess, until I figure stuff out. I want to concentrate on writing again, only this time I won't have any distractions. You?"

"Back to doing the only thing I know, I guess. Although this weekend has made me re-evaluate my life, so, who knows." An hour later, with sore ankles and waterlogged clothing, they both arrived at the one sight they'd both dreaded until now. The large lake, framed in a white border of melting snow, and beyond that, the cottage—their ground zero.

"You really think she's at the cottage?" asked Marcia. Austin shrugged and took a moment to view the landscape, which had changed somewhat since he was a gardener there. The beauty remained, but the sour memories were no less tainted. "Let's find out."

They walked at the edge of the lake towards the cottage, surrounded by flowerless bushes and skeleton trees, not the chocolate-box memory of Twenty-six years ago. They glanced briefly at the wooden boardwalk, which was once the root of this whole nightmare. It was now a twisted and half-rotten wooden structure, semi-submerged and covered in water grasses. Neither of them felt brave enough to mention it.

The January sun struggled to rise any higher than the treetops, but somehow, it felt warming and comforting. Marcia ignored her waterlogged shoes and numb feet as they neared the cottage. Age and the elements had clearly taken their toll on the exterior. Its once white-washed features were now faded, and a green cancer of moss and unattended maintenance engulfed the grey thatch.

Austin stood and gazed at the cottage. "Never thought I'd

be back here. Even yesterday, I couldn't face getting out of the car. But yesterday, I thought I was a murderer. Today, I have my freedom, but it comes with a bitter twist because I've lost all these years to one big delusion. Kind of a hollow victory."

Marcia patted him on the back. "C'mon, let's go see if anyone's in."

Marcia pushed on the iron latch, and much to her disbelief, the door opened to a clunk. Austin drew in a deep breath and exhaled. "After you, please," he gestured to her.

Marcia entered the hallway. It was cold and empty. Spoors of black mould were dotted around the flacking plaster. She turned left into the kitchen, which was bare. The musty smell was strong, and the years of decay had taken hold.

Austin ventured right into the lounge. Moments later, Marcia heard his startled voice and dashed to the lounge to find Steven sitting on a pine wooden chair wearing black waterproof trousers and a green wax jacket with a large monk- sized hood, with a metal thermos flask on his lap.

"Thought you'd come here," he said gruffly. "As predicted. Surprised to see you though, Molly, but since you're here …"

"Where the hell is Becky?" interrupted Austin. "What happened last night, and why is your house empty now? And our lift home, I'm guessing that's not happening either?"

Steven held up his hands. "Questions, questions. Please, one at a time," he joked. "Well, let's start with the house. Yes, it's been mothballed because Laura and I are going to Australia. She's been through a lot, but you already know that, don't you? She's coming with me on my business trip for a bit of R&R," he smiled. But this was the smile of a smug man. He then handed Austin a piece of A4 paper.

Austin screwed up the paper without even a courtesy glance and threw it to the bare concrete floor. "I ain't playing any more stupid games. You've had your fun. Just tell me where Becky is."

Steven pointed to the discarded ball of paper on the floor.

"Answer's right there. I just gave it to you," he said, unscrewing the top of his flask and pouring himself a coffee.

Marcia picked up the paper and unravelled it. A minute of silence followed.

Austin watched Marcia's expression. "What is it, Marcia?"

Marcia looked up from the paper, hooking eyes with Steven.

"So, this is your idea of a choice? How is this a fair choice?"

"What?" asked Austin. "Where's Becky?"

"Ask him," she snapped.

Steven sipped lightly on his coffee with a taunting grin, just as he had done the previous evening.

"Do you know what empathy means?" he asked in his usual condescending voice. He raised a finger. "Before you answer, let me tell you the true definition. It comes from the Greek word *em-pathos*. It means the ability to sense other people's emotions, coupled with the ability to imagine what someone else is thinking or feeling."

Austin stepped towards Steven. "I'm done with riddles and games, just tell me," he raged.

Marcia pointed to the lake. She held out the screwed-up paper, but Austin shook his head. "No, I want him to tell me."

Steven placed his flask on the ground and stood up. "I wanted Becky to experience the true definition of empathy, something she's quite clearly lacking, as she demonstrated very well last night, so I gave her a choice. Walk away from the cottage and back to her very sad and pathetic existence, or experience true empathy by reliving the exact three minutes of
pure panic that you all made my daughter endure."

Austin reached out, quickly grabbing Steven's wax jacket so they were nose to nose. "What have you done with her?" he yelled in Steven's face.

Marcia placed an arm between them. "C'mon, Austin, let him go."

275

Steven was still wearing his silly grin. "She agreed to do it," he laughed.

Austin glanced at the metal flask on the floor. His actions left no room for thought or consequence, and in the blink of an eye, he grabbed the flask and struck it hard against the side of Steven's head, knocking him sideways against the wall. Seconds later, a warm pool of blood spilled down his temple, staining the concrete floor. Steven's eyes faded, and he dropped to the floor like a dead weight.

Marcia stood in awe. Austin was still clutching the metal flask tightly, his breathing heavy and noisy.

Marcia closed her eyes for a second, hoping this was all a terrible nightmare.

Austin dropped the flask. The metallic noise echoed around the empty room.

Tears began to fill Marcia's eyes. "What the fuck, Austin! Read the note." Marcia thrust the note into his chest, and he opened it.

"I, Becky Monroe, agree to undertake a dare which I accept voluntarily, understanding that it could endanger my life, and I place no blame on any third-party person or persons. If I succeed in completing the said dare, the cottage named in Catherine Monroe's last will and testament shall transfer to me as a whole and in full."

Signed Becky Monroe

Austin dropped to his knees and buried his face in his palms. "What the fuck, Becky? Why did you agree to that?" He muttered through his hands.

Marcia's attention was seized by footsteps descending the stairs. She followed the noise until Becky appeared in the doorway with chaotic hair, wearing a thick parka coat and clutching her weekend bag.

Moments of confused silence followed until everyone could fully comprehend the magnitude of the situation in front of them. Becky looked at the lifeless body on the floor. She looked at Marcia, frozen on the spot, and then to Austin knelt next to Steven's lifeless body. She then looked beyond the dead landscape toward the lake.

She turned to the other two, and a smile grew.

THE END

About The Author

Lance Litherland lives in the south west of England with his wife Sharon. He discovered a passion for writing in his early fifties, having written a few short stories throughout his earlier years. Lance released his first book A DARKER WORLD in 2020 which recieved a string of 5 star reviews. Lance writes UK based mystery thrillers with an emphasis on building suspense with a twist. He is currently working on his third mystery thriller.

mysterythrillernovels@gmail.com

Printed in Great Britain
by Amazon